The Arab Season

Alisa Ahlam

Copyright © Alisa Ahlam, 2011
First Edition

The author has asserted their moral right under the Copyright, Designs and Patents Act, 1988, to be identified as the author of this work.

All Rights reserved. No part of this publication may be reproduced, copied, stored in a retrieval system, or transmitted, in any form or by any means, without the prior written consent of the copyright holder, nor be otherwise circulated in any form of binding or cover other than that in which it is published and without a similar condition being imposed on the subsequent purchaser.

A CIP catalogue record for this title is available from the British Library.

Chapter one
The preacher's daughter

Zuleka finished performing her *wudu* in preparation for her afternoon prayers. As she closed the bathroom door behind her the sound of her mother preparing the evening meal echoed around the otherwise quiet house.

The smell of spices and flavourings permeated the hall and floated up the stairs.

On her way down to her room she stopped at the kitchen door. 'Do you need any help, *hooyo?*'

'No, no, you get on with your studies, *habibti*. I can manage. Your attention to your work is far more important.' Her parent's emphasis on academic success equalled their views on observing religion. Everything else was secondary. Their attitude made the Victorians look liberal. Her Yemeni father, an imam at the local mosque, insisted everyone in the house follow austere Muslim teachings. The girls in the house all wore the hijab with abaya or other forms of loose fitting modest clothing.

Her sandals squeaked on the polished hall floor as she walked towards her room. She couldn't help but be pleased with herself for achieving the room swap with her sister. Safi had put no argument forward, thinking she had the best of the deal, and no one had questioned Zuleka's logic for wanting the much smaller room downstairs. They all agreed it gave her more privacy and provided a quiet place for her to study. They hadn't suspected her real reason, her need to come and go without detection.

The flowing abaya she took down from the hook behind the door draped her body in modesty. Guilt nudged away her self-satisfaction as she continued her ritual and laid out her prayer mat, a gift her father had brought for her from his pilgrimage to Mecca. Asking for forgiveness for her ways clothed her in hypocrisy as she knew she could not give up how she lived her life.

As it always happened, her mind strayed when she started to recite the suras. She'd discussed this once with her father and he had made her feel better by saying: "That's the shaytaan, trying to steal the Baraka - *the blessings of your prayers.*"

She made a determined effort to concentrate on God. She had her midterm exams soon and needed his help. Under her breath she recited the verse from the Al Fatiha, the opening sura of the Quran:

> *In the name of God, the infinitely Compassionate and Merciful.*
> *Praise be to God, Lord of all the worlds.*
> *The Compassionate, the Merciful*
> *Ruler on the Day of Reckoning*
> *You alone do we worship, and You alone do we ask for help*
> *Guide us on the straight path,*
> *The path of those who have received your grace*
> *Not the path of those who have brought down wrath*
> *Nor of those who wander astray.*
> *Amen.*

Once she'd finished and with her conscience appeased, she folded the mat, placed her abaya back behind the door, and turned her attention to her studies. The pile of books stacked on top of one another looked daunting, but she resigned herself to the task ahead.

In her last year studying medicine at King's college, the pressure sometimes loaded against Zuleka. Though it helped that from the beginning, much to her surprise, the workings of the internal organs had fascinated her. Not the sexiest of subjects, she agreed, but better than law or accounting, the two areas her sisters studied. Besides, she looked forward to having the title, 'Dr' before her name. Now *that* would be sexy.

A sound behind her made her look towards her open door. Her mother stood there.

'Mashallah', she muttered, 'I am proud to have you for my daughter.'

Her smile and the gracious way she seemed to glide away brought a lump to Zuleka's throat and the conflict inside her brought feelings of desolation. *Why couldn't she be more like her sisters? Why did her sheltered and austere upbringing have the opposite effect on her than it had meant to?* Instead of wanting to practice obedience and piety she had a hunger for experiences and sought ways to express her individuality. At times she felt she burned like a bright, beautiful star that refused to blend into the night sky. She thirsted for adrenaline and frivolous fun.

Her arms made a comforting cushion as she rested her head on them. No answers came to her, but thinking about what Hani had said to her sometime ago relaxed her. *She could have it all.* She could burn the candle at both ends. No one need ever find out. Tomorrow she'd give herself a day off and she'd be the Zuleka she wanted to be.

***

Oblivious to the line of people behind her in Starbucks, and with yesterday's worries banished from her mind, Zuleka leaned forward over the counter and shouted at the nervous barista, 'No! No! I ordered a skinny mocha!

This has cream. Do I look like the type to have cream in my coffee?'

'Just bear with me for a second, Ms. I'll make you another one.'

Her annoyance was replaced by amusement as she waited and watched him in his flustered state struggling to maintain a veneer of coolness.

She dodged the dirty looks and ignored the 'skinny bitch' comment that came her way as she stood aside to allow the others in the queue to place their orders.

With her mocha in one hand and her huge floppy bag in the other she turned in the direction of Selfridges. Her long hair bounced as she walked, its jet-black colour complimenting the light tone of her skin and the striking beauty of her face. Her movements emulated the models on the cat-walk as she swung her body giving her curves just the right amount of exposure.

Meaning only to window shop, Zuleka ditched her empty cup into a nearby bin and walked into Selfridges; for her, it was a paradise of beautiful smells, glittering glass counters, and expensive goods – she belonged.

Bright bold colours and expensive designer brands were her downfall, not to mention the accessories she needed to compliment them. Stashed in Hamdi's flat, Zuleka had an impressive number of shoes, bags, wallets, and watches and a wardrobe of forbidden, but gorgeous outfits.

The only downfall to this obsession came through her letter box every month - her bank statement. Always shocked by the amount she spent but ever ready to allow her shopping-friendly conscience to console her, the offending reminder of her addiction resembled wedding confetti when it floated to the bottom of her bin. After all, most of the items had been on sale or promotion, so she had *saved* money, hadn't she?

'Do you need any assistance, miss?'

'I am just browsing.' Her answer was to convince herself as she tried to ignore the small voice inside her prompting her to buy as she moved from rail to rail.

She stopped in front of one of the many glistening mirrors, straightened her posture, and checked over her appearance. Skinny jeans, a bright red cardigan with the sleeves pulled up to her elbows showing off a set of wooden bangles inlaid with intricate gold patterns that was complimented by the Lois Vuitton pumps. A far cry from the demure, black abaya she'd left home in, which now lay strewn across Hamdi's bed ready for her to change back into. *Like Cinderella after the ball.*

Damn, that thought had dampened her spirits. She needed therapy. She'd treat herself. A few items had caught her eye. She re-traced her steps and grabbed them from the rail. Not stopping to try them on she bundled them together and headed for the counter.

Her mobile rang as she stuffed her credit card back into her purse.

'Hi, are you coming over to AA's? The others are meeting there in about an hour.'

The guilt of her purchases forgotten, her fun elements shook up again, she told Hani she'd be there and left the shop, both arms now leaden with bags.

***

The hot day had left behind a balmy evening and even now, just before 7 pm, the night promised to stay warm and humid.

Edgware Rd – AKA, the Arab Capital of London vibrated with life. She walked in front of Abu Amin, the Lebanese restaurant, or AA - short for - Addicts Anonymous, as she and the others called it and glanced at those already seating at the pavement tables. Smoke curled around them, but didn't hide their leers in her direction.

All men, Arabs in their forties but looking older, the freedom they enjoyed flashed feelings of resentment through her.

Heading through the restaurant towards the discreet door at the back, which those not in the know might wrongly assume led to the staff room, she went through and descended the stairs to a different world.

The sound of high-pitched music vibrated through the haze of aromatic shisha, and the air throbbed with the energy of youth. *This is where the party is at.*

Besides the young, the place attracted colourful characters: from the Turkish man who walked in and out trying to sell roses to students who cared for none, to the Chinese lady, who approached each table and opened her trench coat as if about to flash, but instead revealed counterfeit DVDs hung in their dozens around her body. And, of course, there were the waiters, some of whom they had a love-hate relationship with.

Tonight, thank Allah, Mahad, who only spoke enough English to let them know he wasn't too enthusiastic on them, wasn't on duty. A mean, vertically-challenged man, he wore tee-shirts that looked like they had shrunk in the washing cycle or belonged on the shelves of Baby Gap. He had a major Napoleon complex.

Mohamed, their favourite push-over waiter came over to her. '*Salaam, salaam!*'

Zuleka pampered to his obvious attraction to her knowing this would secure a generous discount, an important ingredient for her and her friends, and permission to plug in her iPod to the back of the stereo so they could listen to some R&B rather than the same Arabic music that was always on play.

Hani called over to her. She and Hamdi sat in their usual corner with Ayan. She hadn't seen Ayan for a while.

After kisses all round she asked, 'What are you guys smoking?'

'Ayan is smoking double apple and this is grape and mint'

'Oh, apple is too strong. I need me some mint, Hamdi, share the love.'

'Do you mean the shisha or my love life?'

'I meant the shisha, but if you must bore us once again by going on and on about you're so called love life, then go ahead.'

Hamdi had picked up her latest man in AA, stealing him from an unsuspecting girl who had needed to pay a visit to the ladies. Upping her eye contact to out and out flirting she'd hooked the poor guy to the point he'd made some excuse, taken his date to the tube station, and hot-footed it back to pick it up with Hamdi. But boy, did he give her trouble and did they all hear about it!

'Excuse me, but isn't this the circle of trust? If I can't talk to you guys about it, who can I talk to?'

'Fine, go ahead. What is it this time?'

'You needn't roll your eyes like that, Hani...

'It's just that your love life has more spins and turns than a revolving door, girl.'

Zuleka laughed at Hani's comment, but at the same time flicked a warning glance in her direction. Hani's wink told her she'd got the message, far better to let Hamdi have her say so the conversation could move along.

'I don't know what to do about him,' Hamdi said, referring to the half Somali - half Italian, Lorenzo, whose exotic combination of forebears made him uber hot. A guy Zuleka thought she wouldn't mind having a few problems with.

'We're still stuck in first gear. No matter what I do he doesn't seem to take the hint to move things to the next level...'

Her words surprised Zuleka, *Hamdi, unsure of herself? And with a guy, too! This had to be a first.*

'Maybe he's not into me as much as I thought he was...'

'Honey, you have only been out on three dates.' Ayan told her. 'Jam your hype and be a lady, sister.'

'Three dates is plenty of time. That's like what, three weeks now? I am beginning to feel like his friend!'

'Three dates is nothing. You need to wait.'

'Nothing?! How can you say that, Hani?'

'Look, girl. I know you bore easy, but you can't live every relationship in the fast lane.'

'Well, I'm telling you all, if Lorenzo doesn't step up his game anytime soon, I'm jumping ship.'

'Just you let me know if you do, that's one good looking boy.' Hani told her.

'What you complaining about, lady? Zuleka asked, 'at least you have a hot man in your arms. I feel like I haven't been on a date in like, forever.'

'I am with Zuleka on this one, Hamdi. I suggest you hold on to your fish, coz the pond is getting dry.' Hani said.

'I've got just the solution to that,' Ayan sipped her mint tea, her expression was of someone about to reveal some very exciting news; 'My cousin's wedding is coming up, and I've seen a couple of her fiancés friends. And, *mash Allah*, praise belongs to Allah, they are FINE!' She hi-fived them, 'And, the reception is going to be at the Hilton so you know it's going to be hot.'

'Oh goody! I love Somali weddings!" said Zuleka, "They are so different from Arab weddings. I hope it isn't segregated? No offence, but segregated weddings are a DUD. I mean, who wants to get all dressed up to hang out with a bunch of females?'

'Please tell us it isn't a religious wedding, Ayan?

'Nah, this one is mixed. So go shopping and get ready to get your freak on ladies!'

'Unlike you spinsters, I don't need a wedding to get a man.' As Hamdi stood up her mobile caught the light, she waved it at them, 'In fact, he just messaged me and invited me to his place now, so I'll catch you guys later'

Wearing tight drain-pipe jeans accessorized with a slim gold belt and four-inch, golden heels, Hamdi looked fabulously sexy as she grabbed her bag and waved her goodbyes.

'Make sure you get some this time!' Zuleka shouted after her. But inside, she felt sorry for Lorenzo. He didn't know what he had coming to him.

She turned back to the other two. 'Well, that's her out of our hair, come on, let's enjoy this shisha before it burns out …'

Chapter Two
Roping in Hamdi

Hamdi set her mouth in a pout. Lorenzo didn't stand a chance. Tonight she would know what he had to give. Impatience had her sitting forward. She clung on to the handle next to the door of the cab to steady her.

The teasing of Hani and Zuleka and the way Ayan had become quite cross had affected her. She knew she pushed the boundaries further than they dare, but not further than they would like to. They were jealous of her carefree life, and the way she could come and go as she pleased with very little care for the societal rules that imprisoned them, but they didn't envy how she came to have that freedom.

Trying to concentrate on the people busying along the streets and the shop windows displaying everything the world had to offer, didn't help. Her friends' criticism had nudged the place inside her where she kept the things she didn't like to visit. In doing so they had evoked memories of another life that had shaped and haunted her, and highlighted a comparison she didn't want to make, but knew to be true: her behaviour imitated the very person she hated the most- her mother.

Born in Somalia, into a society where the sheer numbers of your clan guaranteed your security, others had regarded theirs as weak. They had joked about her father. In the habit of marrying and divorcing multiple women, they said he'd wagered a one man mission to increase the size of their clan. When he divorced her mother she left behind everything of her old life, including Hamdi.

The feeling of utter desolation this had given her throbbed once more through her breast. She closed her eyes. Tried to dispel the unloved and unwanted child from within her, but the open sore of bitterness her parents had gouged into her bled once more.

Like a slide show clicking in her mind she saw pictures of herself. Lonely and unwanted, passed around from pillar to post, whilst her father took care of his own needs and her mother scandalised their community as she threw herself into the liberal society of 1980's Mogadishu. In these moments of revisiting her past the condemnation of the women of the village resounded in her ears as they'd piled her mother's sins upon her little shoulders.

'You see how she plays with the boys, while the other girls are helping out in the kitchen? Mark my words, she's going to end up like her mother, that's all she'll be good for.'

Was it fair that at ten years of age she'd had to endure such talk and prophecies about her future?

Oh, what did it all matter, now?

She'd never be able to get even with her father, he'd lost his life in the civil war and she had no notion of where her mother was, or even if she still lived, though her last memory of her sat heavy in her heart.

Dumped back with her mother after her father's death, together they had walked mile after mile with hundreds of other displaced people. She could still taste the dust and feel the ache in her little legs and the burning sores on her feet. And remember the joy of at last reaching a refugee camp

Nimo, a clanswoman, had tramped with them. If she hadn't done so, Hamdi knew she would not have made it out alive as her joy had soon turned to desolation.

She recoiled against the memory. Saw once more the slime running down the hill between the makeshift huts. Felt it curl its way around her feet, bringing a stink which had made her retch. She swallowed as her throat dried at the memory of the hot ache in her throat for the want of a drink and how, just as she'd thought to scoop up some of the filth and suck the liquid from it, Nimo had returned from the water allocation bay, lifted her up and dripped soothing drops of water on to her tongue.

Still going through the motions of time, Hamdi put her head back as if lifting her face to Nimo and felt once again the cool cloth she'd used to wipe away the mud from her face and the caked matter from her eyes.

Her pupils stung with held back tears; that was the moment she first felt loved. She'd clung on to the thread of hope Nimo had offered and had never left her side. Together they'd fetched their daily supplies of water and their rations of food and had made fires and cooked what meals they could and kept their area clean. Her mother hadn't hung around much. Men would loiter in their vicinity and she would go with them, returning when she needed food. Then one day the gates of the compound opened and Nimo walked through with her in tow, showed some papers to the guards, and was ushered out.

Looking back sure in the knowledge she would not return she'd seen her mother talking to one of the men she'd called 'uncle' and though she'd kept her eyes on her until the truck she and Nimo had climbed onto went around a corner, her mother never once looked towards her. Never once put up her hand to wave goodbye.

Nimo had somehow passed her off as her daughter and brought her to England. They had settled in Leicester, where Nimo still lives. Hamdi shifted in her seat, *she is my mother and always will be and her family are mine, too.*

Thinking of them now she had an overwhelming urge to visit them soon.

***

The television almost shook with the enthusiasm of the football crowd. Their shouts, whistles, and rattles filled Lorenzo's little living room. He made as much noise as they did, jumping up and hollering, either in pain because his team had missed scoring or joy because they hadn't.

Needing to dispel the last of the threads of the veil of memory that clung to her she allowed her annoyance to bristle through; *he'd asked her here for this!* It peeved her further to know she would have to be the one to make the first move. *What kind of man is he?* His indifference upset her.

She leant towards him. His eyes lingered on her face. Excitement tickled the bottom of her stomach as she saw his look held desire. Without moving she whispered. 'It's so hot in here...'

'Yeah, it is hot…'

Her ruse had worked some magic on him. It seemed he had difficulty in swallowing and his eyes bore into hers. But then, he broke the spell. He stood up saying, 'I'll open up the windows.'

Disappointed, but not showing it she murmured her thanks and moved her tactics up a notch by scooping a lump of ice from the many floating on top of her glass of water. Massaging her throat with it caused sensual beads of water to trickle between her breasts. His eyes followed their progress. She murmured, 'Mmm, feels good. Here let me do it to you…'

He didn't object.

Tracing a path from the nape of his neck down his back and around to his chest felt good.

'Come here…' He whispered.

YES! His face moved closer. His lips brushed against hers. The gentle contact deepened into a passionate kiss.

Just as she was beginning to lose herself in the passionate embrace, he pulled away, 'Be patient, Hamdi.' Taking hold of her busy hands he eased away from her, 'Not tonight, okay?'

'Yes, tonight!'

'What's up with you? Relax, okay?' He stood up and put his shirt back on. 'I want a relationship. I want us to get to know each other first. I thought you wanted the same thing?'

'Yes, I do, but do they have to be mutually exclusive?' *How dare he turn her down?*

He knelt in front of her. 'I want to get to know you, the real Hamdi. You fascinate me, you're an enigma, and I need time to discover and understand *all of you*. Rushing things is just going to cloud it all up, trust me I know this. Will you give me that time, Hamdi?'

'I am really not that interesting. If you insist, I can write a short bio and email it to you.'

He winced at her sarcasm, but she didn't let him off the hook, 'Trust me, if anybody is a mystery it's you! In fact, you're frigging crazy; I mean, who turns down a pretty girl like you just did?'

'I want a little more at this stage in my life. '

'Just my luck, out of all the red-blooded Italians out there I find myself one who is practising abstinence. Great!'

'I am not practising abstinence.' His laugh irritated her, but before she could retort he continued, 'Don't make me sound so bad. I have a reputation to keep. I am just looking for something that carries a little more weight.'

'Fine, Lorenzo! I'll give you time to, discover and understand me, as you put it!' She grabbed her bag and stood up. Over her shoulder she shot one last quip, 'But, you'd better be worth it otherwise I will not be responsible for my actions!' The door slammed shut with just the right velocity she'd hoped for as she left him standing gaping after her.

Near to tears she ran down the road, not even sure if she had taken the right direction. *Get to know her! Nobody knew her. Not even SHE knew her!*

***

The sleeping pills she kept next to her bed had assured her a night's sleep, but nothing looked better on waking. A text on her phone told her Zuleka would be here soon. No doubt spilling the contents of the shopping bag she'd arrived at AA with and hadn't bothered to mention. Neither had she or any of the others, come to think of it, but Zuleka's habit caused embarrassment to the point they sometimes pretended it hadn't happened just to stop any friction arising from the subject. They should tackle it and try to help her, but the easy way appealed more. Anyway, it would be difficult with the love they all had for shopping.

A tap followed by the door opening heralded Zuleka's arrival.

'Hey, gorgeous.' This expression always fitted Zuleka, even on the days, like now, when she walked in wearing her baggy abaya.

'Hey, hun, you alright? Sorry to barge in so early, but I want to try these on to see what you think, and then, we can go for breakfast and you can dish the dosh on last night, okay?' She flashed the Selfridges bag. It's scrunched up look told of its night stuffed out of sight in a small place.

'New clothes, what's the occasion?'

'Nothing really, I just felt like treating myself.'

The smell, freshness, and excitement only expensive gear can give off stopped any further worries of the 'shopaholic' kind, as Hamdi picked up each garment.

'Wow, lady, you made some good choices…'

'Wait before you judge, I'm not sure on these hot pants.'

Zuleka gathered them up and took off to the bathroom.

A familiar tone sang out from Hamdi's mobile. "Good Morning, Miss Elusive, You x"

Lorenzo! That man had sure got under her skin. She texted back, *Good Morning, Mr frustrating, you*

Her x went there, but then she deleted it, it wouldn't hurt him to think she's still mad at him.

Zuleka appeared in the shorts that left nothing to the imagination.

Hamdi let out a whistle, 'Wow, you're brave for buying those. But you need the right pair of shoes if you're going pull it off '

Zuleka scrambled around in the bottom of *her* wardrobe reappearing with four inch Jimmy Choo's. The effect when she put them on transformed her into a sex-bomb.

'That better? Though, there's isn't a need to impress anyone. In case you haven't noticed, I am going through a drought with guys. Feisal stopped calling me ever since getting it on with that Kuwaiti chick.'

Hamdi grimaced, but knew Zuleka missed the expensive gifts her rich Saudi ex showered her with, more than she did him.

'So, just get yourself a new buddy for the lonely times, God knows there are plenty of men willing to take his place. And those shorts are drought proof. Wear them and watch them flock in, girl.'

'You're mistaking my needs here.' Zuleka stripped off the hot pants and started her wriggling manoeuvre to don her trademark skinny jeans. 'Feisal came with petrol dollars'

'Girl, your gold digging ways never fail to amaze me! But, if that's the case, then I suggest you wait for the Arab season. Come on, I'm starving!'

Hamdi almost laughed, they'd sat on the tall stools in the brassiere munching breakfast rolls, and drinking mochas for at least ten minutes before Zuleka remembered the man related dilemma Hamdi was in.

'By the way, how was your date?'

'Thanks for caring. No, I mean, well, I know I have been going on about my love life of late, but Lorenzo has me in a place I've never been before. Despite all my efforts we only just moved out of first gear. I had me a kiss that promised big things, but that's it. I've found me a hot Italian who's roped in his emotions so he can *explore the real me!*'

'Someone should tell him he's on to a loser there, girl!'

'Zuleka! Be serious will you. I'm like a kitten purring on his lap and he wants none of it.'

Good. Taking it slow is something you need to learn and I think Lorenzo is good for you. Different, but good.'

'He's got under my skin, I can tell you and, not just because he presents a challenge. He's really sweet, just this morning he sent me a good morning text. Honestly, who does that?'

'Decent guys, but you don't know many of them.'

The turmoil started up again in Hamdi at Zuleka's words. Some part of her knew what she said made sense, but it did nothing to quell her frustration. She'd send a nice text to Lorenzo, anyway. Maybe she'd even apologise.

But then, Zuleka's next words riled her up once more and a rebellion set up inside her, 'You shock me, Hamdi. I can tell you've got it bad. You just don't seem to realise you are in a good place, and one I never thought to see you in. I didn't think the day would ever come when someone succeeded in roping you in, girl.'

Roping her in? Is that what was happening? No way! No one roped in Hamdi Ismail!

Chapter Three
The quintessential foreigner

The sound of her mother wailing as if there had been a death in the family put Hani in flight mode. She made it to the front door and just as she had her hand on the yale lock her mother came out of the living room waving a utility bill like a victory flag and lassoing her with her voice, 'How can they do this? Who is it that allows such robbery? What...'

'Who is robbing you, *Hooyo?*'

A burst of angry Somali told her that British Gas schemed and plotted to steal money from her mother's little purse to further line their fat pockets.

Not again! God, why had she pressed the snooze button instead of getting up when she should have done? She'd have reached safety by now!

'*Hooyo*, you really should learn to speak English better, and then you would understand these things.'

Not learning the language only amounted to a third of the frustrations her mother brought down on Hani. Her insistence on bargaining for everything in the manner of her native country also went in to the mixing pot along with her constant health problems.

Going into overdrive her mother demanded Hani ring the gas board and stop this utter outrage and, didn't she have educated children to do these tasks and to translate for her?! To her credit she did manage some of this in English.

Knowing it would be futile to resist, Hani picked up the phone. Her mother stayed on her heals railing about her being firm and not to mumble.

'Yes, I know *Hooyo*; don't you trust me to make a phone call?'

Like a practiced deceiver she omitted one digit as she tapped in the numbers, rolled her eyes to signify her annoyance as she pretended they had placed her on hold for a whole minute, and then, proceeded to read out the details of the bill and have an argument with herself!

'But, this is outrageous, its daylight robbery! Did you say an estimated bill? Are you bloody kidding! What do you think we do here when you make your calculations, run a soup kitchen for the homeless of London?'

Her mother cheered her on whilst plying her with questions to ask the non-existent customer service assistant.

After a moment or two of pretend anger and frustration, Hani calmed herself. 'I agree, that's a good idea, although you should have someone come in to read the meter before all of this... No, that will be all, I'm sorry I got angry, thank you for your assistance...' *Bloody Hell, she felt sorry for an invisible person now.*

'Turns out it's just an estimated bill, *hooyo*, they will send someone out to check the meter before the next one you have nothing to worry about, anymore.'

Talk about escaping the pan and jumping into the fire. Now I'll have to pay the stupid bill! But better that, than have her mother force her to make another call when the final demand arrived.

'I have to go now, *hooyo*, or I'll be late.'

'When will you be back, I am not feeling well, and I need you to translate at the doctor's for me...'

'I have a hair appointment, *hooyo*; you know I'm going to Ayan's cousin's wedding tonight.' Not a pang of guilt entered her as she said this, her mother more than bordered on the hypochondriac level and Hani knew if she didn't get to the salon soon there would not be enough time for them to deal with her hair. Not blessed with the average soft curls of Somali girls; it took hours to stop her looking like Macy Gray on crack.

'Get Salim to take you, he should be back from work by then.' She escaped before her mother could reply.

Their mother ran her and her sister and brother around when it suited her and had done so since their father had died when they were only children.

Even though countless tests had not thrown up anything more serious than thyroid and blood pressure problems, which were well controlled, she used her supposed ill-health like a weapon to heap guilt on them to get what she wanted.

There had been several changes of GP's. All branded as under qualified whenever they didn't find her elusive illnesses. In the end she'd tricked her way into the care of Dr. Patel, an Indian GP. Their aunt, her mother's sister, had raved about him, so in order to get onto his books, her mother, using the typical 'cheat the system' Somali mentality, had registered using her sister's address.

Their first visit to Dr Patel spread light on why Somali women of a certain age favoured him. The man did not possess the assertive qualities of the other doctors and they could dominate him, even her mother, using only her broken English had him cowering. He caved in to her endless demands for blood tests and easily prescribed her with medications, which turned her room into a mini pharmacy. However, the constant stream of visits to his surgery and the faking of phone calls to utility companies made for an easy trade off – hooyo, busy with these distractions hadn't a clue what she got up to or where she went to have fun.

If only it could be that simple with her brother, Salim! Not wanting to dampen her spirits by thinking of him and his one-man crusade to keep her in line, she thought about her encounter with the invisible man on the phone and laughed to herself. *She must be mad! But, she had to admit, ingenious at the same time!*

Chapter Four
The CNN ladies and weddings

'Hey, Hani, look at you! You look lovely. You'll more than pass,' Zuleka beckoned her to where she and Hamdi had saved her a place. As she'd spoken she'd nodded over to where a group of women sat. Old, overly critical and done up to the nines with heavy gold jewellery hanging from their necks and wrists, they represented Zuleka's and hers worst nightmare. 'You'll be the talk of the gossips. They'll have you lined up for some good marriage prospect in no time.'

Hani laughed, but enjoyed the warm feeling the compliment had given her. Choosing something that would satisfy the restrictions of covering herself in a modest way and yet give her some glamour had worked out well and she felt good in her long black dress which she had complimented with a delicate, shimmering red scarf to drape over her shoulders. To finish the outfit off she'd matched the scarf's colour to her killer heels.

'I don't know who invented high heels, but you owe him a lot. Those shoes make you a ten"

'Thank you, both. You look great too, gorgeous, in fact, but hey, what gives with you, Hamdi? I thought you at least would kick against the expected and turn up in your usual freak.'

'I thought I would have a bit of respect for Ayan...'

'I know me too, but having said that, it always surprises me how relaxed I feel when dressed like this and beautiful, too, in a different kind of way...'

'Watch it girl, you'll turn into Ayan.'

'Who's taking my name in vain?'

'Oh, hi, Ayan. We were just having a laugh at seeing each other looking so demure, and saying how we'd done it for you.'

'Me and the gossips, you mean, Hani. But, you look great all of you. I wish I could hang around with you, but you know how it is'

Ayan stayed a few minutes chatting with them, but soon, like a nervous kitten, she said, 'I have to go. You guys have fun, okay?'

'Is she hiding again?' Hani asked as she watched Ayan tuck herself away in a far corner.

'I think so, poor girl. She's dodged several aunts already and those she hasn't have only one question for her, "when will it be your turn, Ayan, surely you must be next?"'

The loudspeakers booming out Somali music drowned out their laughter at Zuleka's mimicking of the aunts. Hani looked around her at the sea of colourful dresses on the dance floor. She scanned the room for anyone she knew, fighting the claustrophobic feeling which always attacked her at weddings.

She hated them, but couldn't escape them. They were the single most important event in Somali people's social calendar. People took mortal offence if someone did not attend their family wedding. Friendships broke up forever over a missed invite. Unless one had a very good reason not to attend, the wise and polite thing to do was to at least make an appearance.

Summer heralded the season for weddings. This month alone she had attended three and each had been a more lavish affair than the last one, even though few could afford it. Most landed themselves in debt for years, and not only them; invited female guests spent a pretty dime on their *diraacs*, the long silky dresses traditionally worn by Somali women. And, since nobody wanted to wear their outfit at subsequent weddings, it sometimes became a nightmare, leading Somali men to joke: *"Unless your pockets are deep, beware of marrying a woman who likes to attend weddings"*

'Watch out there's a camera about! Duck!'

This exclamation from Hamdi brought her out of her thoughts. She did the same as the others and grabbed her bag and dived for the loo.

'Phew, I think they missed us…'

'This time, but we need a film guard on duty if we don't want to end up being chosen from the DVD as future brides!'

'You're right, Hamdi, and I think we should take it in turns. You go first while the camera man is still at his most active. You'll be scanning the room looking for talent anyway, so you might as well keep a watch while you do.'

'I like your cheek, lady! Talent comes to me, I'll have you know.'

'Either way, no-one is trusted with looking out for this lady,' Zuleka said. 'I'm going to keep these eyes peeled. There's no way I'm ending up as a mail-order bride!'

Their laughter echoed around the tiled room and doubling them over, but Hani knew a truth in what Zuleka had said.

Somalis were the Jews of Africa, their network spread worldwide. Someone in any part of the world could quite easily spot them as a potential as the DVD did its rounds for the purpose of mothers who looked to settle their sons.

As their laughter died, make up repair went into top gear before they stepped back into the main hall.

Linking arms with Hamdi, Hani said, 'what about the spies and the gossipers, who's going to watch out for them?'

'We'll all have to be on our guard. Oh, I don't know, these weddings! They're bloody hard work!'

'You're right, its one round of ducking and diving from the cameraman, steering clear of the ladies who might notice something you don't want them to notice, while at the same time trying to have a good time and maintain the interest or flirt with a guy who may have caught your attention. Why do we give a shit?'

'Do we have a choice? I just hope that talent Ayan promised turns up soon.'

'Oh, come on girls,' Zuleka hooked into Hamdi's other arm. Let's have some fun and to hell with the lot of them!'

***

Around 10pm the bride and groom arrived fashionably late, with the groomsmen and the bridesmaids walking behind them. Everyone stood up. The noise of the clapping drowned out the music, but they didn't need it anyway as some began to chant in a sing-song way.

Hani caught Hamdi's eye and had to resist the urge to giggle at the mischief she saw in her eyes. Ayan hadn't told a lie when she'd said the groom's friends were hot and Hamdi could soon forget her passion for Lorenzo, it seemed.

The crowd parted down the middle for the bride to pass by to take her place on stage. Her visible nerves didn't account for her over-pale look. The make-up she'd chosen didn't match her natural skin tone. Being two or three shades lighter it spoilt the over-all look of her stunning, ivory-white dress.

'Damn', Hamdi said under her breath, 'what's with the geisha look?'

Zuleka strained her neck above the crowd to get a better look, 'It looks like she tripped and landed in a pot of white chalk.'

Hani thought the same, but felt a need to flag up the bride's good points, 'Well, the dress is a nice fit.'

'Yes, but the Pat Butcher eye shadow? Boy, has her make-up girl been watching too much of Eastenders or what?'

'I know. The make-up is hobo the clown wrong, but...'

'Oh, that's just you, Hani. You like to see the best in folk. But despite the gaffs, I bet every girl in this room is wishing it was them walking up to those beautiful thrones.' Zuleka's face took on a dreamlike quality, 'Look at her; she's like a little queen smiling at all her subjects. I would love to have all these people clapping and singing words of praises and a thousand blessings on me, it would be so divine.'

'Only for the attention, not what goes with it and you know it, Z. You're nowhere near ready to settle down. Anyway, you're not hearing the claws scratching, girl? The room's full of cats!'

Hamdi was right. The clapping didn't drown out the remarks of those close to them:

'Mash Allah, he is really good looking.'

'I never would have thought that someone like her was capable of bagging such a man.'

'Where do you think they met? I am sure I've seen him in Blue Bar.'

'I don't know, but his face is familiar to me.'

'Anyways, check out that girl over there, I swear she wore that same dress to the last wedding.'

And so it went on topped only by the gold dripping ladies: *'Nayaa*! That white dress is a little bit revealing isn't it?'

'Yes, I wonder where her mother was when she chose to wear such a thing. *Subhunallah,* what is the world coming to?'

'Puuh! And the father is a hajj, imagine that!'

Hani noticed these remarks changed in a drastic way as the mother of the bride approached the ladies looking for their approval.

'*Mabrouk! Mabrouk!* Congratulations! Congratulation!' they chanted in unison.

'*Mashallah*, a beautiful wedding!'

'She looks the picture of health. May her first born be a son and may Allah protect her from the shaytaan himself!'

Hani let out a sigh of frustration. *Allah, preserve me from growing old like them,* she prayed. She looked around her knowing the comments she heard were only snippets of what went around the room as the various small groups that had formed gave testimony to a similar kind of cattiness taking place out of ear shot.

The suffocating feeling re-visited her—being under microscopic lenses of the ever present, persistence cameraman made her want to escape for some air. Stronger than that, an overwhelming urge to light up a cigarette and enjoy its calming effect took her.

'*Haaye, haaye, kaaleya!* Come along! Come along!' exclaimed the bride's proud mother as she marched extended family members, cousins, aunties and uncles up to the stage to have their pictures taken with the couple. Amongst them Hani saw Ayan hadn't escaped despite her attempts to lay low.

Although, Hani knew it would be impossible to convince her, she couldn't help thinking Ayan looked very beautiful. Her light skin glowed with the hint of bronzer powder, and although her black dress did not cling to her figure it did not hide the outline of her curvy, womanly body. As people shuffled around to accommodate everyone on the stage, the shawl around Ayan's neck slipped a little, exposing just a tiny hint of her full cleavage. She pulled it back into place but the sight prompted another round of comments from the ladies: Halimo, who is the girl in the black up there on the stage? *Mashallah*, she has a good look about her.'

'That's Ayan Elmi; the bride is her first cousin from her mother's side.'

'A very good girl, you only have to look at how she has conducted herself all night to see she is marriageable, very marriageable, I'd say.'

'I can introduce you to the mother if you are of that mind.'

'I am. You know my nephew, Hassan? He is getting on in years, but *Alhamdulillah*, though he is doing very well, his career is leaving him with no time to look for a decent girl. The family tires of waiting; perhaps I will mention Ayan to the boy's mother.'

Hani had a mental picture of the guy, an over educated, middle-aged man with a balding spot on his head. Having no time to look for a girl meant he had zero game and probably couldn't string two interesting words together, poor Ayan.

As everything settled down and the cameras clicked and flashed Hamdi leaned towards Hani, 'Ayan was so not wrong with the fresh talent thing. I've seen some blessed brothers up in this joint and I'm ready to do my thing!'

'Good luck with that, but I need a break, I'm going outside to smoke.'

Not a smoker as such, Hani always carried some with her ready for when the occasion arose and she might need one. That time had come.

The loud music combined with the hustle and bustle made her feel dizzy and the busy-bodies crushed her free spirit.

Outside she looked for a secluded enough space to spark up in peace, away from the prying eyes of those who frowned upon smoking as un-ladylike behaviour.

It hadn't been easy as a lot of young people, albeit more young men in sharp suits than women, had flocked out to do the same, but eventually she'd found a somewhere near to the car park.

She must let Hamdi know where the talent congregated. That boy-crazy girl changed men as often as she changed shoes. This thought brought a smile to her face.

'Hey, how you doing?'

Jeez, can't a girl get a little break! Recovering from her fright she fumbled with her unlit cigarette and debated whether she should try and conceal it. The dilemma paled as she looked round and into the sharp green eyes of the handsome, immaculately attired groomsman. Tall, with light brown skin and hair twisted into little dreads that came down to his ears, his friendly smile exposed cute dimples and a flawless set of teeth. He wasn't Somali, but he was gorgeous.

'I'm Izzy.'

His hand felt strong as it clasped hers, 'Hani, nice to meet you, Izzy'

'So what are you doing at this wedding? I couldn't help but notice how tortured you looked'

'My friend, Ayan, is related to the bride.' *She hadn't realised she'd been so transparent.* 'It's weddings. They're not my thing...'

'Really? This is my first time attending a Somali wedding and I am enjoying it so far.'

'Are you a friend of the groom?'

'Yeah, Zak is my mate so when he asked me to be his best man, there was only one answer. Speaking of which, I gotta get back to my duties, but afterwards a couple of us are heading to Penthouse in Leicester square, maybe you and your girls can join us?'

'Maybe...'

He smiled. 'Great, see you later, then?'

Hani watched him walk away. He had a confident swagger about him. *Okay, so maybe weddings weren't all bad. Not when there was a chance of bagging yourself a hot man!*

Finishing her cigarette she walked back inside. Thank goodness it looked as though the reception had reached a point near to the end as the happy couple prepared to leave. She headed for the ladies' room. Something compelled her to reapply her lipstick and spray her clothes with perfume before adjusting her dress. ... *Girl you think you're in with a chance or something?* She laughed at herself as she made her way back to the main hall.

Zuleka, Ayan, and Hamdi stood with Izzy and the other two groomsmen. As she came up to them she saw Ayan introducing everyone to one another. Zuleka spotted her and turning her back to the group grabbed her before she reached them, 'Oh, my God, he is soo hot! Too, too hot!'

Hani laughed, 'Which one?'

'The tall one, with the dimples, his name's Izzy, let me introduce you,' she grabbed Hani's hand, giving her no chance to say anything and pulled her further into the group, 'Izzy, this is our other friend, Hani,' she said, flashing him a brilliant smile before turning to the others 'and, Hani, this is Tariq and Mohammed.'

'Actually Hani and I met earlier...'

'Oh, okay... That's great.'

'Well, now that we are all introduced we should probably make our way.'

Though Zuleka smiled an acknowledgment of Izzy's suggestion her nervous glance around the room as she did so told of her fear. Hani knew it centred on the gossipers or— CNN ladies – AKA reporters, as they referred to them. She took Zuleka's hand and winked at her as she told the guys, 'We'll meet you in the car park in a few moments.'

Izzy went to protest, but Tariq, a Somali, understood and guided him out whilst making gestures as if to say goodbye to them.

'For goodness sake...'

'Hamdi don't. Okay, you don't have to worry about these things, but we do.'

Though they didn't know any of the old ladies personally, if they suspected you of any behaviour that could be frowned upon they would make it their business to discover your surname. Armed with this they could identify your forefathers, your clan, and what town or village you're family originated from. They may not do it in an instance, they may ponder over you for days until their radar hits red, and pronto they have it! The acid tongues of these ladies had ruined many girls reputation. *God how she hated the CNN ladies, them, and their bloody weddings!*

Chapter Five
Dealing with conflict

'This is the shit! Turn up the music, man.'
The beat boxes thumped and vibrated the heavy baseline in response to Tariq doing as Mohammed asked.

'You want one of these, babe?' Mohammed passed around bottles of WKD. Zuleka accepted one and took a sip hoping it would lift her mood. Hani had scuppered her plans by manoeuvring her way into Izzy's car, and he hadn't been an unwilling co-conspirator. Damn!

'Yo, Tariq,' Mohammed's hyped up mood made the car feel like they had already arrived at the club, 'You need to be producing beats like this man. Shit is popping!' He lit a joint, took a couple of puffs, and handed it to Tariq.

'It's soon coming, my man.'

Tariq inhaled the marijuana and stepped on the accelerator.

Fear clutched Zuleka's stomach. Her head jolted backwards. Her scream rasped her throat. 'Slow down!'

Tariq ignored her, keeping his foot well down. His grinning face in the rear view mirror mocked her fear, 'don't be scared, babe'

'I wouldn't be if you'd stop driving like you think you're Lewis Hamilton and this is a formula one track. Cut the speed before you get us all killed.'

He hit the brake. The tyres screeched. Her body jerked forward then backwards. Pain shot through her neck.

A car overtook. She could see the driver fighting with his steering wheel in an attempt to avoid them. He blasted his horn and hurled abuse she could only guess at.

'Is that better for you?' Tariq asked

'Are you fucking crazy?! Pull over and let me get off now!' The handle did not respond to her struggling with it. Frustration and anger gripped her, 'What's with this fucking door?'

Mohammed laughed out loud. 'Child locks, babe. We use them to stop the girls escaping.'

Were these people crazy? If this is their idea of fun, it certainly wasn't hers. 'Let me get the fuck out!'

'Calm down, girl.' The danger didn't seem to bother Hamdi, but she took up Zuleka's cause, 'and you, Tariq. Chill the fuck out and stop the dumbness.'

He turned his head to apologise, 'I'm sorry, I was just playing that's all.'

Zuleka didn't reply to him, afraid if she did he'd look back over his shoulder at her again to come back with some retort. She'd rather he kept his eye on the road and his attention on keeping the car at a more acceptable speed.

As she relaxed the sweet smell of fresh marijuana smoke tinged her nostrils. This was madness; their first joint still smouldered in the ashtray! She needed Hamdi to wake up to the danger they were in. Seeing she held her mobile in her hand she thought a message would be the best way to do this: *What the fuck are we doing here? We don't know these losers and I think I am getting high on their drugs. This is the stupidest thing we have EVER done!'*

One of Hamdi's, *are you for real s*ort of looks came her way as soon as she'd read the text, but then turned away and busied her fingers on the type pad to reply.

'Jam your hype. We are okay. And it's not like you've never smoked weed before.'

Zuleka seethed, but resisted the urge to send another text to point out the obvious. Instead she concentrated on the road, alert to every obstacle, conscious of every hazard now that she was aware of how impaired Tariq's driving skills were.

Twenty or so long minutes passed before the bright lights of Leicester square came into view. The streets teemed with people having a good time. Some of the tension in her released itself at the sight.

The music outdid the laughter and the chatter of the crowds as they entered the club. It vibrated through Zuleka. She followed Hamdi, her thoughts reflecting how Hamdi's lack of care for their safety in the car had affected her. She saw Hamdi's normal behaviour in a different light and a flash of irritation had her thinking, *its obvious the tramp is having a good time; they'll be no getting her home tonight.*

Her face must have registered her negative feelings. Hamdi looked at her, a question creasing her brow, 'What you looking for, girl? Boy, if its talent, you'd better take that hate look off your face. Come on, chill it!'

Regret and shame at her reaction to her friend cooled her anger. Hamdi was just being Hamdi. It was herself that was all tangled up and moody. She sought to detract from it by brightening a bit, 'Nothing, just Hani hasn't arrived, yet. Anyway, I take it you've noticed Tariq isn't as good looking as Lorenzo?'

'Who cares, he has bad-boy charm in lethal abundance, he'll do for me.'

Zuleka looked towards the door. Izzy and Hani walked in. Hani looked cute with Izzy's blazer slung around her shoulders. Jealousy at the casual way they came across the room chatting like old friends, assailed Zuleka. *But then, she'd known Ayan wouldn't come, she never came to clubs. So with only them in the car they would have had time to get to know one another a bit.*

'Oh, I see, you both have the hots for the same guy? Mmm, interesting. Well, you'd better crease your dimples and lose the Ayan look if you want to come out the win-

35

ner, girl.' Hamdi tugged at the scarf Zuleka still wore around her shoulders.

As it slid off it revealed the plunging neckline of her dress and changed her outlook. *Hamdi's right, her behaviour wouldn't endear anyone to her, at least not the type of guy Izzy seemed to be.* She greeted Hani as if nothing bugged her and gave one of her dazzling smiles to Izzy.

'This is my jam,' Hani said as she came out of Zuleka's hug. 'Old school, Sean Paul, I love it, come on let's dance, I'm not sitting this one out…'

Izzy jumped in before Zuleka had a chance to.

'I'm with you, honey babe.' He said as he wriggled into the same movement Hani made.

'Then come on through…'

Hani gave a sexy little twirl as she said this. Her whole body spoke a flirtatious language, though she did try to keep a respectable distance between herself and Izzy. But Izzy wasn't having that, he leaned forward and whispered something into Hani's ear and their bodies swayed closer, moving in perfect sync. His hands clutched her waist igniting Hani into a red hot dancer worthy of the podium.

When the upbeat Sean Paul track changed into a slow jam, Izzy pulled Hani closer to dance a sensual slow rhythm. Their bodies melted into each other. Zuleka could stand no more. She looked around the room hoping someone would ask her to dance. She needed to erase the image. Something had sizzled inside her at her first glance at Izzy. She'd liked how his persona gave off an aura of arrogant male swagger, which contrasted with his soft, chiselled features –a potent mixture.

Watching him with Hani cemented the feelings he'd kindled in her, and set up longings inside her. She wanted it to be her eyes he looked into.

'Hamdi, I'm going to the loo…' Hamdi waved her hand. *Damn! What's with these bitches tonight? One steals my man and the other couldn't give a jot for my feelings.* She stormed over to the ladies. Playing with her make-up, which needed no repair, she talked to herself in the mirror. *Calm yourself. If Hamdi noticed your cranky mood, then others will, too.*

She knew her mood wasn't all down to things not going her way. The CNN ladies had unnerved her. She'd been reckless in coming here straight from the wedding. She should have gone home first and then left again. Make it look as though she'd returned at a reasonable hour. Though, it's still possible she could get away with it. Her parents did give her a little more leeway when she attended a wedding, after all some of them went on all night. But that depended on whether she'd attracted the attention of the gossips. It would only take one of them to mention she left early.

'You all right, hun?'

Hani's question made her jump. She hadn't noticed the door opening or anyone coming in.

'Hey, I'm not treading on your toes, am I? I'm just enjoying myself. If he's got your knickers in a twist, I'll step right out…'

'No, honest, it's okay. I don't deny he's got something…'

'I'll tell you now, girl, it ain't money! He's a struggling wannabe hip-hop artist'

'Hani, how can you think that would influence me?'

This had them laughing to the point they both had repair work to do. As they leant forward, mascara held at the ready, Hani said, 'Tell you what, we both fancy him, but he doesn't sit in either of our criteria's – he isn't worth a mint and doesn't appear to have the intellect, which presses my buttons. So, how about we toss up for him and the winner gets to have some fun until she tires of him?'

'Sounds good. Lady Luck, look down on me…'

The coin spun high. Zuleka held her breath. It fell in Hani's favour. The jealousy reared inside her once more. Hani looked apologetic, but made a joke, 'Sorry, hun, but you know what they say.'

'Yeah, right. Anyway, it felt good. For one moment we held the power over a man's fate. She hooked her arm into Hani's, 'Come on, let's party…'

***

Glad she'd smoothed things over with Zuleka and on a high because winning had given her the freedom to enjoy Izzy's attention, Hani hesitated before unlocking her front door.

The birds twittering their early morning songs sounded like a full blown disco in the otherwise quiet of 5am. Sure the noise would awaken the whole bloody household and alert everyone to her wickedness; her temper rose up at her thwarted attempts to get into the house. *Who's moved the fucking keyhole!*

When at last she found it and the lock yielded the click it froze her. If her brother heard her, Allah help her. She looked at her watch. The luminous dial caught the fading street light. Her heart thudded. Salim, otherwise known by her and her sister as Taliban, is bound to be stirring to attend to his morning prayers.

Her bag seemed bottomless as she fumbled in it. She needed her perfume and some chewing gum. If he even smelled a whiff of alcohol on her breath or clothes it would send him into a hissy fit.

Crossing the hall, she groped her way to the stairs with the exaggerated care of the intoxicated before tip-toeing up. Each step announced her assent in loud creaks that would wake the dead!

'Relax, Taliban is not here,'

Hani's heart dropped to her boots. 'What the hell are you doing up at this time, Luul?'

'This time? It *is* the morning, sis! I'm heading for the bathroom, like normal people do when they wake'

'It's the middle of the night for me. I need my bed. I've had a wicked time. Tell you about it sometime.'

The mother of all hangovers, heralded by a thousand bells ringing in her head, woke Hani some hours later. Gulping water as if warned a drought would descend on them at any moment, she made it to the sofa. Mobile switched off –this was one lady who was not going anywhere today –she snuggled down for a good dose of 'Sex in the City'.

The front door clicked just as the movie had reached the halfway point. Hani's thumping head registered it must be Salim. Her mother and sister would be at her aunties for a while yet.

Oh, God, here we go.

The harmless scene flickering on the screen preceded one her brother would not approve of. The door opened. He did not speak. Like a sergeant of the haram police, he inspected the contents of the film. His Pakistan-style long shirt and short trousers complete with an Islamic hat added to his holier than thou look.

Hani willed him to go, dreading him witnessing what was to come.

But, Samantha let her down. She chose that moment to spy on her hot new neighbour having sex. Gasps of pleasure emanated from the TV. Naked flesh pounded on naked flesh, hands caressed, and all in full view. Hani remained still. Salim dashed across the room. The screen went blank.

'Sister…'

Oh no, he only adopted this formal term of addressing her before he launched into a lecture.

'You shouldn't watch DVD's that encourage sin, your time could be much better spent educating yourself about Islam.'

'Stop over reacting to everything, Salim.' She got up and turned the TV back on, 'people are sinning all over the world are you going to ban me from going outside too just in case they corrupt me?'

'No, but it's my duty to make sure you don't spend your time watching filth, and that you dress appropriately when you go out.'

Oh god, I've led him to his favourite sermon...

'When you dress the way you do, what message do you think you are sending out there? Sister, it is not right. And by Allah, as long as I am the head of this household it will no longer be tolerated.'

'Head of this household?! According to whom?' She resisted the temptation to laugh out loud at the indignation on his bearded face. *He really believes this crap!*

Something about this realisation sparked the fear of him she denied having.

'According to the Quran and Sunnah.'

'You've lost your mind, mate, and if you don't slow your row you're going to end up in an orange jumpsuit.'

The door banged behind her. She tried to tell herself that on any other day she would have argued and mocked him until he had been the one to leave the room in anger, and that her insane headache hadn't given her a choice, but doubting niggles pulsed inside her brain.

When she reached her room her anger abated a little and something like sadness crept into her at the change in her brother. 9/11 had a profound effect on him and some people he met at his university had influenced him. He'd reacquainted with Islam and practised it with the zeal of the new convert. Their once good and harmonious relationship had deteriorated and was now extremely fractious.

The springs of her bed groaned as she flopped down on it. Her brother's pronouncements had become more and more puritanical and bold. She worried about him. *How far would he go?*

Banishing this apprehension she allowed her indignation to rise. *Head of this household, my ass. What's next? Stopping me eating ice cream in public for fear of inflaming the desires of the general male population in Britain, perhaps? As if.*

Chapter Six
Bridget Jones

It had been Hani who had introduced Ayan to them. At first she and Zuleka had agreed that this one wasn't their type at all, but the girl had gotten under their skin and commanded love and respect. Even though you would think at some point in her life she had discovered the Good-Girl guide book and swallowed it whole!

But, tonight there was something in the air; she was acting a little different Hamdi felt sure of that. 'Ayan, you're dressed up like a dog's dinner tonight, what are you up to?' She asked, waving her hand in an attempt to clear the smoke which curled between them. The crowded AA wasn't all to blame for this, Ayan's nerves showed in the way she puffed her pipe.

'I have a date.'

'Oh, with whom, I didn't know you were seeing anyone?'

'I just met him last week at that Somali concert I went to with my cousin. His name is Mahmud, but his friends call him Mike. He seemed decent enough so I gave him my number.'

'He's Somali, but likes being called Mike? He sounds weird to me. Are you sure you want to date this guy?'

'He's not weird, Hamdi. Though actually, using an English name is kind of strange when you think about it…but whatever. I'll see how it turns out. So, you think I look good, really?'

'You're all woman, girl. I wished I had your curves.'

'You mean I am fat…'

'No, she means you are gorgeous. What is it with you?' asked Zuleka.

'Well, I do stand out amongst you size six to zero girls…'

'Yeah, you do, I'll give you that, but in a nice way. I hope this guy is worth it.'

'So do I. I hope he turns out to be more than worth it. I am sick of the hassle I am getting. I need to meet someone and fall in love pronto, and he has to be presentable and suitable so I can introduce him to the family; my mother and aunt are forever giving me hints. They have heard of someone and are keen for me to talk to him, ugh'

She took a good puff of her double apple.

'Hey, steady on, you're already sending more smoke up than an Indian at a pow-wow. You know what I told you. When you're hot on the heels chasing love that's when you're flooded with losers.'

'I know, Hamdi, that's what worries me. Anyway guys, I'm off. See you later.'

After she'd gone they all fell silent, but each knew what the other thought to the point they burst out laughing at exactly the same moment.

'Do you think she has met her knight in shining armour at last?'

'Your guess is as good as mine, Z. She's a mystery one. How she manages to date and keep her virtue intact, I don't know. No wonder she has so many disasters. I think we should leave our mobiles on the table where we can see them; something tells me Ayan may need us, and fast. Bloody hell, what's the girl thinking of…Mike!'

This prompted a spontaneous eruption of giggles.

Relaxed by the smoke and the music, the sudden jangle from Hamdi's phone almost went unheard, but its flashing and jolting movements demanded attention. Hamdi picked it up, studied the call register, and clicked the end-call button.

'Lorenzo?' Hani asked her.

'The slow boat to China, you mean? Yes, that was him.'

'Still not going so well?'

'To tell the truth I'm growing tired of his Mr Nice-Guy persona and I don't think I even find him attractive anymore.'

'That's a u-turn if ever I heard one. So, him wanting to wait to get to know you don't wash, I take it?'

'No it doesn't, Z, that's just crap. I'm fed up with his saccharine attitude.'

'If he's not harassing you for sex it's a sign of respect, and that maybe there is a future in it? After all, it could signify he's looking for commitment'

'Oh please. It's like dating Jonas' brother. We don't even look right together. He's always smiling and happy. I am telling you guys; he's like a walking type two - diabetes and if I stay in this so-called relationship any longer I am going to be sick.'

To Hamdi's annoyance Zuleka pushed it further, 'It sounds to me like you're the one with the problem, Hamdi.'

'Me?! Look, lady, it's been over a month now, what more does he want to know, and what about all this?' Letting her hand map out her curves she told them, 'this is a prime piece of real estate he should be hungry to get his hands on. Is the dude blind?'

This lightened the moment and as the others laughed with her, she exhaled with relief. She had detected a note of discord in Zuleka's voice. *Man, she knew the girl hadn't had any for a while, but that was no excuse for thinking others should go without. Not this baby, anyway.*

'So what are you going to do?' Hani asked.

'I don't know. He doesn't seem to take the hint. I've hung up on him a few times and... Well, the guy's a nutter. Who in their right mind would try to make a lady out of me? The task is futile. Somebody should have told him he would have had a better chance fanning the sun in the hope that it would turn into ice.'

'You should end it then'

'That's just it. I don't know how to, Hani. Look, guys, cut me some slack here. It's him that's not reading the signs. He's just not getting it and I don't want to be blunt with him. He's too nice for that. Maybe I'll just block his number.'

'Hamdi, you've heard of karma, right?' asked Zuleka. 'You can't just go around treating these dudes like crap and expect to get away with it all the time. Lorenzo is good people, I wish you would just give him a chance or one of these days you're going to end up on the receiving end, just you watch'

'Okay, okay. Don't make me feel guilty about it. I'll find a way of talking to him. It's just…'

Her phone lit again, did its shuddering dance and gave out a tone she kept for her friends. 'Oh, oh, here we go. It's Ayan, alias Bridget.

Ayan's dating exploits had earned her the nick-name Bridget Jones. It seemed she was going to live up to the name, as surely she wouldn't ring to say everything was going swimmingly? Hamdi answered, but put the loud speaker on so they could all hear.

'It's awful and I don't know what to do.' Ayan's desperation stopped their giggles.

'Hamdi, are you there? How do I get out of this?'

'How bad is it?'

'For a start he left me standing outside Bayswater station for ages! Finally he turns up wearing Adidas tracksuit bottoms and a baseball cap! And, to top it all off, he's brought me to BURGER KING for dinner!'

'Are you kidding me?'

'Of course not!'

Hamdi made an extreme effort not to laugh, but the others had to move away a bit as they creased up.

'Fucking hell, Bridget, walk out, tell him you've just remembered your favourite TV programme is about to start or something.'

'I tried that, at least, I said I'd got to go as I was expected in early, but he said: "we just finished eating, and man had some plans." Now he's on about one of his mates having a flat nearby and we should go there to chill!'

'Tell him to do one'

'Oh, I don't know why I even bothered to call you! And stop calling me Bridget!' The phone went dead.

Hamdi beckoned the girls back over, 'Right, you two, its batman to the rescue, yet again! Our Bridget's - oops sorry, Ayan's really in the shit with this one, she sounds scared to death. Save me some smoke, I'll be back soon.'

Hamdi walked into the fast-food restaurant. The so-called, Mike leant over the table invading Ayan's space. A repulsive blob of mayonnaise hung on the side of his mouth. Hamdi's stomach turned over.

She marched to them, 'Hi, I'm Hamdi. Ayan, are you ready to go with me or what? I have been waiting for you for over an hour and we are late already.'

'Oh god, you're right, I had made plans with you. I completely forgot, Mike, I have to go.'

'But... Hey, lady, you can't just walk out on me!'

The table jolted. Half empty cups spilled over. Aggression snapped from every part of Mike's body as he stood confronting them.

'Back off, boy. I know people...'

He scorned at this from Hamdi, 'Yeah, well they'd better be tough'

They made a dash for the door. The queue at the counter parted for them, but closed ranks as Mike tried to follow. He pushed his way through.

Outside a policeman stood across the road. Hamdi looked back. Mike had reached the door.

'If you don't want me to shout him over I'd call it a day, brother.'

'I ain't your bro, lady.' Despite his mean tone he hesitated and didn't step out on to the pavement. Then, he shrugged his shoulders. 'No sweat, babe, you're not exactly...'

'Leave it there, man'

Hamdi waited. Their eyes locked. Mike turned and walked back inside. 'Right, come on, let's leg it.' Hamdi grabbed Ayan's arm.

When they reached the corner they looked back. Mike hadn't followed them. 'I tell you, girl, that's the last time I rescue your ass. Have you lost both your mind and vision? What the hell are you doing setting up a date with a dude like him? He's fugly as hell.'

'I met him at night, it was dark and he looked different,' she said defensively

'Then you should have strolled as soon as he stepped out in daylight. He looks as if he just got up and nipped out to get a pint of milk at the corner shop of a bad neighbourhood. Euww!' A shiver of disgust rippled through her.

'Look guys, what were we moaning about before I left?' The laughter at her description of Ayan's date and her rescue had died down. 'I've forgotten, and that's down to you, Ayan. Your dating antics brighten our lives. You truly are our own Bridget Jones, no matter how much you protest. If things get bad and you have a shit date we know all is well with the world and there's no need to panic.'

'You can talk, your dates with Lorenzo are nothing to shout home about and what you get up to, to bed the poor bloke is more Bridget Jones than Helen Feilding could ever come up with!'

Hamdi winked at Ayan. That was the first time she'd heard her stand up for herself. 'Good for you, girl, now, if you used some of that spunk to get yourself out of a hole, we'd be home and dry.'

Chapter Seven
The blowing of Zuleka's cover

Like a veteran CIA agent Zuleka had perfected her game and lulled herself into thinking she'd get away with anything. Being her father's favourite and knowing of the deep love he had for her made some part of her think he would forgive her even if he did find out about her *other* life. She couldn't imagine any other scenario. Some of the fear she'd harboured of her parents discovering the truth had paled and she had allowed complacency to take hold.

Guilt visited her less and less when she stood demure and saint-like while her mother extolled her virtues to anyone who would listen as she told of her pride in her daughter's achievement of never scoring less than straight A's in any exam she took, how she studied and prayed, how she helped around the house and kept to the strict Islamic teachings, and how she could speak Arabic, even though she'd been born in England.

This second language also adhered her father to her more than ever as he considered Arabic the most refined language in the entire civilized world. He had strived to teach it to his other children, but they had showed no interest and now when with her it had become their preferred language of communication and the seal of their bond.

Going over all this in her mind she could paper over the deep crevices of discord inside her and plan the next outing without a second thought to anything in her life changing. She tidied away her study books and sat back. Her body ached for release. Her thoughts turned to the clothes she had stacked in wardrobes in Hamdi's flat and she remembered the micro shorts she hadn't yet worn. *That is something you have to put right, girl.*

Telling her mother she needed to go out for some air and had rung some friends to meet up with her, she left the house and hot-footed it to Hamdi's. Using her key to get in she changed into her jeans and top, rang the others, found they were already in AA and jumped on the bus. Relaxing in the back seat she ignored the attempt by the guy sitting next to her to engage her in conversation and addressed the restless feeling consuming her. She needed somewhere hot and new to do credit to her hot outfit, but where? She remembered hearing something about a new club on the scene, The Blue Bar. She'd persuade the others they should check it out, it sounded perfect.

'What is this place and why has it got you all worked up?' Hamdi asked as Zuleka put the proposal to them, 'You sure sound very excited about it'

'I am, I want to explore somewhere different, and from what I hear this club is it. It is Somali run, and there's a lot of hype surrounding it. It seems everybody but us has already been. I want to put that right and paint the town red!'

'I have no problem with that,' Hani told her.' They turned to look at Hamdi.

'Don't look at me. You know I am always down.'

'Right, Saturday night it is, then. Pick me up at around, 12ish, everyone should be asleep in our house by that time. And, I have my outfit all ready.' She tapped her bag and gave them a wicked smile.

She'd picked out her stuff whilst at Hamdi's. Every item she intended to wear was so tiny she could easily conceal them in her room. Maybe do as she'd done before and pin them inside one of her abaya's hanging behind her bedroom door. She'd have to make sure it was a clean and freshly ironed one. She didn't want the panic of seeing it trundled off to the washing machine. *Imagine her mother's face when she put in a huge black robe and pulled out the tiny pants!*

Every creak in the house had become a familiar, identifiable sound to Zuleka. A stair cracking alerted her to the tread of a footstep. She dashed to the light switch and plunged herself into darkness. Fear trembled through her at the thought of one of her parents coming into her room. She leant forward and turned the lock.

Her sigh released some of her tension, but having someone awake didn't fit in with her escape plans. She stayed with her ear against the door. *Only five minutes to go before the girls pulled up outside in a taxi!*

The noise of its engine ticking over would have whoever was up looking out of the window. She heard the kitchen light go on, and then, water hitting the base of the sink resounded around the house interrupted by, she assumed, a glass placed under the flow. The light went out and the stair noise told of the ascent of the mystery family member. Floorboards groaned their route to the bathroom above and a clink heralded the medicine cabinet opening and closing. *What a time for someone to wake with a flipping headache!* Or perhaps, worse, one of her sisters with the pain of the dreaded curse! How gleeful they would be to discover her secret. A few minutes passed. Sweat formed little beads on her forehead and trickled down her face. She dabbed at them careful not to disturb her make-up.

At last, the groan of a bed taking a weight told her the unknown had settled down again, but what to do? They wouldn't fall straight to sleep. She decided to climb through the window and make it to the end of the road, that way she could stop the taxi before it got to her house.

Walking along a dark street - her own street - in the sexiest outfit she'd ever worn wasn't her idea of fun, but she made it. Her heart pounded as the taxi turned into her road and she prayed it was the one she was waiting for. How awful to flag down one that had a neighbour in and have them open the door and see her in all her glory! Waving like mad she had to take the chance. At first she thought it wouldn't stop as the driver indicated his, 'not for hire', sign, then Hani spotted her.

For a full minute she could not tell them what had happened, but when she did they reacted as she expected them to and they all slumped on their seats dabbing away at their eyes to stop their mascara running.

Back in control they admired each other's choice of dress. Dangerously high heels, short skirt, skinny jeans, and hot pants, all cooed over and, like a trio of high priestesses for glamour, they agreed they looked fabulous! Zuleka forgot her earlier fears and anticipated the night ahead.

They encountered little traffic on the motorway and arrived in north London in no time. The driver had a problem locating the address of the club so Hani whipped out her smart phone to consult Google maps.

'Take the second left and then turn right at the first set of traffic lights.'

Zuleka looked out of the window. Consternation tickled a dread inside her as trendy parts of North London gave way to what looked like an unsavoury neighbourhood.

She caught Hani's eye and saw the same worry mirrored there. Winding down the window she pushed her head out and looked up and down. The street looked rundown and abandoned - a far cry from the vibrant nightlife they had imagined. 'This can't be the place...'

They passed a bunch of corner shops and fast food outlets that suggested a commercial liveliness during the day, but right now most of the grills were closed. The bright neon sign flashing 'BLUE BAR' confirmed they were at the right place and so did the group of young men loitering outside.

'What do you think?' Hani asked.

'Not much, it looks a bit of a dive. Are you sure this is the place everyone is raving about, Z?'

'Make your minds up, ladies. I have another fare to go to and it ain't back where you come from, have I got to pass the job over and take you somewhere else or what?'

'Let's stay now we're here,' Zuleka said eager to get some fun and conscious that if they travelled somewhere else the night would be over. She regretted her decision the moment the taxi did a u-turn and disappeared out of their sight.

A few girls stood in the line to get into the club, but the males outnumbered them. Unlike other clubs there didn't appear to be a formal dress code. Most of the guys wore fitted, American-style, New Era caps, and some had hoodies covering half of their faces. All gave the impression they had entered a 'tough guy' competition.

Zuleka could see Hani and Hamdi looked as concerned as she felt. Hani whispered her fears. 'Guys, I'm not impressed with this. It looks rough as hell.'

'So this is the famous Blue Bar? Wow, people sure know how to exaggerate. I suggest I call Tariq and see where he's working tonight? Then we can just go and hang out with him. My outfit is wasted on this joint'

One of the guys swaggered over, stopping Hamdi's attempt to get her mobile out, 'Check out the Charlie's angels.'

His demeanour told of him being a 'somebody' around here. His style: baggy, hip-hop jeans and an expensive leather Averex jacket gave off an - *I'm to be reckoned with* - impression.

He positioned himself between Hani and Zuleka and put his arms around them.

'How are you beautiful ladies doing tonight?'

Now he'd closed in on them the ugly scar on his left cheek became visible. It held a vivid message of violent encounters. Zuleka stood still. Her body stiff, fear stopped her moving his hand away. An instinctive gesture had her tug at the leg of her shorts willing them to be longer than they were. Everything about her dress now screamed at her the type of girl she must look. She caught Hani's glance and sensed the dread in her.

One of the young men who'd stood with the guy circled Hamdi like a shark would a prey. He leant closer to her and said something. His face hid inside his hoodie. His manner threatened. Zuleka tried to lighten things by answering the question posed a few moments ago. She forced a casual note into her voice, 'We're good, we just heard about this place and decided to check it out.'

'Oh yeah? Lucky for us, then.'

She felt her body compelled forward as he took them to the front of the long queue. The huge Nigerian bouncer ushered them in without subjecting any of them to a search as he did other people.

The not to be messed with guy asked, 'What ends you girls from?'

Zuleka lied: 'South London.'

'Cool, I know some peeps from them ends' he said. 'I'm Gillette by the way.'

'As in the razor blade of the same name?' Zuleka asked him.

'I like her, she's sharp. Ha, me too,' He laughed at his own pun, 'Posh, too. They don't talk like that down the South, what ends you really from?'

He'd steered them to a table and as they sat down he and five of his cronies sat on the other vacant seats.

'I live in the South, but I don't spend much time there. My university is in the west…'

'We got us some university students, fellas. Isn't that grand?' He turned and commanded a youth who walked by, 'Yo, tell the DJ to turn that up!'

The gangster hip-hop blared in the background at burst ear-drum decibels.

Looking around the club, Zuleka felt like she had walked on to the set of a music video. Girls in super-provocative outfits gyrated against each other on the dance floor and the males could have held regular spots on the BBC's Crime Watch. Their saggy jeans pulled low flashed the elastic band of their designer boxers. Poor man's bling, cheap cubic zirconium, and diamante jewellery hung from sweaty necks and elongated ears of both sexes. Everything about the place and those frequenting it put her so far out of her comfort zone she wished the earth would swallow her up.

Gillette sat in the centre seat like a Mafia Don. He pulled Hani close and swung his right arm over her. His eyes trailed Zuleka's exposed thighs. He placed his left hand on top of her left leg near to her crotch. She stood up. 'I'm for the loo, anyone coming. Hamdi and Hani joined her.

As soon as they closed the door she paced up and down. 'This place is a dump and those guys scare the shit out of me. These stupid shorts! Why did I even wear them?'

'Well, they're hotter than hot, I give you that, but they're not all to blame for our predicament.'

'They're not helping though, are they? What do you think we should do, Hamdi?'

'Well, there are plenty of guys here who look scary, but luckily we happen to be with the ones who seem to run the show, that bouncer just let them push the line.' Hamdi leaned over the sink to get closer to the mirror to fix her makeup as she spoke.

'So? What's your point?' asked Zuleka

'My point is: this place is shitty, but we are here, we have the protection of the tough guys so let's enjoy the experience and make the most of it. Walking out on them would be asking for trouble. Let's play nice and have a good time.'

'Have a good time? Are you nuts?' Hani echoed Zuleka's fear, 'you're not the one with some guy named after a razor blade groping you.'

'He likes you guys. So what's the big deal? Stop being melodramatic and take one for the team and maybe we can get out of here okay. It's the curse of being beautiful, enjoy!'

Calm settled in Zuleka at Hamdi's words. 'I have to agree with you on the beautiful bit, but...'

'Oh well, I suppose it won't hurt to play along, but I think we're mad to do so, we should skedaddle, jump out the win...'

A crowd of screaming girls burst into the tiny bathroom, shocking them all and stopping Hani mid-sentence.

Gripped in panic some of the girls crushed themselves into the cubicles that were barely able to accommodate one, let alone four or five!

Crashing sounds and more screams came from the main hall. Hamdi opened the bathroom door and stepped out. Zuleka and Hani followed.

They clung together in disbelief at what they saw. People huddled in corners and under tables. In the centre of the dance floor the posturing Gillette and his boys stood off another gang. Light glinted on their makeshift weapons - table stands and jagged broken bottles.

'What's going on?' Zuleka asked a girl cowering on the floor.

'A fight just broke out between your mate's boyfriend and another gang. Stupid fuckers, this shit always happens! You can't go out and have a good time without some fuckers threatening to kill one another.'

'He's not my boyfriend.' Hani protested

'I don't give a fuck whether he is or not, you were

Sitting with them; right now that makes you a target. Stay the fuck away from me'

'God, NO…!' Hamdi's gasp took their attention from the girl.

Zuleka stared at Gillette. He stood in command, the space around him suspended. The gun in his hand pointed ahead. The shot echoed around the room. Zuleka followed its direction. Plaster spat dust clouds as the bullet ricocheted off the wall, but thank God, it claimed no victim. Her ears blocked out all sound, and then, a high pitched ringing sang the aftermath as the world around them sank into awful, terrified, hollow screams.

Hell took over as Zuleka's senses tuned into the sickening thuds, the cries of pain, and the sight of blood splattering floors and walls. Bodies landed within feet of them with faces mashed to something unrecognisable.

The Nigerian bouncer didn't appear. The first fleeing crowds who made it to the exit found the door closed. Subhana Allah! Terror bringing the bile to her throat like she'd never experienced before, Zuleka stood paralyzed as the awful truth dawned on her. She, Hani and Hamdi had walked into the middle of a gang war!

Despite it all, the music, like some horrific backdrop to a film, played on. She looked at her loved friends and could do nothing. Seeing the feisty Hamdi stood like a baby needing protection, undid her. Tears escaped from her eyes though she did not cry inside. The impact of the destruction and lack of human feeling unfolding in front of her had severed her from her emotions.

'Oh my God, we are going to die!' The words rasped from her dry throat as they huddled together under a table, 'I am supposed to be in bed, and my dad is going to find my semi-naked corpse in a bar!' Mascara stained her cheeks as the fear of the reality of what that would mean dawned on her. *How had she come to think her dad would be okay with it all?*

'Don't worry, Z, if you die I'll get you out of those shorts and change your pretty corpse into the jeans I am wearing.'

She knew Hamdi attempted to reassure them by making a joke, but it didn't go down well.

Hani screamed, 'what is wrong with you, Hamdi?! Can't you see what's going on? Just for once be serious for God sake!'

Before Hamdi could answer the approaching sound of police sirens gave them all some hope. The fighting stopped. Those gang members who could still move headed for the exit, leaving the floor littered with bodies. The door yielded to a gunshot and desperate kicks. Within minutes, and with the sirens still in the distance, a new sound assailed them. That of screeching tyres as speeding cars tried to get away.

Even with the door now open most on-lookers didn't move. The club filled up with cops who ushered everyone outside.

Local residents woken by the noise stood in their pyjamas and nightdresses gazing from their bedroom windows. Their net curtains flapped in the wind and their open window reflected the red and blue lights of parked police cars.

From nowhere, bulbs flashed and voices shouted, 'look this way, what happened? Were you involved?'

Then one light brighter than all the rest froze Zuleka to the ground where she stood like a rabbit caught in headlights. She shivered as her world crashed down around her. The words, 'UNIVERSAL TV' on the side of the huge camera zoomed out at her. She read them over and over as if they held her death warrant.

'SHIT!' Beside her, Hani grabbed her arm as the expletive left her mouth.

'Zuleka, that's the Somali TV Channel, Oh God, this keeps getting worse! Come on.'

She felt her body jolt. She hadn't needed Hani to tell her what she knew already: Universal TV, the station taking the only Somali spoken news into the hundreds of houses where people who had no, or little command of English, dwelt, had just sealed her fate. The image of her stood in the skimpiest of shorts and revealing top, caught in a sleazy, gang-controlled night club would beam into every one of their homes. Homes like her own and that of the CNN ladies.

Chapter Eight
The aftermath

In recent weeks there had been a marked increase in black on black violence breaking out in North London. The TV network had been there on a tip off to witness it. It seemed like a spiteful quirk of fate that on this occasion Zuleka and her friends had been there, too. Hamdi and Hani had blended into the crowd, but she had attracted the cameraman's attention in her micro shorts. Somali himself, he knew what would capture the viewer's indignation. That shot of a provocatively dressed young girl amid the gang violence was his exclusive.

'I am so dead,' is all she could say as they sat on the bench inside the police station awaiting their turn to answer questions on what they had seen.

After giving their statements, which amounted to nothing of substance, the questioning officers offered them a lift home. They refused. Zuleka's situation would only worsen if she arrived home in a police car, not to mention Hani's if Salim saw her.

'I am so dead.' Zuleka wanted to stop saying it, knew it must grate on her friends nerves, but her lips moved and the words formed without her being involved in the process. Her body shook outwardly as well as inside her. 'Oh, God, I might as well stop breathing. My dad is going to kill me.' Tears rained down upon tears already flowing. Nothing could comfort her. Though the others tried she knew they only gave voice to the right words, empty words that spoke lies, but meant in the nicest way.

'I am sure it won't be that bad, hun,' Hani said, putting her arm around her as they sat in the taxi.

'If only I hadn't been wearing these Kyle Minogue hot pants, I might have found a way to explain it away, but…

Look, I am not going back home.' This last sentence held desperation as her fears mounted with each passing second, 'Hamdi, can I crash at yours for a while?'

'Of course you can but, sweetie, I think staying away will make things worse. I mean, the best thing is for you to be there and at least try to explain to them, otherwise the worst is all they will have presented to them, with no defence put up on your behalf.'

'This is the worst! It can't get any worse than this!'

'Why don't we go to Hamdi's, get something warmer on, and then, find a place that's open and grab some breakfast. Everything will look better with some hot buns and coffee. I don't know about you, but I am so cold I can't think straight.'

'You mean you won't leave me, Hani?'

'No, love, I won't no matter what the consequences of Salim discovering me having been out all night might mean. I'll stay until something is resolved for you.'

They sat in Starbucks in Shepherd's Bush. Zuleka now attired in one of her modest abaya's and the others clad in jumpers and jeans. Steaming coffee blurred their vision and warmed the cold out of them. Hamdi argued the point of Zuleka going home, 'Your father isn't going to kill you. Yes, he's going to be angry and disappointed, but running away from home is just going to add to it all.'

Hani joined in, 'Plus, you can't stay away forever, Z. You are going to have to face them sometime and what about your things, your books and...'

'Okay, I'll go back,' her voice came out in a whimper as she gave in.

'Good, now here is how to play it,' Hamdi said leaning towards her, 'Give them a chance to be mad and angry, then try to explain how it is for you and what you want in your life, but if shit really hits the fan and things get out of hand, don't hang around get out and come to mine.'

With legs that almost refused to carry her she tip-toed to her window before turning and waving to Hani and Hamdi. She knew they wouldn't ask the cabby to drive off until they had seen her climb through.

Different prayers and *dua's* crowded her brain as she called on Allah to help her, and yes, to forgive her. *Oh, why hadn't they left as soon they saw what kind of shitty place the Blue Bar was? Why did she even persuade the others to go there?* Usually they avoided all places that were popular with Somali crowds. *Why had she thought the frigging Blue Bar would be different?*

Her frantic mind gave her no peace.

Around noon, still not having gone to sleep, her mobile rang. 'It's Hani, are you all right? Have you seen the news? Have your parents?'

'No, I haven't left my room yet and I don't think they have seen it. It's rare they put the TV on until the afternoon and I think my dad went out earlier. Oh, Hani, I feel like…'

A knock on her door froze her words. Her mother's voice called out,

'Are you okay, Zuleka? Why are you not up, yet?'

'I… I am fine, hooyo.'

'Open your door, daughter.'

'Hold on, Hani, I won't be a mo. At least it doesn't sound like she knows.'

'What's wrong? Oh dear, you look very pale and tired, Zuleka, are you coming down with something?'

Trying to joke, she told her mother, 'I don't know, I am not far enough along with my studies to self diagnose, as yet. No, I'm okay, hooyo, it's like you say, I am tired.' Suddenly she had a flood of sorrow wash over her as she looked into her mother's eyes and thought how undeserving she was of her love and trust.

'Okay, you have a rest and I'll come and check up on you later.'

'Hani? Sorry about that.'

'That's okay, you sound awful'

'I feel it and it just got worse, my poor mother, I am about to shatter her world. Do you think I should just fess' up now, they are going to find out anyways and perhaps its better they hear it from me first?'

'Well, you have time by the sounds of things as they won't see it until they tune in to the box, but think about it some more. Letting them hear it from you doesn't sound like a bad idea, but you know your parents best.'

Zuleka could sense Hani tried to say what she wanted to hear, but what else could she do? What could any of them do?

'No. I can't tell them.' This dismissed her own idea, but she knew she couldn't do it, 'doing so would sign my own death warrant.'

'I'm so sorry I can't help you, Z. I am to blame as much as you, but I don't know what I can do. What if I came round and stayed with you while you tell them?'

'No, that would tar you with the same brush and give them someone to blame, I don't want that. But, thanks for offering. Look, I'm going round in circles here. I'll call you later when I've figured something out.'

Her agony went on. Her mother visited her every fifteen minutes or so expressing more and more concern for her. The afternoon arrived. The house had settled down to a peaceful quiet. The time for the news passed. Nothing. The phone rang. No one answered it. Her mother must have fallen asleep. No one napped like her mother, often a cause for mickey-taking, but today a blessed relief. The call would have been one of the gossipers. Zuleka felt sure of that.

She tried to guess where her father was. He would have spent some time at business and some at the mosque, but wherever he was the news hadn't yet reached him either, it couldn't have done.

This thought had only just settled in her when the peace of the home shattered and the angry tones of her father bellowing from the top of his lungs let her know the time had come to face the music.

With resignation built in her by the hopelessness of her situation she forced herself to go to him. Each step she took made her know how a condemned man felt as he walked towards the gallows. Like a contained storm her father stood in the middle of the living-room.

'Yes, *abo*?'

'You dare to call me father! You, who is nothing but a common whore, you whose naked body paraded before me and everyone in the coffee-shop? Everyone in the whole world, even... You on the TV screen...' He stepped nearer to her, 'you, a vile creature not fit to step into my house?!'

His hand lashed out. The stinging blow reeled her backwards.

'This is what you do behind our back? You parade here like an angel of sweetness and mercy and when we are not looking you mock us by going to nightclubs and spreading your legs for dogs.'

His screaming had deadened her fear, deadened everything in her. '*Abo,* it wasn't like that, I don't even know those gu...'

Her father, his face purple with rage lunged at her. His punches bruised her small body. His kicks sunk into her bringing agony into every part of her. She vomited. Tears mingled with her snot. Blood oozed from her nose, deep cuts opened up exposing her bones. Her screams turned to moans. Trying to shield her face and body proved useless. She cowered on the floor. She had turned into an animal, a lowly beast from the gutter. A filth-ridden rodent. She deserved nothing less.

The door opened and her mother came in. Zuleka knew in doing so she would be defying her husband's orders. She had a blurred vision of her mother pulling her father. She heard her plead with him to stop.

'Subhannallah! That's enough!' She crouched on the floor next to Zuleka. *Did she know what had happened? Would she protect me like this if she did?*

'Ya rabb, Oh lord, what have you done? Why…?'

This question whispered close to her cheek answered the first part of her question.

'Believe me, madam, this is not enough, but it's the only thing I can do.' Her father didn't sound like her father, his voice held disgust and hate now he wasn't screaming. This broke Zuleka more than the beating had done.

'She has shamed us beyond repair! She is in no child of mine. Get her out of my sight. GET HER OUT!'

'Not until you tell me what is going on. What has she done?'

'I sat in my local coffee shop playing dominoes. The TV played in the background. I took no notice until the room went quiet. I looked up and there was our daughter, her semi-naked body filling the screen. She stood outside a night-club…'

As the story went on Zuleka saw her mother's face twist into disbelief, then horror, and then stretch into an ugly bitter picture of someone not capable of loving again as the impact of what her husband told her registered.

'Oh the curse! The shame!' she cried as she walked up and down, the injuries of her daughter forgotten, or not cared about anymore. Her ranting told of her position in the community, the centre she ran, how she had become a leader amongst the women, but now those same people she wanted to lead and advise were going to whisper about her and look at her with pity.

Zuleka felt loneliness engulf her. Unable to move, the only blessing she could count was her father had stopped kicking her to death and had turned his attention to consoling her mother and himself.

They left the room. Nothing happened. The silence emptied the space around her. Not even her sobs filled it. The door opened. Safi walked in, she had a bowl of water, and despite Zuleka's protests she dabbed and bound her wounds before helping her to her room, 'Oh, sister, how could you? You have brought shame on us all...'

Through her bruised lips she tried to say how sorry she was, but Safi surprised her by saying, 'There, there, *habiba*. I forgive you. I have the same feelings as you, but would never have the courage to do as you do. I've known for a long time and I prayed you wouldn't get caught.'

The next few days passed in a haze. Zuleka's body took over her mind. Pain wracked her. Fever shook her and then, boiled her. Nothing passed her lips. Cracked and dry, she could not open them enough to take anything. Safi tended to her, cleaned her but rarely spoke. But, once when Zuleka had tried to protest she said, 'It's alright, *habiba*, they are not stopping me from helping you. They think I will learn a lesson from it, but little do they know I hate them for what they have done to you. Why can't they see we no longer live in their world? If they wanted us to, they should not have left Yemen.'

These words gave her hope as well as fear. For some reason the last thing she wanted was to influence her sister to follow the same dangerous path she had trodden, but it helped to know she understood.

'Cou...could you get my phone, Safi?'

'I can't, they have confiscated it.'

Sinking back into her pillow it seemed to her the Zuleka she had been had gone forever. She allowed the darkness to descend like a comforting curtain, hoping it would carry her off to a far distant place they called heaven. In lucid moments she wondered what Hani, Ayan, and Hamdi were doing. In others, she thought about the eventual outcome for herself, but the veil that blanketed her mind also let in happier memories of her uncomplicated childhood.

After a week, her weeping mother came into the room. Zuleka thought if she had died in an accident or of an illness her mother would cope better than seeing her fall from grace in such a spectacular manner.

'I…I am sorry, hooyo, I…'

'What good is that? Your reputation along with ours has gone. Your father has resigned from his position at the mosque.'

'No… Why?'

'His role was to be the moral compass of this community, to lead and instil the correct Islamic values, but how can he do that when it's clear to everyone he cannot lead or instil those same values in his own house?'

'What will happen to me…?'

'You…You? We have plans. Nothing will mend what you have done, but people need to see you have turned a new leaf.'

Zuleka watched her mother leave the room. A pain, different and more damaging, settled in her heavy heart. Her mother hadn't shown a shred of pity or love for her. How could that be? She'd spoken of Islamic values, but what about the forgiveness taught in the Quran? Or has the judgement of the community become more important to her?

A scream of frustration rose to her throat, but she didn't release it. If she did she would not be able to stop screaming until she breathed her last breath. She didn't want to die. Her dreams of heaven had come from her desperation. She wanted to live. She wanted to fight against whatever punishment they were dreaming up for her. She had to. She had to do something.

Chapter Nine
Planning Zuleka's escape

The month since Zuleka's confinement had passed without much enjoyment for Hani, Hamdi, and Ayan. When they did meet up they found nothing else to talk about other than Zuleka's plight. Even Ayan had stopped her dating antics, which testified to the truth of what Hamdi had said and further put a damper on everything.

'Look, you guys, I know it is not a good thing to do, but we have to get our lives back to some normality'

Hani looked up and took the pipe out of her mouth. Not even the double apple had any appeal these days. 'How do we do that, Hamdi?'

'Well, I've made a start. I bumped into Tariq, you remember, that guy we met at your cousin's wedding, Ayan?'

'Yes, but what about him? I know you girls went off with them, but I thought nothing had come of it.'

'It couldn't with the way things are, but Zuleka wouldn't want me to live like a hermit now, would she?'

'What have you done, Hamdi?' Hani could sense Hamdi had done something without consulting them. Part of her wanted her to have moved things on, but another part of her didn't think they could whilst Zuleka remained in the fix she was in. They'd had no contact and had no real knowledge of what had happened to her. Rumours told of a terrible beating amongst other speculations, but no one seemed to know for sure. Ringing Zuleka's mobile had proved fruitless.

'I invited Tariq and his friends here.' She looked up at the clock, 'They should walk through the door anytime soon.'

'Oh, no. Not for me. I'm off.'

'Ayan, wait.'

'No, I'm sorry. You enjoy yourselves, but me? I've had it with guys'

'What about that guy, what was his name? Siddiq, that's it. The one your cousin introduced you to?' Hamdi asked.

'Especially not him'

'But, what's wrong with him, you have to kiss a few frogs before you get your prince, Ayan. You can't give up that easily. Give him a try at least.'

Hani smiled to herself, no one believed Siddiq was a prince, but to have Ayan not dating on top of everything was a disaster and the reason she suspected Hamdi persisted in trying to persuade her.

'If you fall off a bike you just have to get back on it as soon as possible if you are ever going to learn.'

'Oh, Hamdi, give it a rest. I don't want to date him or anybody else at the moment. If you guys think he's got so much potential, then one of you can go out with him. I'll be happy to arrange it.'

If Ayan didn't have such a determined look on her face Hani knew Hamdi would have pressed the point further, but whatever was on her mind troubled her too much for them to press the point.

In the aftermath of Mike and the subsequent losers that followed him Ayan had declared she would take a break from dating, but none of them had thought it would go this far. She got up, said her goodbyes and left.

'Well, she said she needed time out to recuperate before she lost faith in mankind all together, but it's sad to see she means it and, by the sounds of her, means to keep it up for a long time.'

'I know. With no Zuleka, and no Ayan and her dates, life stinks at the moment. I don't even think I am in the mood for meeting up, even with someone as dishy as Izzy.'

'I suppose how things are it would seem like you are taking advantage?'

'What, because Zuleka had the hots for Izzy, too, you mean?'

'Yes, I know we use the old adage all is fair in love and war, but well…'

'Oh, we sorted that; we tossed a coin on it'

'What, you mean you actually tossed a coin to see who should have him? I like it, lady. Yeah, right on'

'Well, he's not a serious prospect for either of us, but…'

'You both fancied the pants of him, right?'

'Yeah, but that's all it was, none of us has his type on our CV as part of our ambitions for the future.'

'Way to go, girl. The more I hear the more I like. Men are for us to use not the other way around.'

'Shhh, they're here now.' Hani had seen Tariq with Izzy close behind him entering AA and she indicated as such to Hamdi.

This being their first meeting since the wedding reception, Hani thought Izzy looked just like she remembered him, but unlike that day when his appearance had been impeccable he now sported a six o'clock shadow, which made him look even hotter. *How was that possible?*

'How are you ladies doing?' Tariq strolled over to them. He had a toothpick hanging from the side of his mouth, with that and his trilby hat and stylish clothes he looked like he was making a bid for the GQ magazine cover. 'So, this is the place you've been hiding in. I wondered why we have never bumped into one another before.' He sat next to Hamdi and she moved a little to the side to further accommodate him.

'Yeah, we kind of love Abu Amin. It has so much…character.' Hamdi told him.

'Character?' Izzy looked around AA's shabby interior decor with distaste, 'if you say so, but I would not have predicted you guys to hang out in a place like this.'

Hani thought their opening words probably marked the difference between Izzy and Tariq. Tariq seemed charming and always ready to flatter, which she imagined lead girls to adore him. Whilst Izzy did not hesitate to say what he thought, even if it did offend, and gave the impression he knew they would adore him anyway. But both, she suspected, wouldn't bat an eye at breaking a girl's heart. This observation put her on her guard.

'What's your flavour?' Izzy asked.

'Apple and mint.' Hani passed him the shisha pipe.

'My favourite.' His eyes held her gaze as he exhaled. Thick grey smoke covered his face. *Is he flirting with me?* She couldn't tell. At that moment her mobile lit up, its chime hailing a text message. She fumbled in her bag for her specs. *Fuck, why couldn't she wear contacts like others did? Even though her glasses were stylish they still made her look nerdish!*

'What are you looking at?' Izzy hadn't taken his eyes off her.

'Nothing…Well, you actually, you look very geeky in those glasses. Try contacts.'

'And you are the epitome of cool, I suppose?' The uninteresting message concerning downloads she could have added to the irritation she felt at having admitted an interest in him. And as for flipping a coin to win her right to his attention, she must have been nuts!

'Uh, uh, don't go there,' Hamdi came to the rescue, 'you're on to a sensitive topic.'

'Sorry I didn't know that,' his laugh told her he was far from sorry. He leaned forward. Holding her gaze he whispered, 'Anyway, I am a long way from cool. Tariq is the cool one. He's got your girl tuned in already.'

Hani turned her head, glad to break the spell which held Izzy's eyes on her. Far from how it looked, she knew Hamdi's actions of listening intently to something Tariq had said was part of her act when it came to flirting.

'Smooth, very smooth, nice change of subject just when most needed, now if you don't mind.'

'Look, we've got off on the wrong foot.'

'Hey, Hani, don't forget you need to cash in on that win,' Hamdi winked at her.' She smiled back and felt better. Yes, she needed to conquer this one, just for her own satisfaction. She'd cool her irritation.

'What was that about?' asked Izzy.

'Oh, something and nothing...' She looked into his eyes, 'Anyway, what have you been up to since I last saw you?'

She could turn on the charm when she wanted to. She'd pull this arrogant sod down a peg or two. Lead him on and...

'Babes! I didn't expect to see you here!'

The loud exclamation cut into Hani's thoughts.

A petite blonde with an Essex accent and perky assets bouncing around her chest with her every movement, plonked herself down next to Izzy.

'I don't usually come here, in fact up until this evening I hardly knew about this place'

Hani saw embarrassment creep into Izzy's flushed cheeks and wondered if being caught here or bumping into the girl was causing it. He introduced her as Emma, an old friend of his.

'You old dog! I've been demoted to the rank of an old friend, now?' Emma poked him in the ribs. 'How long has it been since I heard from you, huh? That's no way to treat a lady, Izzy.'

'Busy times. You know how it is.'

Emma might have been many things to him, but 'friend' was not one of them, Hani decided as she watched her flirt with Izzy while ignoring the rest of them. The way she went on about friends they had in common and what they were all getting up to it seemed to Hani, Emma had no intention of leaving anytime soon, which left her feeling like a third wheel.

Exasperated Hani grabbed her coat and said her goodbyes. *Izzy, the arrogant sod, didn't even acknowledge her leaving!* Angry beyond her own understanding she stormed out of AA.

Outside she fumbled for her phone. Her anger had made her walk straight out without asking them to ring a cab for her.

'Hani, Hani…'

Hani reeled around at the sound of the urgent whisper. She could see no-one. A finger of fear crept up her back. The female voice had sounded afraid.

'Hani, it's me, Safi, Zuleka's sister.'

'Where are you? You scared the shit out of me…'

'Over here, just around the corner of the building. I daren't show myself in those bright lights someone might see me.'

Hani walked in the direction of the voice. Her heart pounded her hope this was not a trap. She'd heard of girls lured by another female into a dark alley and finding a gang waiting to mug and rape her, but then, if that was the case, why would the girl use Zuleka's sister's name and how would she even know she knew Zuleka? When she reached the corner, she saw the unmistakeable outline of a Muslim female.

'Zuleka needs your help. But, I am very afraid. They may be watching me as I am tending to her. You see, at first my parents thought it would teach me a lesson, to see what they would do to one of their daughters for showing such disobedience, but now they are beginning to suspect me of sympathising with her. I have to be careful. I have to treat Zuleka rough when they are about.'

'I understand, Safi. What can I do? How is Zuleka, is she hurt badly?'

'Yes, but she is getting better. Much better than we let our parents know. Hani, please meet me in the café near to the university Zuleka and I attend. It is called, Babylon's.'

'I know it. I used to go there when I was at uni. When?'

'Tomorrow, I will come out of my lectures at 2pm. And, Hani, wear the hijab. And if it is possible, if you have a spare phone, can you bring it with you?'

'Yes, I will. Don't worry, Safi. And, thank you. Give my love to Zuleka.'

'I will.'

As she said this she turned and fled up the alley. Hani watched her go then stood alone for a moment unsure what to do. She hadn't asked if Hamdi could come along and Safi hadn't mentioned her, but still, she felt she should tell her about it all. Besides, Hamdi is likely to have a spare working mobile.

Why hadn't they thought of that before and smuggled one to Zuleka somehow? But then, it was all right to think like that now she knew the situation, but before, if she had admitted it to herself, she hadn't really known if Zuleka was still in this country or not. Relief sank into her. The news hadn't been good, but it hadn't been all bad. Zuleka was still alive, she was still here and what is more, she was ready to put up a fight, why else would she contact Hani?

Hamdi's reply to her text came just as the taxi arrived. *Bloody hell, this is serious. What do you think she is planning? Where are you, can you meet me at home, I am leaving right now.*

'Can you wait a minute driver, there's another passenger…'

Hamdi pushed open the café doors. 'Oh, you haven't gone!'

'No, jump in. Safi met me outside here before I'd rung for the cab. Let's get to yours. What have you done with lover boy?'

'I made a quick date with him and left telling him a friend was in trouble and needed me. It was a wrench I can tell you, girl. That Tariq already showed some good signs. He's hot for me! Zuleka had better be worth it!'

The atmosphere in Babylon buzzed with noisy students. Remembering it from old, none of it came as a surprise to Hani. Every nationality, culture, and religious persuasion piled in with no heed for any normal conventions. Here you could say, lay the true spirit of a multicultural society.

'There she is, Hamdi.'

'How can you tell? You can only see her eyes'

'I just can. Anyway, she nodded her head at me and she was staring at the door when we came in.'

Hani adjusted her head scarf. As she did so, she reflected once again how comfortable she felt wearing the traditional dress.

'Safi, you know Hamdi don't you?'

'Yes, hi…'

Safi appeared relaxed, but then she was in her comfort zone. Somewhere acceptable and as she and Hamdi joined her they did not stand out from the rest of the crowd. To all appearances they looked like three Muslim girls gathering for a chat. They wouldn't attract attention or be commented upon.

'How is Zuleka?'

'I have to tell you, it is not good for her. My father beat her badly. She was in and out of consciousness for many weeks with only me to tend her. But now she is much better.'

Shock held Hani silent. Poor Zuleka. So the rumours had been true! But for her father to beat her so ferociously as to render her unconscious?!

'She has to escape. My parents are planning to marry her off to a cousin in Yemen'

'Yemen!' Hamdi and Hani spoke at once and not in the hushed tones Safi used.

'Please, you must keep quiet. I do not know for sure, but I think my dad may have asked some people at school to keep an eye on me, this business with Zuleka made him really paranoid. Talk about something else for a moment. Start to laugh or something.'

Beginning to feel like she had a clandestine meeting with the KGB Hani's skin pebbled, she looked around. Hamdi seemed to find the whole thing funny and fulfilled Safi's wish by laughing out loud, but not in a pretend way.

'For goodness sake, Safi, this is Britain. There are no spies here. If there were we wouldn't be sitting here now, they would have hung, drawn and quartered us years ago. Wouldn't they, Hani?'

Safi looked taken aback.

'Oh, don't mind her she doesn't live under any restrictions. She doesn't like to cause a scandal though and is the first one to avoid it. But, I know what you mean, Safi. What does Zuleka think of your parent's plan?'

'She doesn't know. I overheard my father speaking to my uncle…'

'You mean it has gone that far? My God, this is serious. If Zuleka refuses, how can they save face after having arranged it? Zuleka *is* in trouble, *big trouble.*'

'I know. I am not pleased with my sister, but I love her and I understand her, even though I could not do as she did. I know it would kill her to be sent to Yemen.'

'It would kill Zuleka to send her to rural England let alone Yemen!'

'Hamdi, making wise cracks isn't helping. What do you propose Safi; you have obviously thought this through?'

'I don't have a specific plan, but I thought if she at least had a mobile and could contact you, my parents look at mine all the time and scrutinise the bill when it comes in, so we daren't use it to get in touch with you. But, I know when they tell her of their plans Zuleka will go mad and may even provoke my father into beating her again or even…Well, he could kick her out and if he doesn't she would run away. I wanted her to have somewhere to go.'

'That's easily sorted, she could come to mine. I don't have a spare room, but she could sleep on the couch until we found her somewhere. And here, take this mobile to her. I have loaded our numbers on it for her and put £20 credit on it. I can top that up from my phone if ever she needs it.'

'Thank you, Hamdi.'

'Tell her we are with her every step of the way. Don't wait until your parents give her the news. Put her in the picture as soon as you get home. That way she can have time to get her head around it all and maybe pretend to be pliant, so she doesn't get beaten, and then escape. Tell her we'll have a taxi at the end of her road the moment she texts to say she needs it.'

'I will. Thank you, Hani. Now, cover your faces as you leave, no one must connect me with any of this. I…I mean, if ever they caught her with you in the future. It must not be that I am known to have been with you. There are a lot of people in here that know me and keep looking over. They haven't seen your faces as yet. None of them would mean me harm, but a word in the wrong place that I met up with some girls they didn't know…'

Poor Safi. Her body shook. Her anxiety leaked from her every gesture and in the tremble in her voice. What she'd done today for her sister took a lot of courage. Zuleka could be proud of her.

Outside, neither Hani nor Hamdi spoke. Hani felt sick in the pit of her stomach, like when a scene in a horror movie really scares her. They walked towards the street where they knew there was a bus stop. Keeping their faces covered they remained silent until they had turned the corner and were out of sight of the café.

'For God sake, look at us, Hani. This is a joke!'

'It is anything but a joke and you know it, Hamdi. Zuleka could…'

'Don't say it… Don't. Things like this don't happen to us.'

'Not to you, maybe, but…'

'Not here, surely?'

'Don't you read the papers or listen to the news? It happens, girl.'

'You're scaring me. If she comes to me…'

'Yes, you could be in danger, too.'

'Well, fuck it. Let them try. Let them try'

'I know you mean well, but Hamdi, you should try to suss out a place for Zuleka. There is no point in both of you being in danger.'

'I know. My place isn't big enough for the two of us anyway, but how will she afford it?'

'We'll cross that bridge when we come to it.'

Hani's mobile rang a dozen times over the next few days. All calls from Zuleka. And she knew the same happened for Hamdi who'd already had to top up the credit on Zuleka's mobile. One moment she sounded strong and in control, the next she wept and Hani couldn't lift her. But, the moment her mother and father confirmed to her what Safi had told her, the call for the cab came through.

'Now, Hani, now. Come at once. Don't let me down.' Her sobs made it difficult to understand her.

'What has happened, Z...?'

'They...they had me in the living room and told me. They had airline tickets the lot! I... I told them I would not go through with it, that I would go to the law, or if I couldn't I had friends who would. My...my father called me a whore...a whore, oh, Hani!'

'Did he hurt you?'

'Not physically, but...but how can he have lost all the love he had for me? He...he told me I had to leave his house and never call him father again... never... How could he... I thought he loved me...'

'He does. He is hurting as much as you, I am sure. They must be thinking the same as you, love. Wondering how you could have brought such disgrace on them. They had a different upbringing , it is all so alien to them, but at least he isn't taking it any further than throwing you out and maybe in the future...'

'No, I know once I walk out of here I do not have a family. How will I cope without them, Hani?'

'We will help you, Z. Just get out of there before he erupts again and forces you to go to Yemen. You know what he is capable of now, so don't give him the chance. I am on my way to you and will meet you at the end of your road in about fifteen minutes. Just make sure they do not follow you. We have to protect Hamdi. You can trust Safi, can't you?'

'Yes, she will be fine. The way it has happened, with my father insisting I go, they won't question her. I am glad really. Thinking about it, if I had played pliant as I had planned and then left, they may have thought she had something to do with it.'

'Good. I wouldn't like to think she would suffer.'

'No, she has been the best sister to me. I am going to miss her. She is so brave, Hani.'

'So are you, Zuleka, so are you, love.'

Chapter Ten
New relationships

'Getting Zuleka to come here is a no-no, Hani. I've tried, but she is too scared. And, I for one don't blame her. You know we have to dodge in and out if we see someone from the community pass by as it is, she can't take that risk.'

'I know, but she is settling down with you, that's one thing. Has she sorted anything out about how she is going forward?'

'Yes, she went to university yesterday and she can still catch up, they've given her CD's and reading material and there are some lectures she wasn't scheduled for, but they have suggested may be useful. The change in her is amazing since she found out about all of this. She worked at home today and intends going in tomorrow.'

'What about money?'

'Well, it will become a problem, but she can't look for a job, yet.'

'I can help, Hamdi. I have a decent amount in savings. I can loan her from it and won't need it for a long time.'

'That's great, Ayan, and really kind, you're some lady, full of surprises, girl. I'll tell Zuleka. And don't worry, I don't think she will be spending it on flippery, she is a changed girl.'

'Well, that's the practical side of her life sorted, what about the fun side?'

'I've thought about that. I've kept in touch with Tariq. He seems to have his finger on the hottest parties in town, and I mean hot, the crème de la crème of society, kind of parties. I'll ask him to fix something up for us. Something really different where no-one knows us. That should bring the girl out. She has to get her freak on sometime, it keeps winking at her from her wardrobe.'

Hamdi loved how Hani and Ayan laughed at her. It made her feel they were all turning a corner.

'Well, that's me. There's some more apple in that pipe if anyone wants it, I've got a dinner date to attend.'

'Ayan! You never said, who is it?'

'It's you know who. But I swear to god if he turns out to be lame then I am swearing off men for good.'

'Siddiq?'

'That's the one, Hani'

'I am sure it will be fine.'

Hamdi heard the note of glee in Hani's voice. She didn't blame her. Did this mean everything would come right again? It was a start anyway. 'Good luck, Ayan. I really mean that.' She told her.

As the door closed behind Ayan both girls giggled. It felt good.

'Do you think he will take her to McDonalds for dinner?'

Hamdi's giggle turned to a belly laugh, 'I hope not. That would just be too much, but if he does and if shit hits the fan I will not be the one rescuing her again. It'll be down to you, Hani.'

'We'd better keep our phones in view anyway.'

'Actually, Ayan has scuppered things a bit for me. I did have another date with Tariq, but I can't leave you alone…'

'Another date?! I thought you meant you'd kept in touch by phone.'

'I know, with everything going on this last week I just let it slip by. You didn't want to be listening to tales about my love-life.'

'Trust me, I do. I want everything to return to how it was, annoying bits as well.'

They laughed at this, but Hamdi knew what Hani meant and she wanted exactly the same thing.

'Well, it was just one date. He took me to this divine place. He had to work. He's a DJ as well as an events promoter for a number of exclusive clubs. You should see him with his too cool for the office swagger. He's a real party animal and promises to have traits of that in other ways, too.'

'Promises? You don't know, then?'

'One thing I learned from Lorenzo is that the longer you make them wait, the keener they get. I would have dumped his ass long ago, but his taking it slow always left me wanting more. That was a good thing, and I am goner put it on play here.'

'I hope it works for you, and it's good to hear. You go, hun, I'll pop round to yours and have a chat with Z and I'll text Ayan to give me a call, not you, if she needs help.'

***

Not able to describe the feelings inside her, Hamdi let herself into her flat. She couldn't believe the clock down the road only chimed twelve times. But, though it hadn't lasted long as she hadn't felt dressed enough to go on to the nightclub Tariq headed for, the evening had been great. This guy did something special to her. Made her tingle inside, and yet, he smacked of trouble. She could read that much.

She had a moment's disappointment as she realised Hani had left and Zuleka had curled up on the sofa. Her small snores told she'd drifted off into a deep sleep. *Damn, I needed to have me a gossip session.*

Feeling unsettled she welcomed her phone ringing as she reached her bedroom. The screen flashed Ayan's name. *She can't want rescuing this late, surely?*

'Hamdi, sorry. I had to ring. I've had a long chat with Hani, but it wasn't enough. I have to say it all again!'

'What? Do you know what time it is, Ayan? Oh, never mind. I'm not ready to settle, dish the dosh.'

'He took me to a lovely Indian restaurant and we talked and talked, like old, reacquainted friends. And we had so much in common and shared the same sense of humour. Oh, Hamdi, it was wonderful...'

'Really? Actually I...'

'Yes, really, it was so good I didn't want to go home after dinner so we drove around London and ended up in Westminster. Oh, Hamdi, it looked beautiful at night. And we walked around until we reached the Millennium Bridge...and then... Well, we kissed...'

'You mean he kissed you?'

'No, well yes, he did, but then, I kissed him back!'

'Ayan, you fast lady, you!'

'I know. I'm dizzy with happiness. But, we did have a fright. I forgot the time and we had to race back to try to beat my father home. We only just managed it.'

'Thank goodness for that. I couldn't go through a repeat performance. You may be in love, lady, but you make sure you stick to your father's rules.'

'How do you know?'

'Know what?'

'That I am in love, I never said that. That was coming next. But it's true, Hamdi, I am. I'm completely and utterly in love.'

'No more Bridget Jones, then?'

'No, no, unless, well, you do think he will feel the same, won't he?'

'Without a doubt. And you know that, girl. Now, say goodnight. I need my bed.'

'Goodnight, Hamdi. I hope you soon find someone to feel like this about, I hope everyone does.'

I have, girl, I have.

Chapter Eleven
The clouds begin to lift

AA had a relaxed feel about it. Hani looked around. The few people in the room sat chatting, but not in a noisy, intrusive way. In their group, Ayan held the attention telling them she understood the expression: walking on air. Hani thought she had a new glow about her as she recounted every minute of the latest glorious date, relating everything Siddiq said and did, what he wore, what she wore. *This man sounded too good to be true, they needed to meet him:* 'Come on, Ayan, it has been two months now, time to wheel him out and introduce him to us. There is no way we could jinx the relationship, if that's what you are thinking.'

'I don't know...it's still early days yet.'

'It's me isn't it?'

'No, Zuleka, don't you even think that. It's, well... You're all so beautiful...'

'For god sake, Ayan, stop thinking of yourself as the ugly duckling! We, the so called beauties, envy you. You, girl, have found what we want. Enjoy your moment of triumph; don't taint it with unfounded fears,' Hamdi hardly stopped for breath before she turned on Zuleka, 'And as for you, thinking every little thing is your fault, you need to get over it, lady. You've had a bad deal. Your life has gone down shit loads to what it was, but only you can turn it around. We've lost Bridget Jones, we've lost fun-loving Zuleka, there's only me holding the side up with my love troubles.'

'Well, good luck with that, Hamdi. But, remember what I told you about karma. Don't let this be the time it fires back at you.'

Hani held her breath expecting Hamdi to counter attack Zuleka, but it didn't happen. Hamdi just took hold of her pipe and sucked in some good smoke.

Not given to saying much these days, and when she did it was something cutting and killed the conversation, Zuleka didn't seem to notice how her words had upset Hamdi. Hani wished something good would happen. Something that would bring back the Zuleka they used to know.

'Changing the subject, Hani,' Ayan's look told Hani she wanted to fill the awkward gap in the conversation, 'you should have someone in the pipeline by now, girl. You are letting your time tick by.'

'Oh, Ayan, I don't subscribe to that Muslim thing about a girl looking around the field during her uni years and being ready to get engaged and married as soon as she graduates. I'm enjoying my life and my job. I didn't tell you, did I? I'm going to help copy edit the latest book of one of our established authors instead of being consigned the wannabies. I'm really excited about it and besides, I'm not ready to settle down, yet.'

'That's great, well done you, but we graduated over a year ago! A career doesn't have to end when you find your man. You can have both you know. I intend to carry on and I am even planning to do my MBA in a couple of years. Anyway, you said you want to meet Siddiq. Well, I have a plan that would achieve that and might serve you well, too. Siddiq has this friend. A well set up man, and I have told him about you. We could arrange a double ....'

'Oh, no you don't. I have sampled one of your blind dates before. I am more than happy to meet Siddiq, but with no strings attached, thank you.'

'But, this one is just right for you. I know he is. And, I have a duty to help you in the marriage stakes.'

'Since when? Oh, okay fine, drop the puppy look. I'll agree to meet up with this guy if it pleases you.' The moment she'd said the words she wanted to snatch them back; *fuck, why do I always let Ayan persuade me? Now I've got to go through what will most likely turn out to be a bloody farce!*

The breeze lifted pieces of wrapping paper, plastic carrier bags and pages of old newspapers and scuttled them along the ground. Her choice of a slim fitting, knee-length skirt meant she did not have the same problems other girls had in trying to anchor down their clothes.

A shop window reflected her appearance; she liked the affect she'd achieved with her new purple, silk blouse and the Ferragamo heels Zuleka had given her as a birthday present last year.

As she turned into Upper Street, the Thai restaurant they'd agreed to meet in came into view. Nerves attacked her, clenching her stomach.

Oh, why had she agreed to this? She tried to tell herself the attraction and the motivation to carry through with the blind date hadn't come from what Ayan had told her about Abdi. Though she had to admit, the fact that he was apparently intelligent and very successful in his field of business as head of marketing for Arsenal football club, did mark him as above most other Somali thirty-something's. *That made him worth checking out, didn't it? But then, that implies I'm looking for a husband, and I'm not, am I?*

A waiter greeted her as she walked into the restaurant. She looked around. Ayan sat opposite the entrance. The clean shaven, well dressed, and with a cute factor of ten man, sitting next to her must be Siddiq. *Not bad, Bridget!* She indicated her intention to join them hoping the absence of a second guy didn't mean she'd have to face the embarrassment of her date standing her up.

'Hey gorgeous!' Ayan got up to greet her with a kiss. 'Siddiq this is Hani, my best friend'

His hand felt warm in hers, 'It's good to meet you.' Her mouth dried leaving her unable to continue as his look compounded her nerves. It took in her outfit and showed a brief moment of disapproval before he pulled it back into a smile, but it was too late, she'd already noticed. His cute score dropped to zero and the full marks she re-awarded for ignorance.

'It's nice to meet you, too. Ayan talks a lot about you girls.'

Hani knew Ayan hadn't missed the look. Her embarrassment showed in the flustered way she tried to settle them into place whilst explaining that Abdi had called to say something had delayed him, but he would be here soon.

The drinks menu handed to her by the waiter caused a distraction. Not daring to ask for a glass of wine, which she would have loved, Hani ordered a coke.

A more relaxed Ayan asked, 'So, how's work coming along? Have you started working on the new book you mentioned?'

'Not yet, but I can't wait to start. It's going to be an exciting project and I expect to miss a couple of sessions in AA because of it.'

'How did you end up working for a publishing company?' Siddiq placed a hand behind Ayan's neck caressing her earlobe with his fingers as he spoke. She snuggled closer to him, completing the happy picture suffused with warmth between them. Hani did not doubt their mutual affection. *Has Ayan found love at last?*

'It happened by accident rather than design. I found my degree in English Literature didn't lead to many opportunities. Out of hundreds of applications this was one of the few that came back with an offer of a position. As it has turned out I love the work,' she explained. A glance at her watch told her Abdi's slight delay had turned into half an hour. *She should have known better than to trust Ayan to set her up. He'd better show up soon otherwise I am going to kick your ass, Ayan.*

As if she'd conjured him up, he appeared. Ayan had caught sight of him first. Her voice held more than a hint of relief as she exclaimed, 'Oh, here he is!'

Hani turned to look in the direction of the door. *Fuck! Ayan had been so busy highlighting his resume and good credit, she'd forgotten to mention his looks.*

A balding, verging on clinically obese, teddy bear of a man approached their table.

The introductions saved the day as Abdi's charming apology overrode her first impression. Hani's relief allowed her to make an effort to enjoy the evening. *But still, she was relieved that it was a foursome and she didn't have to spend time alone with Abdi.*

When Hani entered AA she found Zuleka, Hamdi and Ayan had already arrived and sat in their regular place. She knew to expect a grilling about the disastrous set up from the night before, but she was not in the mood for it. It happened as soon as she sat down. Ayan leant forward and asked her opinion of the double date.

'Are you out of your frigging mind? Isn't it obvious from the fact that I left half way?'

'I thought you were being honest when you said you weren't feeling well? You mean you lied?'

'You left half way?' Zuleka asked, 'and to think I almost didn't come here today. Well, go on, dish it out.'

'The man she kept raving about happened to be a prime candidate for weight watchers,' she said accusingly.

'Oh c'mon don't be a superficial bitch. He's an absolute sweetheart, just give him a chance, he really likes you.'

'Oh, I know he likes me,' said Hani, 'With the heavy breathing characteristic of the morbidly obese, he leered at me several times to tell me so. That sweetheart, big brother act he shows you, Ayan, manifested as sexual aggressive and an over inflated ego, boosted by the confidence of someone who has money and expects girls to reciprocate the attention he gives. If he'd placed his hand once more near the top of my thigh I would have tipped the contents of my bowl of soup all over him.'

'Oh, do tell...'

'Back-off, Hamdi, it wasn't anything to titillate over. He soon stopped when I told him if he touched me again I would stab him with my fork in places he wouldn't dream of. Anyway, he's just not my type,' Hani leant forward and touched Ayan's hand as she said this, 'look, hun, leave my love life to me, hey? I don't think you have the picture of the sort of guy I like.'

'Well, the sort of guy you do like, has asked about you a lot lately,' countered Hamdi, 'how about you give him a chance?'

'If you're talking about Izzy then I am not interested, and I wish you would stop trying to push him on me, Hamdi. I suspect he is the same as Tariq, but, unlike you, I don't have a penchant for so called bad boys.'

'I don't blame you. Dating Tariq is exhausting,' replied Hamdi 'He's always pulling stunts and disappearing for days on ends with no phone calls and then when he's back, we get into explosive arguments.'

'You should walk away now' Hani warned

'I don't want to walk away. I can handle his shitty attitude. Just watch how I'll have the boy eating from the palm of my hand in no time. He's a real challenge, I love that he's not swooning over me.....yet.'

'I'm with Hani on this one, Hamdi. You're mad. That boy is heartache on legs, I tell you. You'd save yourself a lot of trouble if you just walked away now.' Ayan told her.

'Where's the fun in that? I do agree with you that he's trouble, but that's why I want him so badly. No matter how much he pisses me off, I just can't seem to get enough of him!'

'I'll give you a couple more weeks.' Hani suspected the simmering power struggle between them kept Hamdi interested in Tariq. The moment Tariq showed a genuine interest in her she knew her friend would discard him with no second thought.

'Have faith in me, dear, plus there is plenty more to explore with him, if you know what I mean?'

'Well, whilst you lot haggle over your love lives, here's one babe who is sorting out her life… If any of you are interested - I have a job!'

'Zuleka! That's amazing, where? And what about uni?'

In the manner she was used to these days, Zuleka had jumped in with this total surprise and changed the conversation around in an instance.

'It's in the Cartier department of Harrods, and I can fit uni around it. I have to. I need to get a place of my own and getting a job is a good place to start. Ayan, is that loan offer still good? I need a fair bit, enough for a deposit and the first month's rent.'

'Sure. No problem.'

'Thanks, you're a star and a true friend. I won't let you down, but it may take me some time to pay it off, maybe even until after my junior doctor internship. So we're talking four to five years…'

'It's not a problem, really. It just sits in my account and there is plenty of it. You let me know how much and I'll get it for you.'

A silence followed this and Hani noticed Zuleka wipe a tear from her eye. She knew she'd have found it easier if it had been herself or Hamdi who could have helped her as she had taken a long time to let Ayan in and even now had an occasional go at her. But, above all that, the asking must have been very painful. Zuleka, the big spender, the have it all girl, reduced to this…

'Hey, girl, that's one massive corner you just turned, don't spoil it by blabbing.'

'I know, Hamdi. But, when you are down and your friends help you out it's a big thing. I'll never forget what you have all done to help me'

'Well, you can thank us by cheering up. From now on, all is positive, right?'

Zuleka smiled and Hani felt relief. It had been a hard couple of months, eventful for them all in one way or another, but always there had been a cloud over them. She hoped Zuleka's smile meant it would now lift. She had a long way to go, but she had taken steps, small ones, but definite ones on the road to recovery.

Chapter Twelve
The house-party

'Hani, I don't know what to do…'

'What is it, Hamdi? You sound really stressed, not another row?'

'No, well, yes in a way. I think I've got myself into something I can't get out of… Tariq thinks I'm a virgin!'

'WHAT!'

'I know… don't, it's bad enough as it is without you laughing at me.'

'I'm not laughing at you just the situation, and the preposterous idea that anyone could think of you as virginal! How did that come about?'

'Every time he tried to move things to another level I found ways to delay things. I teased and tantalized him but never gave in. I meant to build his anticipation so when we did have sex it would be mind blowing insane, like nothing he'd ever had before.'

'What did you think that would achieve, him declaring his undying devotion to you?'

'Something like that, but instead he told me last night that he *respects me!* He said I am so different from the other women he's known and he never thought girls like me were real. When I asked him what he meant he said: "Girls who stick with their traditional values the way you do. I had you all wrong when we first met, but now I see that you have that balance. You're modern, sassy and yet you keep it real, the way a home girl should. I really appreciate that in a woman, and truthfully I thought they were all extinct."'

'Oh dear, he thinks you are an Ayan!'

'Stop laughing, Hani, this is serious. Tariq *respects* me, I don't want him to respect me, I want him to make love to me, but now I feel like I am living a lie and don't know how to put it right. Arrrrghhh! This is a disaster!'

'I just can't believe it. Your whole persona screams sex. You might as well have the words 'I love sex' tattooed on your forehead. It beggars belief that the streetwise Tariq could make such a blunder. Are you sure you understood him, hun?'

'He made it crystal clear. He said he knew that I didn't believe in sex before marriage, and he respected that."

Hani lost it and couldn't speak for a whole minute despite Hamdi's pleading voice coming down her phone. When she could get a word in she said, 'Oh, Hamdi, It's more like you don't believe in marriage *before* sex. What are you going to do?'

'I don't know. I need time to think, to make him like me for me. Then I'll tell him the truth. Until then I guess I am a virgin. Don't you dare laugh again!'

'I can't help it. The situation is hilarious. You, who views sex as equal to bread and water, as being an absolute essential to your well being now have to wear a self imposed chastity belt!'

Hani's sides hurt, she could hardly hold the phone as her body went out of control and gave way to hysteria. The silence on the other end cracked as Hamdi at last saw the funny side and joined her. Neither could speak; only splutter as they tried to calm down. Hamdi managed it first, 'Anyway, Hani, that's not the only reason I rang. It's a lovely day and Tariq has arranged an impromptu garden party at his and Izzy's house. Can you make it? I could pick you up around two-ish.'

'Sounds good. Are the others coming?'

'No, Z is working and I don't think it's the kind of scene to invite Ayan to.'

'Okay, yes, I've nothing else to do. My mother's gone on her usual Saturday bargain hunt, dragging sis with her to interpret, and Salim is probably prostrate in the mosque begging Allah to look favourably on him, so there's no one to object. I'll be ready.'

Hani's thoughts went to Izzy as she dressed. He'd no doubt be strutting his stuff like usual. He and Tariq had become a regular part of their social lives. They're involvement in the entertainment industry meant lots of invitations to clubs, after parties and gigs followed by barbeques and chill out sessions during the day. The whole whirlwind social calendar had helped Zuleka and they'd all had a ball, even Ayan had attended the odd barbeque when she didn't have a date with Siddiq.

Despite Hani's initial attraction to Izzy things hadn't moved on further with him. She suspected he'd like them to as he paid her more and more attention, but she no longer felt interested.

Hamdi's relationship with Tariq had shown him to be a health hazard best avoided, she had no doubt Izzy would prove to be the same. Both were big time players, but unlike Hamdi, Hani had no fondness for drama and so Izzy had become a no go for her.

Time getting to know him had done nothing to change her mind it had only confirmed her early estimation of him as an arrogant and egotistical man who always had two or three women on the go. He could be in the most random of places and girls would gravitate towards him without any effort on his part. The fact that she and Zuleka had pretty much reacted in the same way now made her cringe and contributed to the dismissive attitude she had adopted towards him.

Scorning all invitations to his gigs, she hoped, gave him the message she remained unimpressed by his musical ambitions. Though there were some invitations she couldn't refuse, like the house party today. *After all poor Hamdi needed her support!*

Admiring the effect she'd achieved, loose fitting harem style pants, strapless top, her tamed hair pulled up and clipped into a bun and with, as usual, ridiculously high heeled, peeped toe shoes revealing freshly manicured nails, she sizzled inside with anticipation, but what of, she couldn't say.

'Hey, look it's all in full swing.'

Hani looked out of the window of the taxi at Hamdi's exclamation. A lot of people hung around outside and she spotted Izzy talking to a pretty mixed-race girl. She decided to ignore him and followed Hamdi inside. There they found another throng of people. The living room, with the furniture pushed to the side made a make-shift dancing floor and music belted out from the DJ decks manned by Tariq.

'Wow...' Hamdi's excitement pulsated through Hani. Everything looked set for a great afternoon's entertainment. 'Let's get us a drink, girl, and get us into the party mood'

Before she could answer Tariq spotted them and jumped down from his self-built little stage. He grabbed Hamdi and squeezed her, 'Hey, baby, you look good, where you been? Now, the show is on!' Hamdi snuggled into him.

'C'mon the bar's outside, that track'll play on and keep them all happy for a while. Hi, Hani, cool, girl, like it.' His eyes travelled up and down her, appreciating how she looked, 'what you having?'

'I'll just have a Bacardi.'

As Tariq pushed his way through to the bar Hani told Hamdi, 'I didn't expect there would this many people here. Hope the neighbours are okay with it!'

'They're probably here, too, and I guess with the trade Tariq is in he just knows a lot of people. I've seen some familiar faces, but there's a lot I don't know. Hey, it wouldn't do for me to throw a party only you and Zuleka and Tariq are likely to attend.'

'True, but then, with me and Zuleka there that's all you would need to have a good time!'

'What's the joke?' Izzy came up behind them.

'My lack of friends,' Hamdi said as she took her drink from Tariq and handed it to her.

Tariq led her away, 'I've someone I want to introduce to you, Hamdi…'

Left standing with Izzy the moment held silence. Hani stood looking over his shoulder acutely aware Izzy's eyes lingered on her body.

'You look good.'

'Thanks'

'So what were you up to today? I mean, the party has rocked for some time and you girls have only just arrived.'

'I have stuff to do. Some of us have real jobs you know.'

'There you go again, why are you always so damn judgemental and condescending? You're acting as if graduating from university puts you head and shoulders above everyone else, but you don't know shit.'

She had been unnecessarily rude but she was not about to back down. She crossed her arms across her chest before rolling her eyes: 'At least I graduate from university'

'Actually, I have an undergraduate degree in Economics from LSE, but I chose to pursue what I really wanted to do.'

He turned to go as if he couldn't be bothered to continue the conversation any longer. But, almost as an afterthought he looked at her again and said, 'And oh, I did I tell you that I also did a Masters in English literature at SOAS?'

Left standing alone she felt unsure what to do next.

'That doesn't prove anything other than that you are confused!' *God, why had she shouted like that, people were look-*

ing at her! She stomped across the lawn. *What an ass!* How dare he throw his degrees on her face? And what did he think it proved? If anything it made him even more of an idiot for pursuing two degrees and using none of them.

Izzy made no response and continued to ignore her as he appeared to have a wail of a time dancing away the afternoon and evening with some girl.

Her anger increased with every passing hour as she spent most of it on her own, only getting snatches of Hamdi's time. At one point she contemplated finding a dancing partner of her own to show him that two can play that game, but she couldn't be bothered so decided to leave.

'Hamdi, there you are. I know you want to be with Tariq, but you could take care of me more. You know everyone is a stranger to me. And besides, how could you leave me with that idiot, Izzy! I'm going home, I've had enough.'

'Honey, what happened? I saw you talking to him and thought you'd pick up again, you know you have the hots for him'

'I do not! I find him loathsome. Look, I'll catch up with you in a couple of days.'

As she turned to go she saw Izzy, *Fuck! That bastard is making a meal of some tramp right in the doorway; she'd have to push past him to get out.*

Just as she reached them Izzy put both of his hands on the girl's backside. His mouth covered hers.

Hani nudged him, 'Excuse me, I need to pass.'

'You leaving?'

The girl pulled Izzy back towards her as if to ignore Hani and continue where they were at before her interruption.

'Hold on a second, Danielle… Hani, it's late, how are you getting home?' He followed her as she went through the door.

'I am a grown woman. I can find my own way home; go back to your girlfriend.'

'That's reading a little too much into it,' he flashed a grin, 'she's not my girlfriend. Look, it's past midnight there are no trains and it'll take ages to get a taxi. Let me drop you off home… There's no need for us to talk. I'll drive in silence.'

She had to admit defeat. She needed to get home and the options she had didn't give her much hope of doing so for hours. She couldn't stay here a moment longer.

'Fine.' She couldn't even accept with graciousness. *What was the matter with her?*

The black tinted windows of his car concealed a random array of stuff he'd thrown onto the back seat: books, a football, a large bottle of Evian water, and a grey Nike sports jumper. 'Is this where you call home?'

'Second home.' The engine jumped into life, 'And, you know what they say about sarcasm, right? It's the lowest form of wit.'

'Why bother giving me a ride if you are just going to insult me?'

'I thought that accusation fitted you rather than me. I offered to drive you home in silence, but, if you choose to start poking at me you should be able to take it when I respond.'

He leant forward and turned on the radio. Ten minutes of awkwardness passed before Izzy spoke, 'What is it about me that pisses you off so much? Or do you just enjoy arguing with me?'

'Oh, there's plenty I don't like about you.'

'Okay, so when did this dislike kick in?' The amusement in his voice irritated her, 'I know at one point you flipped a coin for me.'

'What?! Who the hell told you that? I swear to god I am going to kill Hamdi! And, there's no need for you to look so pleased with yourself. It was a long time ago and I didn't care either way if I won or not!'

'Look, I am tired with these games.' The car slowed and then came to a stop in a lay by. Hani held her breath. The atmosphere changed. It now held a sensuous aura. She didn't move. Izzy touched her shoulder, 'I like you, Hani, I really like you, and from the first time I met you I've been trying to get to know you, but you keep pushing me away. I am putting it all on the table now, so let's do it like we grown folks.'

'Do what exactly?' His admission had completely thrown her, but she recovered when the picture of him pushed up against Danielle, or whatever her name was, came back to her. She had no desire to be another one he could chalk up.

When he didn't answer she said, 'Look Izzy, I appreciate what you have said, I really do, but I just don't feel the same. I am sorry.'

His eyes searched hers for a few seconds then he shrugged. 'If that's how you want it then its fine.'

She couldn't define the note in his voice, but his anger showed in his clenched jaw and stony silence as he drove her home.

His 'goodnight' sounded surly and final. For some reason this hurt. He couldn't even be bothered to try a little harder. Saying he really liked her had been what? She thought, a ploy to make her yet another of his conquests?

Chapter Thirteen
A clash of ambitions

Zuleka watched the droplets of rain hit the bus stand and trickle down the Perspex shield of the shelter. Her mind gave her the game she and her sisters used to play on wet days when they were children. Kneeling by the window they would each pick a bead of water and then compete as to which one would get to the bottom of the pane of glass first. The sound of their little fists banging to encourage theirs to go faster and their squeals of delight when it did filled her head and triggered her sadness. She mentally shook herself and checked her watch. Damn! The bloody bus was late again!

A steady stream of buses pulled in, but none displayed the number 52 the one that ran from Notting Hill to Knightsbridge where she worked. If it didn't arrive within the next five minutes she'd be late for work, again. She groaned inwardly and rolled her eyes.

Marta, her uptight Ukrainian supervisor ran the shop like a communist factory manager and Zuleka was not her favourite person. She had no idea what she had done to get on Marta's wrong side and she didn't care. As long as her cheque went into the bank at the end of the month, Marta can scowl at her all she liked.

She tapped her foot and contemplated whether to cross the road and jump on the tube or whether to hail a cab, but decided against it. The bus didn't cost as much as either of those two options and she had to watch her pennies, her budget remained very tight and cash flow caused her a lot of problems despite putting almost full time hours in at *Cartiers*.

To try to ease things if any overtime or covers for other's holidays came up, she signed up for it. Marta should be grateful to her; she had stepped in save her ass on numerous occasions when staff shortage occurred. As a result she'd had to cut classes more than she'd liked and her university grades had suffered. Trying to pull in extra studying after work had left her exhausted and dark circles ringed her eyes, but she stuck it out and never complained. She consoled herself with the thought that soon the term would be over. *I'll still have to work hard, but the pressure will ease, when the new term starts again, but maybe things will have changed by then, who knows?*

She arrived at work ten minutes late and found the Iron Lady, her private nick name for Marta, waiting with her arms crossed. No customers ever needed attention at this time of the morning so it wasn't as if she had let the side down. The first hour of the day usually entailed checking around with a duster and re-filling the displays from the safe. Work, needing very few hands and done before she arrived for her shift anyway.

'What time do you call this, Zuleka?'

'When the small hand is at ten and the long hand is at two, we usually call it ten past,' she thought with a flash of annoyance. Always the last one to leave the shop, often volunteering to stay behind with those pesky customers who dawdled at closing time and doing all the cashing up, surely meant cutting some slack for the odd time when she arrived late?

'I realize I am ten minutes late, sorry Marta.'

'Time keeping isn't your strength, is it, Zuleka? I have spoken to you about it before. Consider this your final warning. If you are late again you are sacked.' Her tight smile did not reach her eyes. Zuleka gritted her teeth.

'What is up with that bitch?' she said to Sam, the other Sales Associate who stood behind the glistening counter. 'Ever since I started here she has been on my case.'

'Don't pay her any attention, she probably just feels threatened. You're pretty good at your job and you haven't been here long, so...' she shrugged her shoulder as if that said it all before adding, 'not to mention how good you look in the uniform.'

'We are all good at the job. It's not exactly rocket science,' Zuleka did a twirl in front of the mirror. The formal black trousers and fitted black jacket, worn with kitten heels did do her justice, 'and thanks for the compliment, it's a pretty cool uniform, actually. Probably the best bit about the job.'

'You're welcome. Anyway, on top of that you have outsold all of us, including Marta, since you joined. She's angling for the managerial spot and you are making her nervous.'

'Ugh. I have no interest in managerial or supervising positions. I am doing this to support me through uni; the bitch can relax. I am going to be a doctor for Christ sake; I've no ambitions what-so-ever to carve a career in retail.'

She joined Sam behind the counter and took out some paper work regarding an order she had requested for one of her customers. She smiled at herself for using the 'her' in her head. Now that Sam had mentioned it, she could see why Marta might have felt threatened.

'Sam, if that is what is making Marta act like such a cow to me then the first opportunity you get, can you please put her straight? I am not here to steal her bread.'

'I will. Oh-oh, here comes the first customer.' Sam as 'first sales' approached the lady browsing around the cabinet containing men's watches.

Left on her own, Zuleka searched the database for the ordered product. As she did so her mind mulled over how things must look. She had turned out to be a surprisingly good Sales Associate. She knew all about luxury products and could give customers candid advice on purchases. Especially the men looking to buy gifts for their girlfriends and wives, more than once a grateful male customer had stopped by to tell her that the gift had been a hit. Many even asked for her personally when they wanted to purchase something again. She didn't think anybody noticed or minded, but apparently Marta had. It made her smile to think of her feeling threatened, but as much as she enjoyed working here, she could never escape the fact that she belonged in front of the counter: not behind it. She didn't want to sell expensive jewellery, she wanted to *wear* it. One of her biggest bug-bears at the moment centred round the staff discount. *Thirty percent off and she never had any money left over to take advantage of it!*

How she envied the Eastern European ice maidens and the Arab princess who shopped at Harrods! They looked so beautiful; long flowing tresses, (no doubt layered with extensions) manicured nails that never did a day's work and immaculate clothes that were always up to date with the latest trends.

As if on cue, a trio of young Arab women dressed in long black abayas entered Harrods leaving the scent of heavy designer perfumes trailing in their wake.

'All hail, the Arab season is here.' whispered Sam, rubbing her hands in glee.

Zuleka didn't have to ask the meaning of that. She'd enjoyed a relationship with a petrol-rich student in the past, which had taken place in the Arab season, but she looked quizzical anyway.

Sam laughed. 'Sometimes I forget you're still new. The Arab Season starts from July and ends in September when the Arabs from the oil rich Gulf States come in their packs and flood Knightsbridge. With your selling skills, you'll make a killing in commission.'

'Big spenders, huh?' *As if she didn't know.*

'Big doesn't even begin to describe it, girl. The amount of money these people have is obscene. All these expensive apartments nearby are empty for the rest of the year until they come and snap them up like cheap hot cakes just to be near the designer stores.'

A few minutes later a different group of Arab women walked past. They had multiple bags from the various outlets.

'Lauren from the third floor told me they tend to buy the *sexiest* outfits,' Sam said with a heavy emphasis on the word sexiest.

'Of course they do.' It amused Zuleka to think that sales assistants were fascinated and gossiped about the Arab ladies across the stores.

'But what's the point? I mean nobody gets to see it.'

'They do, actually. Those women dress up for women, not men. What straight man is going to notice whether you're wearing Dior or Gucci from this season or the last, or even care? He's not going to desire you any less, but the women from the same social classes as you will notice, *and* care enough to point the fact out. It's the same for all women; the Arab sisters are no different. Hidden from the prying eyes of men at female only parties or weddings, they flaunt, revel, and annoy one another with their latest purchases.'

'I guess that makes sense.' Sam turned her attention elsewhere.

Zuleka watched the Arab girls walk out. They looked excited and probably were not much older than her. She hadn't said so to Sam but, she was willing to bet that when the night fell a few of them would try their purchases on and party the night away in some club. *Well, if they did good luck to them and I hope they never get caught out.* She wouldn't wish that on anyone.

These thoughts brought into her mind the notoriety she knew now wrapped around the very mention of her name because she had been the one who hadn't got away with it. By running away she thought she would escape the wagging tongues, but she had made her situation even juicer to the gossip mongers and her reputation had taken a further battering. News spread that she refused to get married to her cousin and people cited it as lack of repentance and as evidence that she was trash through and through. She knew that over the weeks and months the few minutes captured on film outside the club had grown into a long titillating tale worthy of a Hollywood production in which she starred in many different roles.

Hani had told her she had heard a variety of versions and with each new telling the facts changed and the description became more and more lurid. Zuleka sighed; she didn't want to become an urban legend with mothers using her as an example to warn their wayward daughters of what could happen if they didn't behave properly.

Not long ago she'd bumped into a woman she knew. The woman had spat on the pavement in front of her and before crossing to the other side had said, "Huh, you tramp, you thought you would get away with your harem behaviour behind your parent's backs. But you can't hide anything from Allah; he will always expose and punish those who are doing wrong unto themselves or unto others."

Zuleka hadn't been able to take it in. The incident had shaken her to her very roots. The woman had been a close neighbour who had known her personally. How could she be so unforgiving in her judgement?

But then, all the community had regarded her as the ideal daughter; dutiful, polite and kind, and to them she must seem like the embodiment of the worst kind of sinner -a hypocrite that pretended to be one thing when in fact she was another. But if that is so, then in tripping over themselves to condemn her, they forget that hypocrisy is a valid charge only if you have a choice, an option to be something other than what society expects you to be, but with no voice or choice, hypocrisy became the only way for her.

The feelings provoked by these thoughts kept her spirits down, but she didn't show it to the outside world.

Sam didn't notice anything, or if she did she hadn't commented. The end of the shift had never been more welcome than it was when it finally arrived. Every part of her body ached. Hani had texted and said they were meeting somewhere for dinner, but she had declined. A hot bath and a plate of whatever she could scrape together from the left-over's in the fridge was all she could face.

Walking up to her place, she was stunned to see the small figure of her mother waiting outside. 'Zuleka, my daughter…'

'Hooyo?'

Zuleka's heart pounded against her ribs. Her mother stood on the pavement outside the house where she rented a small flat.

'Is everything all right? Are you all right? How did you find me?'

Her mother cringed from the kisses Zuleka went to bestow on her.

'Never mind all that, and no, nothing is right and I doubt it ever will be again.'

Zuleka unlocked the front door. 'Do you want to come in? I mean, if you took the trouble to track me down, you may as well…'

'Of course I do. I want to talk to you, daughter. I went to the university, but you weren't there. Others told me you are hardly ever there. What are you doing? Why are you not keeping up with your studies?'

'Hooyo, I have to live! What do you expect of me? Did you think that I could carry on and exist off fresh air? I have a job. I work long hours and study at night. I go to uni when I can and they let me have materials through the internet, which I access through my laptop, I am behind, but nothing will stop me graduating.'

'But how can you? You will fail, you are bound to.'

Typical that my education, even now, is taking precedence in her mind over everything else!

'Graduating is something that is taken over the whole of my years at uni, not just one part of it. My average grades are so high that I can afford a few lower ones. Okay, I won't get a distinction, but I should still attain a first. And, I have already secured a junior doctor's post in a South London hospital for when I finish uni next year. You have nothing to worry about on that score, Hooyo. You can still boast about your daughter's achievement-- that is if you ever speak of me at all.'

'Don't you see? None of it atones for what you have done. Come back home and beg for your father's forgiveness. You have broken his heart, but he still loves you.'

'And what about Yemen and Abdul Rahman? Are you telling me he won't force me to get married to his nephew?'

'That's the only way to wipe away your shame, Zuleka! I am sorry it is such a repulsive idea to you, but you should have thought about that before you took off your clothes and went into discos. You have ruined your life! Who do you think will want to marry you now?'

'I don't care!'

'Have you heard what is being said about you out there? Do you not care how your actions affect us? Are you that selfish that you can only think of yourself and what you want?'

'Haven't they said enough, hooyo? What more can they say? How else can they hurt you or me? And why must we care what they say?'

Even though it hurt to see her pain she knew there was nothing her mother could say that would persuade her to go back home. She had only been living by herself for a short while, but she had tasted freedom and she liked it. She came and went as she pleased, she wore what she wanted and the thought of going back to the old ways of living, even if they no longer tried to make her get married, was just not possible. She had resolved never to go back, but she tried to make her mother understand even if her father never would, 'honestly *hooyo*, I don't care what anybody thinks. I want to live on my own. I must to do this for me. I am a grown woman, but until this happened, I had never spent a week without you or the family telling me what to do or making me account for myself every time I wanted to go out. I can't live like that; I need to find myself in order to know who I am.'

'Find yourself? I didn't know you were lost! Do you hear yourself talk? My dear child, you may fool yourself into thinking that you are white, but you are not!'

Zuleka could see her mother's strength seeping out of her body as she looked at the daughter she no longer knew. The feeling inside her brought down her own spirit at seeing her mother like this, but she could not give in. From somewhere deep within her, her mother found enough voice to deliver a final blow, 'Your father is right, you are dead to us. Should we pass over to the next world before you, don't come to our funeral, or visit our graves.'

Without another word her mother left. Zuleka watched her walk down the street from her window. When she could no longer see her she flopped into the nearest chair. Her mother, usually a great one for theatrics, always declaring herself to be on the verge of having a heart attack or something equally dramatic, had displayed genuine pain. Zuleka had seen it reflected in her eyes and knew she had meant every single word she'd said.

Zuleka had long fantasised about living on her own and had always thought when the time came she would be jubilant, ecstatic and over the moon. In her imagination she had seen herself screaming from the rooftop, no more curfews or the what, whys, when and where's, every time she came home late from a night out.

The restricting culture and customs would be behind her, her destiny no longer written in stone by her family. That day had come, she had broken century's old tradition to be the first woman in her family to live on her own prior to marriage; but instead of feeling proud she felt a severe sadness. She had fought a battle, but had a hollow victory. Freedom, never bestowed as a benevolent gift, and she wondered what price she would pay.

Chapter Fourteen
The Grime and the Grammies

'What gives with Zuleka, Hamdi, have you any idea?' Hani stopped in the process of rubbing sun cream over her exposed stomach. She had hired a deck chair, and relaxed back into it, but Hamdi preferred to lie on her towel on the grass. Although crowded with fellow sun bathers, they had managed to find a quite spot in Hyde Park that was shrouded in greenery and calmness.

'She's still smarting from her mother's visit. She'll get over it, she's a tough cookie. The Arab season should sort her out. Nothing short of having more money or a rich boyfriend will do the trick. Be patient, girl, and mark my words. The time is only a week away to when the streets will seem like they are paved with gold.'

Hani laughed. She knew Hamdi had it right. Even through her gloom, Zuleka had shown some signs of anticipation. Besides, uni had closed for the holidays so that took some of the pressure off her. Zuleka only needed her results to come in good so she could go forward into her final year with a chance. Things would change for her then.

'Yo, babes.' Tariq came up to them.

Hani squinted up at him shading her eyes with her hand. A trickle of disappointment at seeing Izzy wasn't with him annoyed her as it wormed into to her gut. *For God sake, get over it, you idiot.*

She hadn't seen Izzy since the night he'd driven her home. What had happened had since churned over and over in her mind. She'd had to admit his admission had pleased and flattered her, but then, it would have any woman, but on reflection it changed nothing.

If he could claim to have feelings for someone and yet hit on every girl that came his way, it clearly did not mean much to him. *And I don't care anyway.*

She had to admit though, him going AWOL made her suspect he was avoiding her and that did rankle.

Hamdi spent virtually every day at their place and to her discreet probing always said Izzy was just busy in the studio and that she rarely saw him at the house. As if reading her thoughts, Hamdi asked Tariq, 'How is it going in the studio, baby,'

'Oh man, we've been working on some dope materials,' replied Tariq as he applied sun cream on Hamdi's back, 'the tracks are almost ready to drop, and then we are off the hook.'

As it turned out, Hani had to admit that Izzy was not wasting his time with the music business. Those who knew the UK hip-hop scene, which she did not, thought he had great talent.

Like Tariq he had started as a DJ for local pirate radio station and so the underground circuits knew him well and his demos and mix tapes proved very popular with the garage and grime crowd. She knew he currently worked on another demo tape with Tariq collaborating on the beats. All this she had found out once she had decided to listen instead of walk away whenever a conversation led to him and what he did.

'Sounds cool,' Hamdi said.

'Yeah, it does, actually. I'd love to hear some tracks soon.'

Neither Hamdi nor Tariq commented on this change of heart, but without moving her head Hani thought she saw a look pass between them. After a few moments of silence, Tariq said, 'Hey, Hani, Izzy's performing one or two tunes at one of the toilet circuits tonight, why don't you come?'

'What's a toilet circuit?'

'Tiny, shitty venues. Hamdi knows the one, you know, babe, where we were at a couple of weeks ago.'

'Yeah, it rocked. Let me know if you want to go, Hani.'

'Thanks. I might check it out.' Feeling a little embarrassed but not knowing why she should, Hani picked up her book and buried her head in it. *That titter had nothing to do with her, she was being paranoid. Hamdi and Tariq were just having fun together.*

Underground raves or 'toilet circuits' were not her scene but a small part of her wanted to see Izzy again. Her position had not changed, but she had decided they should at least be friends. Not to mention her curiosity over his music.

Once inside the dingy east London club Hani regretted the urge that had brought her here. It seemed the organisers had squashed a million people into a very small space.

They'd had a job to get a taxi to take them this far so arrived after the performances had started. This meant they had to stand at the back near to the bar where artificial fog light added to the poor view they already had.

'What happened to fucking Health and Safety laws? They must be breaching them, I can hardly breathe! Ouch, ouch.'

'Chill out, girl, let the music do it for you…'

'Fuck, Hamdi, you didn't tell me it would be like this!' After treading on her toes, the offender now turned and spilled his drink all down her front. Hamdi laughed.

Resigned to the fact she'd get no sympathy from that direction she decided to concentrate on the music. Having never listened to Grime, an offshoot of Garage music, before, let alone attend a live performance of it, it took her a while to adjust to the deafening and erratic beats. Soon the pure energy and vibe emanating from everyone had her gripped. Without realising what happened she found herself at one with the crowd and totally immersed in the fast beats.

'This is different from what I had expected!' She shouted to Hamdi when Izzy came on stage and continued with the fast, frantic pace. If she had thought about it at all, Hani realised, she had expected Izzy's music to be like the sugary hip hop tracks that she often heard from Kiss 100FM. But the futuristic, electronic beats and dark harsh bass lines totally blew her mind.

Hani roared as loud as any of the mesmerized crowd as Izzy unleashed his lyrics over the aggressive beats while moving on the stage with a compelling aura of confidence.

'Is this is what they call grime?!' Hani's throat hurt with the throbbing of the beat and having to shout.

'Yeah, I think so!' Hamdi shouted back

'Damn, it's intense!'

Hot, sweaty and exhilarated, Hani allowed Hamdi to pull her though the crowd. Izzy had finished his set and they were all to meet in the small room at the back, used as a kind of dressing-room by the performers. She tried to tell herself she found it hard to breathe because of the crowds and the frenzy she'd allowed to take her over, but some of it she knew could be down to her worry that Izzy would ignore her or still be angry with her. She didn't know anybody who coped well with rejection so knew she should prepare herself for his snub.

Standing in the middle of the room, Izzy had taken his shirt off and had a white towel draped around his neck. His toned stomach glistened with sweat.

'Baby, that was friggin awesome!' Hamdi leaped into Tariq's arms and congratulated him on the role he'd played behind the scenes.

'Well done, that was good.' Hani kept her gaze on Izzy as she said this.

'Thanks for coming.' Izzy chugged down half a litre of bottled water before pouring the rest on his head to cool himself down.

Hani tried hard to not look at the water that trickled down his stomach. Her mind gave her a comparison to a river rippling over even, beautifully polished cobbled stones.

'Did you enjoy yourself?'

'Well, it's very different.'

'That's diplomatic. But okay. Grime isn't for everybody. Here, take the demo. There are a few tracks, which are a little bit more laid back and you might enjoy more.'

'Thanks, so how did you get into music?' she asked, trying to make conversation.

'I've always been fascinated by language and word play, you know, the manipulation of rhymes and couplets. Anyway, changing the subject, I'm always hungry after a show so I'm going to grab something to eat, you want to come?'

'Sure.' Something in Hani fluttered a nerve. She dismissed it.

Tariq and Hamdi didn't want to join them. They had their own plans.

The local restaurant he chose buzzed with activity. Hani felt glad of this as a quiet place would enhance any silences between them. Izzy ordered a feast of dishes, but she stuck with a chicken dish and some salad.

Curious about Izzy's music and why he would choose to be a struggling musician over a lucrative career in the city, which his LSE degree would have given him, she paved the way to question him on the subject, 'Can I ask you something?'

'Fire away…'

'What was the point of going to university and spending all that money, time, and effort, when you weren't going to use it?'

She had a moment's relief when he didn't attack her, but leant back on his seat and smiled. 'To get my father off my back. In our house, his word was law and education the be all and end all. He busted his balls to pay for his engineering degree and no kid of his would ever opt out of university. Besides, since there are no guarantees in this industry it made sense, plus my grades qualified me for a scholarship so I had to do it or suffer a major ass whooping.' He laughed. Hani liked the sound and felt more relaxed.

'I admire your father for his foresight and pushing through the many arguments he must have had with you. If it doesn't work out at least you can walk into a well paid career.'

'I don't know about admire him, you even sound like him.'

'I was just saying...'

'I know what you were saying, but it *is* going to work out. I can't imagine doing anything else. I love what I am doing right now. There is no substitute for bringing my creativity to life in the studio or spontaneously free-styling on stage. That feeling of winning over a tough crowd and getting their heads nodding to your words or leaving them thinking: damn, how did he come up with that one. Man, that feeling is ace'

'I hope it does work out for you, I mean that. It was refreshing to hear something different. To be honest, I was expecting to hear gun totting, gangster crap in the style of 50 Cents. I was pleasantly surprised.'

'Nah, that gangster shit is played out; it's not my style or experience. I don't have a taste for bullshit, just straight up lyricism, that's what I'm all about. That's my biggest beef with major labels though, that gun shit sells so they show interest in my work and then try to change my style.'

'So what's the plan? If major labels want you to change your style isn't it better to compromise?'

'Do you know how many people listen to my shit on YouTube? Check it out, the numbers speak for themselves, people want something authentic, and I am trying to bring it to them. I won't change, but those record executive and station managers will; mark my words.'

Hani downloaded Izzy's CD onto her laptop and then onto her iPod and listened to it on the tube on her way to work. After skipping a few hardcore tracks she stumbled upon one track with soulful beats, which prevented her fingers from pressing the fwd button. It was titled: 'The Revolution'.

The fluid lyrics tackled social issues; war to pollution, terrorism to immigration. She could hardly believe she listened to Izzy. Was he really capable of writing such introspective and thought provoking lyrics? The gig had left her in no doubt that he was a performer, but this was something else. His words, poetical and holding social comment came from his heart. He had a message that demanded people listened to. How could she have dismissed him as a being just a player and a party animal?

This one track opened her mind to the others. She paid more attention to the lyrics and found the more she absorbed them the more they grew on her. Feeling very impressed and wanting to tell him so, she arranged to meet up with him for coffee at the Cafe Nero in Holborn.

When Hani arrived, Izzy was already seating at a table opposite the door. She ordered a skinny Mocha from the counter before approaching his table.

'Hi, how was your day?'

'You know the drill, another day, another dollar, and yourself?'

'Fine. I've listened to the demo you gave me all day today,' she said, pulling out a chair and sitting down. 'I really liked it. Some of the lyrics are very deep. Did you *really* write them yourself?'

He laughed, but the sound held a cynicism. 'Why, don't you think I am capable of deep thought?'

'That's not what I meant. It probably came out wrong. I didn't mean to offend you.' His dimpled smile that was always with him told her she hadn't. 'I was just curious that's all.'

'I write all my stuff.'

'So, what happens with the demo now? Do you send it off to any labels?'

'Yeah, it's been sent to a few. I had a meeting with the people from Virtual Entertainment, they requested more material, told me they liked it and then, like I told you before, they asked to me change my sound. Same old shit really.'

'But, couldn't you have gone along and then later when you are established bring out your own stuff? After all, Virtual Entertainment is a big label and just the association with them could have a good impact on your career.'

'Nope, I told them to fuck off. I don't own a gun or drive a Lamborghini. So how can I write about that shit? But they keep yapping on and on, telling me that's what's hot, that's what's relevant right now. Fat cats don't know shit.'

'Oh, I'm sorry.'

'Why are you sorry? A lot of people think like you, it's nothing. My time will come without me prostituting myself by writing stuff I don't have a sense for or toeing anyone's line just to make it.'

'Well, I know I gave lip-service to the sentiment, but in my heart I agree with you. Stick to what you do best.

They will come round in the end,' wanting to capitalise on calming him and letting him see she intended to bat on the same side as him, Hani raised her cup, 'as I believe your time will come, lets us raise a toast: *To the Grammies!*' But, even as she said it, she couldn't help thinking him insane to turn down such a label.

'To the Grammies' he replied, and raised his cup, lightly tapping hers.

As they laughed together Hani had a good feeling. Izzy may be a lot of things, but she knew without doubt, he would be a good friend and really good company. But why did this thought leave her feeling something would be missing. Did she want him to be more than a friend? Surely not... *Keep it real, girl.*

Chapter Fifteen
Trouble in paradise

'Have you seen anything of Ayan, lately, Hani?'

'No. She's got it bad, Z. She did ring me the other day. She's still on cloud nine – I think – She said to say hi, but she spends most of her spare time with Siddiq. She hasn't introduced him to her family, yet. Which I find strange given she clearly things he's the 'one''

Something didn't sit right where Ayan was concerned for Zuleka and she thought she detected some of the same feeling in how Hani had answered her, too. Holding guilt over the money she owed Ayan made it more comfortable when not in her company, but still the gesture of the loan had bonded them and she couldn't say why, but she felt all wasn't well. 'I'll call her. See if she'll come and meet us later.'

Zuleka and Hani sat outside a café not far from where Hani worked.

'I doubt if she will, but you can try. So how are things with you? You seem more cheerful lately.'

'Well, I've something to look forward to. The Arab season coincides with the end of term. So I can concentrate on the job and have a potential to earn a lot of money in commission on the massive sales I'm going to make at work. It just feels good to have something positive to look forward to for a change.'

'Great, it's good to see you looking more upbeat and with some hope for your future. Look, I have to go, lunch break over, but I'll see you in AA later. Hope you can persuade Ayan to come, I haven't time to ring her to back you up with that, but I doubt you will need help.'

'Zuleka, it's good to hear you. No... I'm fine. Well, you know. I'm scared sometimes...'

'Why, hun? What's going down? We haven't seen you in ages. Why not have a break and come and meet up with us later?'

'I don't know. I suppose it would do me good. But there's nothing wrong. You know I've always believed that if something was too good to be true, it usually was... that's all it is, I am still very much in love. And, Siddiq is the first guy I've ever been with who's not scared of commitment; in fact he hungers for it. And do you know what's funny? I even pray to Allah to protect this relationship. Do you think that's daft?'

'Not if you don't, but then, it depends on why you feel a need to. Are you feeling insecure?' she gently prodded, 'If so, think hard, girl. I mean, we three are already looking out for some outfits to wear to your wedding, but that shouldn't happen unless you are sure. Look, we'll see you later. And, don't let anyone talk you out of it.'

As she snapped her phone shut, Zuleka felt even more afraid for Ayan. Her parting words to her had seemed to hit a note. Was Siddiq preventing Ayan from seeing them? No, she agreed to come along. Surely she wouldn't have if that was the case? She hoped with all her heart Ayan did turn up. The daft girl could drift into something that wasn't right for her just to save face... No, Siddiq was right for her. They'd all liked him, hadn't they? Well, she knew one thing; she'd probe some more tonight and try to find out for sure that all was well.

But as they sat smoking and chatting, it become clear things were not as they seemed with Siddiq. It took some time getting to the bottom of it, but cracks had begun to show for some time though Ayan had chosen to ignore them, or perhaps love had blinded her, Zuleka thought as she listened to her.

'I do love him and I know he loves me, but there are issues. He is possessive. Oh, he says he can change, but I am not sure...'

'The thing is, can you love him despite this, and how much of a problem is it causing?'

'Some days I think I can, Hani. But, we really fall out when it comes to... Well, like I say there are ongoing issues.'

'Can't you tell us?' Zuleka asked, 'After all, we might be able to help. I knew there was something wrong...'

'It's not really wrong... Just difficult. It concerns all of you. I'm sorry, but he thinks that you are a bad influence he resents my friendship with you.'

'What!'

'Let her finish, Hamdi. Go on, Ayan, don't be afraid. We only want to help.' Zuleka told her.

"Are you sure you know them well enough?" he asks me all the time. "They just seem too fast. You are not like them, and they ...well, I am just not too sure they are the right friends for you." Things like that,' she laughed. Zuleka detected a nervous tremor in the sound, she looked around at the others, caught Hani's eye and saw the concern in her.

Ayan continued, 'I tell him that I know you come off as a little slippery, but you are good girls really and told him he must give you a chance, if he does he will come to love you as I do.'

None of them spoke. Zuleka didn't know what to say and the other's silence indicated they had been shocked too. She felt her anger rising. *The fucking cheek of the man!* She couldn't say as much though as that would cause conflict with Ayan. 'Go on, hun, give us the full picture.'

'He talks about not liking Tariq and, the rapper guy, as he calls Izzy, he thinks you club hop with them endlessly. And he thinks I don't really know you.'

A prickle of embarrassment caused Zuleka to feel hot. She was glad Ayan was able to be frank with them, but the last comment felt as if Siddiq meant her in particular and referred to her scandal. She couldn't think he would see anything wrong in what the others did.

'It has all caused some rows and made it difficult for me...'

'Look, we can see that, but you have to stand up to him. Tell him you are coming out with us at least once a week and he can put that in his pipe and smoke it!'

'Hani is right, by not doing so you are confirming what he says and allowing him to dominate you.'

'I know it looks like that, Hamdi, but I don't think like that, honestly, I still think it is early days and I am working on helping him see my perspective whilst respecting his.'

None of them spoke for a moment after this and Zuleka knew, that far from them teaching Ayan anything they stood to learn from her. Her respect for Ayan deepened and with all her heart she wished she could play things her way, but they had fundamental differences. Something inside of her would never accept how Ayan did things.

Hamdi broke the silence, 'look, let's put bloody men aside for a bit and have us some fun. How about a real girly night in at mine? Get some drinks and we could grab a take away and... Well, pick up a movie, or ring up Macie, even. She's a girl from work who does make-up demo's in the evenings. If she isn't booked we could get her around to give us all a makeover. What do you think?'

'Sounds great, just the kind of evening I could do with.'

As they got up to leave Zuleka's worry for Ayan compounded as after saying this she heard her whisper to Hani, 'It makes me feel nervous here, Siddiq knows I am out with you and I am afraid he will turn up later to see me home and we'll have another row.' But she felt better when Ayan laughed and said, 'Ha, I'd like to see his face when I'm not here. His mind will work overtime thinking I've gone clubbing with you or something. Well, it will serve him right.'

That's the spirit, Ayan, Zuleka thought, *so, all was not lost; Ayan was fighting back.* She knew now she could enjoy the rest of her evening.

Chapter Sixteen
The deal

'Oh, My God! Are you kidding me?' Hani squealed down the phone at Hamdi, 'that's friggin amazing!'

'I am not kidding you, girl. It's true! *IT'S REALLY TRUE!* Now stop getting so excited and tell me, can you make it or not?'

'Yes, yes, but it's unbelievable!'

'Shut up and get ready and don't take too long. Get your ass here soon, girl!'

'Okay, okay! I'm on my way to the bathroom as we speak…'

Hani couldn't understand why she felt so elated. Yes, she liked Izzy now, but him getting offered a record deal shouldn't have this effect on her. Her body shook with excitement for him. Tariq was throwing a party for him and she couldn't wait to get there.

She rummaged through her wardrobe, *damn, what am I going to wear - what do people wear to such a party anyway? Shoes, I have to start with the shoes, they always determine an outfit.*

Box after box found itself strewn around her bedroom as she looked at and discarded one pair of shoes and then another, some she had never worn. At last she settled on some and decided they cried out for a chic look, so on went a pair of skinny jeans and a black silky vest top that had a little bit of lace around the neckline. To compliment the outfit and bring it all together she donned a burgundy pashmina around her neck. A quick check in the mirror confirmed she looked good, so she called a taxi and headed out.

On the way she thought what all this would mean. Izzy would be famous! It all seemed so unbelievable and simple, but she had to remind herself she was new in his life and hadn't witnessed all of the difficulties he must have faced to reach this point.

A little disappointment seeped into her as her thoughts went on; only a tad, but she wished he'd called her himself. But then, it isn't as if he is supposed to be in love with her or anything! Granted, they have seen a lot more of each other, the odd coffee and longer than usual chat when she'd visited their place with Tariq, that sort of thing. The least he could do was to call and share his good news personally. Still why should she care...*Oh come off it girl, you know you are crazy for this boy... What?! Where did that come from?*

The inner voice so shocked her she felt her cheeks blush and had a moment of feeling like a silly teenager. Annoyance at herself made her rummage for her mirror. She checked her make-up to make sure she applied it okay; after all she'd been in such a rush.

The house bulged with people. It was obvious from conversations she heard that some of them were his family. Others she thought were friends of his and some might even be from the industry, but all expounded the same message of how well he'd done, how proud they were and how all their hard work – distributing his tapes and following him around all his gigs - had at last paid off for 'their boy.'

Their enthusiasm lit the place up and Hani felt thrilled and excited to be a part of it.

Izzy's own music blared from the stereo. People danced, laughed, drank, and clapped Izzy on the back to congratulate him so many times she thought he must have bruises as medals. He beamed. He deserved to. This was his night.

He stood in a far corner talking to a group of people. Hani tried to push her way through to get to him and add her praise when loud noises coming from the kitchen stopped her. Curious she pushed the door open to take a peep.

Not prepared for what she found Hani stood in the doorway in amazement. Zuleka downed two straight shots of tequila, banged her glasses down before swiftly picking up another. Liquor spilled down the front of the tight blouse she wore soaking it and whipping the mostly male crowd gathered in the kitchen into frenzy as they loudly cheered her on, 'Go Z! Go Z! Go Z!' *My God, she's in a competition!*

'Wohooo!' she screamed with her hands in the air after her opponent dropped out. Completely smashed he slumped against the kitchen sink. The only thing Hani could think was that he must have started drinking early in the night otherwise Zuleka would never have out drunk him.

'You, my dear, are completely nuts.' Hani jumped in when she saw Zuleka reach for another drink. 'I think you've had enough'

'Don't be a party pooper; we're celebrating a record deal here.' Zuleka picked up a bottle of wine that was almost empty. She drank the last of its contents straight from the bottle before turning to the group of boys who were leering over her.

'Right boys, who wants to play spin the bottle?!' Her voice was loud as she spun around holding the empty bottle up in the air like it was a trophy.

She had no shortages of takers. *Well, on her head be it.* Hani left her to it. That was Zuleka, the life and soul of any party. Hani walked out of the kitchen and bumped straight into Izzy.

'You made it!'

Before she knew what was happening she found herself enclosed in his arms.

'No. YOU made it! Congratulations buddy.' But before she could say anything else a stream of new arrivals interrupted them. A trace of the feeling of his arms holding her stayed with her. She wanted to experience that again. Her whole body yearned to.

Izzy acknowledged everyone and spent a moment chatting to each before taking hold of her arm and saying, 'Let's go outside.'

His grin creased his face. His green eyes sparkled as they sat on the steps. 'Man, times are good right now.'

'I can imagine. Getting this deal is no mean achievement.'

'It's the right label too, that's why I am so psyched.'

'So how did it come about?'

'We sent in the demo; they requested more material. They liked what they heard and called me in and that was that, really' he said, his words coming out fast and holding excitement. 'It's a small label and the exec there is into the urban sound. He's not afraid to take a chance on something different. Of course, it helped that I have an established number of fans on my MySpace and You Tube'

'I am happy for you.'

A few second of silence passed between them. Hani's eyes met his. She felt an irresistible force pulling her towards him. Tiny charges of painless electric currents shot through her body. His eyes never left hers, his dark pupil expanded. She thought he could see into her very soul. The touch of his hand tracing the outline of her face tightened every muscle in her stomach. She closed her eyes. His fingers reached her parted lips and then, drew a slow line down her throat. The heat of his breath told her his lips were close.

A delicious sensation enhanced the tingling as his lips covered hers.

Opening her eyes a second or two after the kiss she found him still close, still looking her.

'Hey.' She couldn't think of anything else to say. She knew her cheeks had blushed.

'Hey, to you too. I have wanted to do that since that night in the parking lot at the wedding reception, but you really know how to keep a man waiting.'

'Really? That far back?'

'Hell, you looked so damn hot. I just wanted push you against the wall and do some things. Then a few days later you changed gears on me and went totally cold. What was that all about?'

'What were Emma and Danielle all about? What is with you and girls? Every time I see you, you have your body pressed up against one. I mean you can't blame me for brushing you off that night in the car when you drove me home.'

'So you were jealous?'

'Far from it— try repulsed.'

He laughed. 'Emma's an old fling and as for the other girls, well I am single guy and the only girl I liked kept dismissing me. And I can tell you, rejection sucks. I was glad that there were some women out there who were attracted to me. Anyway, what's with now?'

'I don't know. It's not one thing. Actually, it's many things, getting to know you. ... I don't know...'

'Well, whatever it is. I am glad. Like I said before, I really like you, and kissing you felt good. So good, I'd like to do it again and again and again.'

His voice lowered every time he repeated the word. His lips came closer to her. Nothing lightened from the first time. The intensity of feeling closed in on her just as it had before. She wanted him to kiss her. And when he did she drowned in him and never wanted him stop.

Someone called his name causing them to part. Hardly able to form the words Hani told him, 'You have guests; we should probably go back inside now.'

'Yeah, we probably should.' He stood up and held his hand out to her. They walked back inside together, but the party had gone up a notch in their absence and Hani found herself on her own again as the crowd pressed around them and dragged Izzy away. A small part of her welcomed this. Her mind was in a whirlwind with what had just happened between them.

The rest of the night passed in a blur. The only thoughts crowding her centred round their kisses and what they had said to each other. She knew she had never in her life felt so deliriously dizzy with happiness.

Chapter Seventeen
Dear God, please make me skinny

Ayan twiddled her handbag strap between her hands. Siddiq would be out at any moment. Something inside her didn't want him to be. If one of the girls came out of the bank and told her he couldn't make it for lunch as happened on occasions because of a sudden pressure of work, she thought she would jump for joy. And yet, part of her wanted to see him. What she didn't want was more accusations. She knew he had insecurities; she would help him with them if he let her, but instead he projected them on to her by slowly undermining her confidence.

She could do no right in his eyes. He accused her of flirting with guys, and of wearing too much make-up and, of all things, walking too 'wavy', whatever that meant, when she went out with the girls.

"Excuse me. Come again? You better tell him: Negro, it's the wavy walk that had you after my honey. Better yet, tell him to get lost. I can't believe he is speaking crap like that." Hamdi had snapped in amazement when she'd told them.

She'd tried to defend him by telling them that he was under a lot of pressure at work, and it was she who needed to be more understanding, but they argued otherwise. She'd protested that the bad times were minute compared to the good times, but stood here; anxious over meeting up with him she wasn't so sure.

The glass doors of the bank glided open and Siddiq came through. 'Sorry I'm late, babe, shall we grab a bite to eat before we hit the shops? I'm starving.'

His smile and the way he took her hand and kissed her cheek dispelled her misgivings. But still, she wished he'd not insisted on accompanying her to help her choose a new outfit to wear to his friend's wedding. It felt as though he didn't trust her choice. She'd taken the afternoon off to give her a chance to look around without him, but when she'd told him, he'd come back with this idea of him taking an extended lunch period so he could help her to choose.

As they walked around looking at this and that, laughing at silly jokes and making purchases none of them really wanted, Ayan relaxed. Siddiq had loved what she'd chosen, a, silky diraac in midnight blue with a pale turquoise scarf threaded with silver, from a shop specialising in Somali traditional dresses. His eyes had lit with appreciation when she'd picked it up.

'I'd better head back,'

He sounded reluctant and Ayan knew a moment of not wanting him to leave her. She took his hand. 'I wished you didn't have to.'

Siddiq pulled her into an alley way. 'Ayan, I love you. You are beautiful.' His illicit kiss thrilled her. Feelings awoke inside her she didn't want to deny.

'Oh, Ayan... We need to make this official, girl; its messing with me and making me think all sorts'

Her heart thumped with joy. *Was that a proposal?*

'Come on.' Siddiq grabbed her arm and almost jerked her back into the main street. I'm sorry, forgive me.'

'There's nothing to forgive, you know I feel the same way.'

'We can't discuss it here, babe. I'll pick you up tonight. We'll go somewhere nice for dinner, eh?'

Ayan nodded. They walked on not touching. The atmosphere was heavy with feeling. As they turned a corner they came across one of Ayan's favourite shops. Stocking fashionable clothes in a variety of sizes, she could always find what she looked for here. On a high she had a sudden urge to treat herself to something up to date. She loved dressing in traditional clothes, but when with the girls she loved to emulate their way of dressing, too.

'I won't come back with you, Siddiq; I'd like to carry on shopping. I need some new jeans and fancy getting a couple of tops, I'll…'

'What do you want to go buying jeans for? They don't suit you, Ayan, you look better in your Abaya than these western clothes.

'But I like wearing jeans sometimes.'

'I know, but a figure like yours just looks better in something loose fitting, that's all I am saying. You did bring me shopping for my opinion.'

'*I* did not *bring* you shopping. You manoeuvred things so that you were with me! And what do you mean a figure like mine?! Are you saying I am fat?

The couple in front looked round, she didn't care that they had heard her, *how dare he?* 'If that's the case, Siddiq, you can forget dinner tonight and use the time to find yourself a twig. Don't you dare presume you can tell me what I should wear!' Leaving him standing there she stormed into the store. Tears stung her eyes and humiliation burned her cheeks. *She hated him!*

Ignoring his calls she met up with the girls the next evening.

'The nerve of the bastard!'

'He should be so lucky, the insensitive fuck!'

Unanimously they agreed Siddiq had to go, but as the week passed and he continued to harass her with phone calls and friends told her they had seen him walking around areas she frequented, looking like a mad man and asking everyone to relay messages to her she agreed to talk to him, for five minutes only, and met him on the corner of the next street to hers.

'Please, Ayan, just come and have a coffee with me, give me a chance to explain.'

In a bid to avoid causing a scene too close to home she agreed. As he argued that she had misunderstood his words, reassured her that he loved her the way she was: how could he not? And confessed, what a sheer hell the last couple of weeks without her were for him, she fought an internal battle with herself.

No longer blind to his fault, he was flawed, she could see that now, but wasn't everyone? She didn't doubt that he loved her. The way he had been chasing and harassing her all week was, to her, proof of that. She had invested too much time and energy into the relationship to walk away over a stupid remark… Forty five minutes later she melted in her resolve to stay away from him.

Announcing the news to the girls she had the reaction she expected, but was ready to fight them down.

'Girlfriend, I know you love the boy, but you need to drop him like he is hot coals and you need to stay away from him. Don't you know that you can't let him disrespect you like that? For every loser there's a lame excuse, don't be buying his.'

'I agree with Hamdi, you don't need him. Seriously, Ayan, you can do better.' echoed Zuleka. 'Forget all that crap about the time you've invested in him, your young for god sake. Just move on.'

'Don't you see how he's been undermining and picking on you for a while now? You need to leave him, before your dignity leaves you, hun. People like him don't change.' Hani added for good measure.

Surprised at how, what they saw as caring about her angered her, she hit out at them: 'That's easy for you guys to say. What do you know about relationships, any of you? Nothing! You walk around as if life is one big catwalk and you're the supermodels, moving from one boy to the next. Well, guess what? It's not like that in the real world!'

'Ok, don't attack us. We are on your side here.'

Zuleka, whose friendship she had come to value more and more, looked hurt and embarrassed as she looked around to see if anyone in AA was looking at them because of her loud voice. But she didn't care about that. They had hurt her by not supporting her.

'What I need is for you lot to get off my case. Who I date is no one's business but my own.'

Hani stood up to stop her from leaving. 'Ayan, don't go. We only expressed our opinion. We have always freely discussed our relationships and accepted constructive criticism from each other but, if you love him and are willing to put up with his bulls— these anomalies in his character, then so are we,' she said, referring to Siddiq's shortcomings a little more politely than originally intended.

Ayan sat down again and allowed them to make their peace and the atmosphere to get back to normal with them all joking and not discussing any further sensitive issues.

But the tiny seed sown that day of the shopping outing hadn't gone. She could ignore it no longer. She had to lose weight. Oh yes, she knew she could trim a few inches off by jogging as she did at the beginning of most summer seasons, but this was different. She wanted to be slim.

The happiness she had attained before the row over the jeans had not rekindled. She could do nothing but change her figure in the hope that things would get better. In her head, thinness now equalled happiness.

Google threw up a few dieting sites. She picked one and started her diet. With the same fervour she tackled dating and finding Mr Right, she set out her strategy to lose the lbs and stones.

The results were too slow. After weeks of starvation she'd only lost a couple of pounds. She remembered one of her friends once mentioning the maple syrup diet which consisted of surviving on nothing but detox drinks. Giving it everything she could she took it on, but starvation pangs drove her crazy. Chocolate bars began to look the size of loaves of bread and reached out for her at every corner making her life a misery. Not giving in had her jumping for joy. She was already beginning to feel lighter and trimmer after seven days.

Somehow, the regime cleared her mind too. Deep down she knew her relationship with Siddiq was doomed. Things were just not the same but still she hoped her new strategy would save things.

Feeling irritable, she wished she hadn't agreed to meet the girls for lunch. They gobbling down burgers and fries while she sipped on a cold diet-coke compounded her misery.

'This is madness, girl, you don't have to do this. A few chips is not going to hurt you, in fact they will help you, nourish you a bit and set you up for the next bit of your regime.'

'It's not like that, Hamdi. I can't break it. I must stay on liquids only. It's the only way.'

Hamdi didn't seem to listen. She pushed her plate towards her, 'Just have a chip, hun. Please…'

Her irritation erupted into anger before she could stop it, 'You probably like having a fat friend, don't you? It makes you feel all the more saintly and contributes to you looking good. Well, you should find someone else to fill that gap because I refuse to be your confidence booster anymore.'

'What can I say? You are right. I liked you a lot better when you were fat.'

'Hamdi!' Hani jumped to her defence.

'It's true. At least then she wasn't always so miserable and snapping at people all the time.'

Though shocked Ayan felt a smile creeping up from somewhere deep within her, 'You're such a bitch, Hamdi…'

They all smiled at her and she could see the relief in their faces. Just as she went to apologise for her tardiness her phone rang.

'I am having lunch with the girls.'

'What have I told you about them…?'

'Don't start, Siddiq.' Once more her temper snapped. 'Come to think of it, what have I told you? They are my friends. I won't stop seeing them just because you want me to!'

'You never listen to me!'

'Oh, shut up! Look, I am too tired to deal with this right now. I'll talk to you later.' she snapped her phone lid down.

'Lover boy on your case again, huh?' asked Hamdi 'I don't know why you even bother with him. He's an A-class loser.'

'Just leave it, Hamdi, I didn't end one annoying conversation only to start another one. I'll see you guys later.'

'Ayan, don't go. You're just not seeing things how we mean them at the moment. None of what we say, even the teasing, is aimed at hurting you.' Hani turned towards to Hamdi, 'though, you get too near the mark at times, Hamdi, and should be more sensitive to Ayan's predicament. We have no right to push her one way or the other, no matter what we think.'

'I agree.' Zuleka chipped in. 'We don't want to push you into a corner, Ayan, and force you into a tug war. You have enough conflict on that score with Siddiq. Whatever you decide to do we are here for you, whether it is to pick up the pieces or celebrate.'

'Yes, sorry, Ayan. Hani and Zuleka are right. No more criticising from us. We are with you, no matter what.

Even if we have to become secret friends. Ha, I quiet fancy that. I had a secret friend when I was little. She...'

'Thanks, guys. Can't stop to hear about your little friend now though, Hamdi. It feels good to know you are there for me, I had begun to wonder. I'll see you later. No, I'm fine... Honestly. You carry on.'

She didn't feel fine. Not really. A battle to rival that of any in history waged inside her. She needed space; space from Siddiq and space from the girls. At this moment she did not know how her future would pan out, but the decisions regarding it had to be hers and hers alone. She turned towards home. She would make *wudu*, then go up into her bedroom and pray.

Chapter Eighteen
Coming to a head

'**W**hy don't we move in together? I'm getting tired of the uncertainty and I want to be with you 24-7.'

'Don't you think it's a little too soon for that?' Hani rolled over to face Izzy and snuggle further into his strong body. 'Besides we have to keep this real. You know by now that isn't how things are done in my culture.'

'I know, but I miss you when you are not here.'

His fingers found her scalp. The deep massaging movements and the playful tugs of her hair relaxed her. 'I miss you, too. You're sexy and gorgeous, but how can we be sure about what we feel for each other? For all I know we could just be having a good time. Which is okay, but I want to be certain before I take drastic steps.'

'I've never asked a girl to move in with me before...'

'That's because you've always had girls available on demand before. You have never needed to commit to anyone, and I am certainly not asking you to. Despite the chemistry between us, you're not in love with me and nor I, with you. As long as we're clear on that nobody can get hurt. Let's just enjoy now, ok, Izzy?'

'You know, just when I think I have you figured out you find new ways to surprise me.'

'Let me guess, you thought when you suggested moving in together I would jump at the chance?'

'Yeah, I kinder did, hey, don't leave.'

'I have to. I need to shower, and you need to ponder on the issues with your ego that need sorting out.'

'Thank you for that compliment – I don't think…' His laugh followed her to the door, 'Hey, you show me a good time and then you bounce. You know who you remind me of? *Me!'*

'It's called control, and it's an awesome thing to have. You've never had a woman turn you down for anything before, well now you have.' *Not one that wanted to though...* She thought as she reached the bathroom. *More, one who has no choice.* As it is Salim would be the first one to go berserk if he found out what she did on her odd nights away from home, which so far she'd got away with by telling them she was working late and stopping over at a girl friend's house. But if she dared to move in with a man she hadn't married, all hell would break loose.

As the water slipped off her smooth silky skin, her thoughts turned to the hype surrounding Tariq and Izzy since news of the record deal. There were more girls on the scene than ever, another reason why she had played it cool. So far, she felt sure it had worked. With what he gave her he had none left for others and didn't show any interest in having.

Tariq, showed different signs. Hamdi was a fool to keep up the pretence, but she had backed herself into a corner. On the one hand she couldn't admit to her lie and on the other, though Tariq said he liked a traditional thinking woman she felt sure he was getting sex elsewhere. And now her misgivings had reached the ceiling with this new thing of Tariq's. Over the last couple of weeks or so when his phone rang he would excuse himself and leave their company to take the call saying it was about business. Then he would disappear. Hamdi faced a quandary, not wanting to confront him on mere suspicion alone she stewed in doubt and...

A scream shattered Hani's thoughts. Goosebumps rippled her skin. She grabbed a towel and ran back into the bedroom. Hamdi's voice screeched through the floorboards, 'Who is this, you rat! You fucking low-life cheating bastard!'

'Oh, my god, Izzy, what's happening...?'

'Oh, it's just those crazy cats, they're always fighting. Take no notice.'

'That's not *just fighting*...' A crashing sound had her pulling on her jeans and jumper. She ran down the stairs. A demented Hamdi lunged at Tariq with the ferocious force of an animal. Hani tried to stop her, 'No, Hamdi, calm down, what is it? No...'

'Get out of my way, Hani. I'm not going to let him play me like that!'

Reeling from the shove, Hani landed on the bottom step. Winded, she couldn't move or speak. Nor could she believe her friend had acted with violence towards her.

Hamdi showed no remorse nor did she stop to take stock of her actions as she sprang at Tariq, clawing at his face before pummelling him with her fists.

'What the hell is wrong with you?' Tariq managed to grab both her hands and pin her back against the wall, 'Baby, calm down and talk to me...'

'Let go of me...Let go of me!' Hamdi twisted and turned like a crazed animal.

'Tariq let her go!'

'No, Hani, not until she promises not to start lashing out again.'

With one movement he flung her towards the living-room. Leapt in after her and closed the door.

Hani sat still, strewn around her a broken hall table and a shattered ornamental guitar. Hamdi's screaming, fish-wife voice assaulted her ears and shifted her body as a dread of what might happen panicked her. She ran back upstairs shouting to Izzy to come and help. She met him on the landing, 'What... What's going on...? Christ, it sounds bad this time...'

'Hamdi's going mad. She has a photo. I think it's of Tariq with another girl'

Another crashing, splintering sound took all reason from Hani. She looked at Izzy. He grabbed her and held her close, 'Babe, you're shaking, are you hurt?'

'No, I'm alright, but we have to *do* something.'

'I don't think we can. Tariq and I, we give each other space. We have to. It's the only way to make living together work. I don't think we should interfere…'

'We must, Izzy, please, something really horrible could happen…'

Hamdi's screams took on a sinister pitch. Half muffled – half demented as if Tariq restrained her, but then she broke free. Horror gripped Hani. Had Tariq resorted to violence?

The thought had her descending the stairs two at a time. Izzy followed her. They were halfway down when the living room door opened. Hamdi came out blindly groping for the door, sobs wrecking her strength. Hani went to go to her but she turned and gasped, 'No… no, leave me…' The door slammed behind her.

Izzy pushed open the living room door. The sight that met them made them both draw in their breath in horror. Tariq slumped in a chair his face covered in blood. His shirt ripped and oozing more blood.

'What the hell happened, man?'

'She's fucking nuts.' He sat down on the sofa, looking weary.

Izzy took his cigarettes out, lit one and handed it to Tariq.

Hani's whole body shook. Never before had she witnessed a grown man almost reduced to tears.

'She… she had a picture… a fucking old one that someone, jumping on the bandwagon of all the hype around us, must have dug up and put on facebook to raise their profile, honest man, that chick was long before Hamdi.'

Feeling embarrassed for Tariq and wanting to get to Hamdi, Hani told him, 'Look, Tariq, I've never known Hamdi to go this crazy. She must be really hurting. She's had a lot of insecure feelings lately. If it's any consolation it shows how much she thinks of you. Not that I agree with what she has done here, no way. I'll go after her and see what I can do.'

Neither of the men answered her. Still trembling all over and with a sick feeling swimming around inside her she left.

On the way over to Hamdi, Hani phoned into work and lied about not being well enough to go in.

Hamdi took a while to answer her door. When she did she fell into Hani's arms. All she could do was hold the distraught Hamdi close and try to soothe her, 'Come on, hun. Let's get inside. I'll put the kettle on.'

'Oh, Hani, how could he?'

Hani left her for a moment. Hoping she would compose herself so they could talk.

'Here, drink this.' A calmer Hamdi took the steaming mug from her.

'Hamdi, what got into you? How did you get that picture? Did you even look at the date it was taken?'

Izzy had texted whilst she'd been in the kitchen, *'Tell Hamdi to look at the picture again the date on it proves Tariq is telling the truth.'*

'It doesn't matter if the picture is old. I know he's cheating.'

'Don't you think it's time you told him the truth? It might give you guys a clean break to start over.'

'Don't you think I want to tell him?! I have thought about it a dozen times, but he's making it so damn difficult! He has complimented my *values* so many times, and he keeps telling me I am different, that he's never met a girl who knew how to have fun but still maintained her

143

traditions and all of that crap. I just don't know what do to.'

'I really don't understand why you torment yourself like this. Just tell him the bloody truth, and if he can't take it, so what? What have you lost?'

'Put like that, I suppose you're right. The lie has gone on for too long. I hadn't imagined it would have gone this far, I'll go over to see him now and I'll tell him the truth.'

'Ring first. Give him a chance to decide if he wants to see you. He's hurting bad, and not just from the injuries you inflicted on him.'

Hamdi reached for her phone. As she did so she looked up at Hani, 'Hun, I'm so sorry I pushed you. Can you forgive me?'

'It's forgotten. Don't worry, love. I know you were not yourself.'

Hamdi's phone lit up on Tariq's name. She pressed the call button. It didn't ring out for long. It was obvious Tariq had refused the call. Hamdi collapsed back into her chair. 'What have I done, Hani? Oh, My god, what have I done?'

Chapter Nineteen
Zuleka hits rock bottom

Zuleka woke to the sound of her shrill alarm. *Damn the bloody TFL for holding the City to ransom and robbing me of much needed sleep.*

She dragged herself to the bathroom and had a quick shower before applying a heavy load of concealer to cover up the dark circles underneath her eyes. She dressed and dashed out of the house.

You have got to be kidding me! So much for getting up early. There must have been upwards of thirty people standing at the bus stop. She looked at her watch. Seven O'clock, surely she would make it on time?

Within the next few minutes several buses, all packed, drove past without stopping.

When she at last managed to get on to one, fighting others off as if waging a one-man war, she knew she'd be at least half an hour late. Her only hope lay with the fact that Marta would experience the same difficulties and would either arrive after her or understand what had delayed her. Phoning in to say she was on her way and would get there as soon as possible was a no-go. With passengers squashed into every space around her she couldn't even retrieve her bag from where she had put it at her feet, let alone get her mobile out.

The smell of cheap perfume and stale body odour permeated her nostrils. Bile rose to her throat. Wriggling from side to side, she managed to lift her cashmere scarf and wrap it around her mouth and nose, she didn't care what people thought. She'd pass out if she didn't filter the foul stench somehow.

Arriving nearly an hour late she found Sam alone on the shop floor. *Is it too much to hope that Iron Lady hasn't made it in, yet?*

'Hey, girl, sorry I am late. It's bloody chaos out there.'

'No need to tell me about it, I just got here myself. Ron just called to say he doesn't think he'll get here for another hour at least. I hate these strikes.'

'You are not the only one. The bus was that full, it reeked!'

'Zuleka, can I see you in the staff room?' Marta's voice cut across their chatter like a sudden icy wind.

Sam and Zuleka exchanged 'uh- uh' looks.

Zuleka followed Marta into the small staff room that also served as a delivery room and led to the department manager's offices. Marta held the door open and waited for Zuleka to enter before closing the door behind them. She stood a few feet from Zuleka, her arms crossed over her chest.

'Zuleka, you have been a valuable member of staff. Your sales record is exemplary but you have a problem with time keeping and with authority. I have asked you numerous times not to be late but you pay no attention.'

'Marta, there's a bloody strike going on. Half of London is late for work, not just me.'

'I wasn't late.'

She had to grit her teeth to restrain herself from slapping Marta and wipe the smug look off her face as she asked her, 'What are you getting at?'

'You were on your final warning. Coming into work an hour late is not acceptable, Zuleka. Regrettably, you leave me no choice. You're sacked.'

'You can't sack me! You're just a supervisor, Marta. Get over yourself.'

'Marc is on leave. Until he returns from holiday I am in charge. That means I can, and *I have* sacked you. Collect you're belonging and leave the shop floor.'

'But everybody else was late. Are you going to sack them, too?'

'They were not on a final warning.'

'I think a tribunal will have something to say about this. You won't get away with it. There are extenuating circumstances…'

'We don't have unions here'

'No, but there are employment tribunals I can appeal to. And, I am telling you, lady, I will contact them. You have made a mistake – a big mistake.' Zuleka stomped out of the department store impotent with rage. Red hot hate for Marta burned her. *The stupid, conniving bitch had waited for Marc to go on holiday and pounced on her chance to get rid of her.* Knowing she had a case against her gave no consolation, those things took so long. What was she going to do in the meantime?

She called up Hani praying she could see her. She needed to bitch. Then she needed help. *Thank God Hani had a free lunch hour.* They agreed to meet in a café near to her office.

'What am I going to do, Hani? I don't have any savings. The gas, electric and phone bills eat up my money, not to mention the rent. Losing my job halfway through the month like this has left me with nothing to fall back on.'

Hani's arm came around her, 'It's going to be okay, hun, really it will. Don't let it get you down. You'll find another job. It's summer; all the shops will want extra staff.'

'But who will take on someone who has had the sack! It's hopeless. I just don't know which way to turn. I've manage by paying a bit off here and there and keeping everyone at bay as best I can. The rent bothers me the most. I'm already behind and promised my landlord I'd have something for him this week. I thought my commission would come in and cover it, but it hasn't. It all seems so hopeless.

'Can't you sign on? I know there is something about not getting much if you have lost your job through your own fault, but as you haven't I think they would even help you to fight your case.'

'It's an idea. It's one I hate, but I suppose I may have to. Look, thanks, Hani. I don't mean to be rude after having begged you to meet me, but all of a sudden I just feel like I need time alone.'

'That's fine. You know where I am if you need me. I can help out a bit'

'No, you've done enough. The last thing I want is for you to think this was an excuse to put you in a position to offer me more. I have to sort something out myself this time. Thanks though, for offering.'

Trying to work out a budget pounded a pain around Zuleka's head. Threatening letters lay scattered around her. Credit card bills, utility bills, bank statements showing her balance over her limit and, worst of all, her open rent book with the arrears clearly marked in red.

She looked around her bedsit, the thread bare carpet left by the previous owner had taken her days to clean as it had stunk of stale urine and rotting food and, the old sofa she unfolded into a bed at night and a table and a chair she had bought in a second-hand shop, all looked shabby. Yes, a bright red throw, a gift from the girls, cheered the sofa up and a lace cloth from a charity shop covered the table giving a semblance of home, but the corner-makeshift kitchen fitted with two cupboards and an old gas stove gave an over-all picture of poverty.

A tear trickled down her cheek. She thought of her comfortable home and her family and her tears increased. Desperation suggested many things. She could sell some of her clothes and jewels, but it's a known thing that you can't get anything like what they are worth. She would probably raise enough to pay one weeks rent, but what good would that be? There would be other weeks to pay and more bills and demanding letters and all to face with nothing decent to wear!

Loneliness engulfed her. She'd already refused Hani's offer and she couldn't go to Hamdi again, either. She owed them shit loads as it is and God alone knew when she would be able to raise enough to pay Ayan back.

Heavy with despair she walked into the bathroom. The bathtub, chipped and stained looked anything but inviting, but needs must.

As the steam began to fill the bathroom she searched her cabinet for something soothing to add to the water to help her to relax. Her eyes caught sight of the aspirin bottle on the top shelf. Meaning only to shake out two to ease her headache something compelled her to empty the bottle into her hand. The tablets lay in a little heap in her palm calling to her, offering peace – a way out. She tore a tissue from the loo roll and let the tablets trickle on to it.

A hot bath first. Dress and make up her face. She must look beautiful when they found her.

The scolding water made her wince but she plunged in welcoming how her body numbed it out. Tiredness weighed a ton on her shoulders. Mentally and physically everything had drained from her. No matter how hard she tried to make a go of her life, nothing she did was good enough.

She couldn't even rely on her grades coming up to scratch to enable her to take up the Junior Doctor post as she had fallen so far behind by the end of term. She'd had no choice but to sign up for more and more hours at work and even burning the midnight oil studying and managing to get everything in by the deadline, she doubted had saved her.

She slid her head underneath the water. Briefly she wondered if her parents would miss her if she died. Would they feel guilty? Or would they hold their heads up high at the shame once more brought down on them by their rebellious daughter, before thanking Allah that she was not able to do any more damage.

That's not fair. She came up for air. Her parents were many things but she knew they had loved her once, maybe they still did. It was her fault that she couldn't be the daughter they wanted. She was a disappointment to everybody, including herself.

God must be angry with her. Her beauty and intelligence had meant everyone had adored her and everything she had tackled she'd succeeded in. All of a sudden that had changed, now she had nothing while everyone around her had something or *someone*. The misery she felt wasn't just because she'd lost her job it was a culmination of a long list of things that shook her confidence and made her question herself. If that wasn't divine punishment she didn't know what was.

Before she took the pills she would write a letter telling her parents she accepted full responsibility and she knew they had done what they could. She would write one to each of the girls telling them what they meant to her and how grateful to each one she had felt just before her death.

None of these positives lifted her resolve. They only made it easier. Inside her head she had a white cloud. It cushioned her. It blocked out all the bad and only filtered in the light of where she knew her spirit would go.

Her body shivered, the water had lost its temperature. She got out of the tub and wrapped a huge fluffy towel around her. Picking up the tissue, careful not to drop any of the precious pills wrapped in it, she headed to the kitchen.

As she leaned over to get a glass out of the cabinet she caught sight of the bottle of wine Hani had bought her for a house-warning present. A couple of glasses of that would help. She would have one then get herself ready then take the pills with another glass.

No fear lay in her. Her body floated through the motions. She took the bottle to the table. Gathered up the bills and shoved them back into the folder she kept them in and put it back in the drawer of the table. Pouring herself a glass of wine she sat down on the sofa.

She wouldn't have minded some food, a kind of last supper. But she had nothing in. The thought of her favourite pizza set up a longing in her. That's what she would ask for on death row. Well, she was there now. She picked up her mobile and dialled the number. The voices – hers and that of the pizza man - sounded a long way off.

As she picked up her glass the crude buzz of the intercom shattered her inner peace and catapulted her back to reality. She froze. It could only be one person.

Loud irate bangs reverberated around the room. 'I know you are in there. Open up or I will let myself in.'

Her heart thumped against her chest as she collided with the real world. *Her landlord, shit!*

On legs that shook and didn't seem to know how to walk she made it to the door. Taking a deep breath she opened it. 'Good afternoon, Mr. Patel,' she forced a smile.

'How are you, Zuleka?'

How was she? Hovering somewhere between this world and the next. She foraged in her clogged brain to find an answer and to appear normal. 'I've seen better days...' She stood aside to let him enter. What did it matter now? He could say what he wanted to, she had her way out. *But it did.* This rude interruption to the state of bliss had taken the beautiful cloud away and forced her back to face everything once more. All her fears and desperation crowded back into her.

'Zuleka, you know you are behind with your rent. I cannot tolerate this any longer. You have to pay me the amount to bring you up to date. Otherwise I will have to evict you and take you to court to get my money.'

'I can't… I have nothing… I've just lost my job. Please give me a few more weeks and you'll have your money. I promise.'

'I am sorry to hear that you have lost your job,' his eyes scanned the room. Then rested on her, 'At least you are a good tenant in how you keep my property in good order and clean. I am not used to that with students. But in every other way you are not good. You have to pay your rent.' As though he saw her for the first time his eyes travelled up and down her body. They simmered an appreciation of the picture she presented to him. His voice deepened, 'You are a very beautiful woman… There may be other ways in which you could pay…'

Zuleka read the look in his eyes and knew the alternative he offered… Could she?'

The buzzer sounded again, 'My pizza. Excuse me.' She fumbled in her bag. Her hands shook. The inference had been clear to her and he knew it. Again she asked herself, *could she?*

Returning with her pizza, she looked at her landlord. Aged around forty he wasn't a bad looking guy. His clothes and expensive aftershave all said he had good taste and a bit of money. In ordinary circumstances she might have fancied him. Had thought along those lines a couple of times as it happened. But, no. Not that. Not sex for payment. A voice jarred her as it shouted in her brain, *Why the fuck not? It won't be any different to any of the numerous one night stands you had in the past! Anyway, what else could you do?*

'I'll just put this in the oven.' She brushed past him as she went over to the kitchen area. When she turned towards him her towel had slipped a little.

He ran his tongue, bright pink against his brown skin and white even teeth, along his lips moistening them. His eyes smouldered as they looked into hers and then lowered. His voice hoarse, he whispered, 'I want you, Zuleka. I have wanted you for a long time.' He sounded nervous, afraid even.

Somehow this put things on a different level for her and banished the thoughts inside her that told her this was wrong, she moved closer to him. The towel slipped to the ground.

'You're beautiful…' The words breathed on her cheek. She told herself she wanted him. Not as a payment for her rent, but him as a man. This wasn't bad. She wasn't bad. This was just a woman and a man who fancied each other. Two consenting adults...

The kiss tasted good. His hands on her naked flesh heightened her need to a pitch she couldn't deny even if he said she would still have to pay her rent.

Between his hungry kisses and exploring caresses she helped him to undress. Then taking his hand she led him to the sofa. Together they unfolded it.

Asif had left the apartment ten minutes earlier, but Zuleka remained snuggled in her duvet, thinking about what she had done. All the while he was there she kept telling herself she hadn't prostituted herself. He liked her. He'd fancied her. That's all it was. He didn't think of her as a whore. *He didn't!*

She had tried to dress it up, but the reality of it being a transaction reared its head when he'd told her he would not want any rent for two months and her arrears were now clear. On top of that he'd left a wad of notes on her coffee table.

She had wanted to protest, not wanting to taint what had happened, not wanting to let in her guilt and her shame. When he left, she picked up the money. Counting how much it was, she felt a load lifting from her.

She clasped the notes to her chest. It wasn't bad, she wasn't bad, she repeated in her head. Anyways, what choice did she have? And it's not like anybody was ever going to find out. Her rent worry had gone – dissolved, just like that. All of a sudden, she wished she could perform the same vanishing act on her other bills.

A plan was growing in her mind. She refused to listen to the small part of her that protested at her own thoughts; she was tired of always being strapped for cash, tired of drowning in a sea of red letters otherwise known as past due bills or of being afraid to open her bank statement.

Taking the pizza out of the oven and tearing off a good slice she sat down at the table. With the glass of wine now an appetiser not a mind duller she sank her teeth into the squishy, delicious tomato and cheese and quashed the part of her that told her she couldn't sell her body and spoke back to her dissenting conscience.

She wanted no more aggressive phone calls. She wanted to have money to lavish on clothes, jewellery and to get her life back on track.

When she finished her pizza, she walked over to her wardrobe she dropped the tissue wrapped tablets into the bin. Her body shuddered at what she had nearly done. Banishing the feelings she opened her wardrobe. If this was going to work she needed to look knockout.

Her eyes scanned the designer outfits. Her blood pounded the adrenaline around her body. A short slinky red dress and six inch black Loubotin heels won her vote. She showered and taking her time to get everything right, she applied her makeup and straightened her hair. A dash of Channel No 5 on her neck and the insides of her wrists put the finishing touches to the stunning young woman who looked out at her from the mirror. She looked like class, and she was. Men paid well for class. *Perfect... Ladies and Gentleman... She's back!*

Chapter Twenty
The past and the present

Hamdi walked out of the railway station in Leicester and turned into Hollowam Road in the direction of her old home. The nostalgia of the journey hadn't lessened her hurt. She hoped being with Nimo would – that's if anything could after the latest blow Tariq had hit her with.

Making up had not given her the chance to tell him the truth in the way she had wanted to. Tariq had forestalled her by telling of his needs and how he thought he'd come up with a solution – God had he?!

Some part of her acknowledged Tariq had tried to be fair. Well, fair in the way a man saw things. Convinced she wanted to save herself for marriage he'd told her he couldn't wait. He had urges and boy being with her had really fired them up. Thinking he might pop the question her, world fell apart when he asked her permission to assuage his needs with other women. They would mean nothing to him, he told her. *Fuck, how could he have come up with such a hurtful suggestion!* But, the aftermath had been worse. She cringed inside as she thought of the look on his face when she'd gone ballistic and screamed her lie at him. It was a look she knew would stay etched onto her soul forever. A constant reminder of how she'd lost him. *She had never meant to tell him like that. Not using the fact she'd slept with others as a weapon against him...Oh, God, why had she... Why had she?*

The convenience store came into her view. She'd stop off and get a few things to take with her. Nimo always needed a helping hand, besides it would provide her with a distraction. Give her time to calm her feelings.

Nappies for the baby, two litres of milk, and a few other random things went into her basket. Shopping for Nimo switched her focus and she wondered what it was Nimo wanted to tell her. Her call asking her to visit as she needed to speak with her face to face couldn't have come at a more opportune moment, but until now she hadn't given much thought to what it was all about. She hoped whatever it was, it wasn't anything serious.

Memories of growing up in the neighbourhood came flooding back as she approached the house. Her former secondary school stood at the bottom of the hill and on the opposite side of the road, the bus-stop where she'd tasted her first kiss as an eleven year old. Barely able to speak sufficient English she had agreed when the little white boy held mistletoe above their heads and said it meant they had to kiss. Once the deed had been done she'd run back home burning with shame and secret pleasure.

Outside the house, Fahad and Mahad kicked a ball with other kids from the street.

'Hamdi!' shouted Fahad, the younger of the two boys. His hug felt delicious.

'Fahad!' The laughter bubbled from her, 'Oh my god, you have grown so much. Has it been that long? And you, Mahad, don't tell me you're too much of a man to give me a hug now?'

'Hey, Hamdi.' Mahad came over. He placed his hand over her shoulder with the feigned coolness of a teenager. At fourteen he towered over her.

'Don't hey me, mister,' she said, reaching up and messing his carefully groomed hair with her hand, 'Is your mom home?'

'Yeah, she's inside, are you staying the night?'

'Yep, we'll catch up later. You carry on with your game.'

She hadn't planned to spend the night there, but it would be good to put some distance between her and London. Everything there reminded her of Tariq, as much as she hated him, she also knew she was in love with him. An admission she felt comfortable sharing with no one but herself. *How had she allowed it to happen?* Anger rose in her at the power she'd let him have over her. Even now, after hurting her so deeply, he still occupied most of her thoughts something no ex-boyfriend had done for more than three days post the breakup period, let alone an entire week!

The front door yielded to her push. She walked in. 'Nimo?'

'Hamdi, is that you?' Nimo appeared at the top of the stairs. Her face lit with the wide, loved-filled smile Hamdi knew so well. Tears pricked the back of her eyes. She blinked them away just as her tiny body sank into the ample bosoms, made for comforting.

'I am hugging you, but really you deserve to be smacked. When was the last time you came to visit us, huh? And I can feel your bones. You need to fill out a little bit, girl; otherwise you're never going to get a husband.'

'If I was ever going to fill out it would have been while I lived here feeding on your delicious cooking, Nimo, besides, many women would kill for this figure so I am over trying to gain weight'

Nimo frowned. 'Unless you plan to bring us a blue eyed adaan, you should know Somali men like their women with a little bit of curves, so keep trying. Anyway how have you been?'

'I've been good.' They'd reached the kitchen and Hamdi put down the shopping bags. The familiar smells clinging to the very fibre of the house set up a craving in her for the mouth-watering rice and suqaar Nimo used to make. As if reading her mind Nimo whipped up hot plates and served her some of the fragrant rice with a side dish of suqaar and chapattis.

'Heaven! You really should go into the catering business. Your food is awesome, walaalo.' Hamdi smiled at how naturally she called Nimo, sister. It had always been so, even though the paperwork had declared Nimo her mother and Hamdi thought of her as such.

'Maybe when Sabah has grown a little more I can think of something like that. I am done with having more kids now, Alhamdulillah, god has blessed me enough.'

'I really hope you mean that, you know what the doctor said.'

A series of miscarriages in the last trimester had left Nimo's body weak, but she never gave up trying, arguing the point that if she couldn't have the big family she always wanted, then she at least had to try for a girl. The doctors had shown their concern at her insistence: didn't she already have two healthy boys and a girl? They had all sighed with relief when Sabah entered the world screaming her femininity and robust health.

'So, while you eat, tell me, what's been keeping you busy in London? You seeing anybody?'

'Well, I was talking to this one guy, Tariq. But that's gone the way of all the others. He turned out to be a bit of a *nacaas* in the end.' Hamdi cleared the last morsel of rice on her plate and went to the sink to wash her dishes, 'You would have liked him, though. He's Somali and real cool.'

'So what was the problem?'

'Different expectations. Anyway, what did you want to talk to me about? It sounded serious on the phone.'

'Well…'

'It is serious, oh, Nimo, what's wrong?'

'It's about your mother.'

'My mother! Has she died?' No emotion assailed her as she asked this. She hadn't any knowledge, nor wanted any of where her mother was. And if Nimo had known she hadn't said so. They rarely discussed what had happened.

'No, she's alive. Word reached me some time ago about where she has been living all this time. She's in Garrisa.'

So, the old glamour-puss is alive after all, go figure.

'Where the hell is Garrisa?'

'It's near Kenya's border with Somalia. A lot of Somalis fleeing the war have settled there. A clansman visiting his relatives recognized her, and he told her you were with me in the UK. She sent you something.' Nimo got up and went to the living room.

She returned with a miserable looking package wrapped in a brown paper bag. Hamdi took it and opened it. A red, silky *Dirac*, beautiful, but old and probably worn by her mother in her heydays unfolded in her hands. From inside it fell a couple of black and white pictures. Hamdi picked them up. An image of her mother, young, wild, and rebellious, exactly as the gossips had described her, looked out at her from one of them. The other was of a little girl. For a moment Hamdi wondered if it was herself, but when she held it up to the light she saw that, though there was a likeness, this was not a picture of her.

'Who's the kid?'

'Your mother re-married. It must be your little sister.'

'Another half-sister... Lucky me.'

The brown paper crackled as she folded everything away.

'What does she want, Nimo? There must have been a message with it. Besides, knowing what I know of my mother she wouldn't go to the trouble of getting in touch just to send me her hand-me-downs and a picture of her new family.'

'She's in trouble, Hamdi, and she needs help. There is a severe drought in the region. It's bad, real bad. They have lost everything.'

'She needs help? What I am supposed to do? I don't want to hear anymore, it's not my problem. Tell her to pray or go and ask her other family members for help. I don't want anything to do with her.'

Nimo winced. 'I understand your anger. As a mother I cannot imagine leaving behind any of my kids. I would fight off hyenas to keep them safe. But though I knew how you would react I had to pass on her message. Here, she also sent you this.'

Hamdi looked at the cassette tape Nimo held out to her. She knew this was the old Somali way of sending messages. For the illiterate, nomadic society recording a message presented the perfect means of communication.

'Take it. Listen to it when you get a chance. There's a number written on the outside. It must be a number you can ring to get to speak to her.'

***

Whenever she left Nimo's house she always felt rejuvenated and ready for the hustle and bustle of London life. But not this time. She had avoided thinking about her mother all weekend, but the rhythm of the train home had throbbed an internal argument through her mind: *What did she want this mother of mine? She can go to hell. Why contact me now…why…why…I won't listen to her plea…Yes I will, No I won't. No I won't!*

A long tunnel had helped to change the tempo and a silent scream had broken the thread. With her head banging a pain through her, her hands shook as she set up her iPod, desperate not to allow the beat back in when the train emerged. It had done the trick. But winding through the streets of London in a taxi the thoughts had trickled back in.

She didn't want to listen to the tape. It would just open up a can of worms. She threw it into a drawer full of bits and bobs she might someday need, but never did.

Her mother could not explain away the hurt and she didn't want to listen to a bunch of excuses all because she was now hard up and needed help. The nerve of that woman! She had made a brand new family and more than likely forgotten all about her first child. *That is until the moment came when she thought I could be of use to her.* Well, now it is her turn to know the pain of abandonment.

Where was she when I needed a saviour? It wasn't my fault that she had married a tyrannical loser. All the other wives had taken their children when they decided to leave. She caught sight of herself in the mirror. The way she ran her life went through her mind. The relationships, the one night stands—well, the gossipers of the day had been right about one thing as they'd slated the way she'd played with the boys instead of being a dutiful little girl.

She did enjoy sex and she was damn good at it. And as if she spoke to Tariq she lifted her head high, *but, it will always on my terms. No man will ever use and abuse me!*

What did it matter anyway? She didn't need a man, not one in particular, anyone of them would do for her pleasure. There was nothing else she wanted from them. She had no problem supporting herself. After leaving Nimo's and coming to London a series of menial jobs had seen her through college and she now held a PA position and ran the human resources department in the main branch of Johnsons and Herbert's a major financial and insurance firm. She certainly didn't need a man to support her financially.

The ringtone she'd set up for Tariq jarred her from her thoughts. She had ignored all his calls since the row, but now could not do so. Cross with herself as much as at him, she snapped, 'What do you want? I thought I made it clear that I don't want to talk to you.'

'Well, I need to talk to you. Are you at home?'

'No, I am in Leicester.' She lied; talking to him on the phone was one thing, seeing him… Well, she couldn't cope with that.

'I really need to talk to you. Is it ok if I drive up to see you?'

She contemplated letting him drive all the way up there only to find out she had left, but thought better of it. 'No, whatever it is you have to say can wait.' She hung up the phone.

She needed a drink. A couple of glasses of wine would send her to sleep then she wouldn't have to lie awake for hours remembering and replaying things she would rather forget. *Oh, if only it was that simple!*

.

Chapter Twenty One
Surprise, Surprise

Since the last lunch date when Ayan had thrown a wobbly, they hadn't all met up in one place and no one had seen Ayan. Hani thought she would rectify this. She rang them round and wouldn't take no for an answer.

'AA, Friday night. We need to catch up on things, Hamdi.'

'You mean you want to wallow in my misery and Ayan's disaster, and God knows what with Zuleka so you can preen yourself and show off that you are the only one in clover at the moment?'

'Hamdi, you've got to sort out that chip on your shoulder, girl. What's going down with you? What happened in Leicester?'

'Oh, just a little matter of a long lost mother suddenly thinking I'd be there for her and forgetting how she'd fucked up my life in the past, sending a present and a message.'

'I don't know what to say. Oh, Hamdi... Do you want to meet and tell me about it? I know you have a history, but you've never shared it. I thought, Nimo...'

'I know, I've never told you the full truth. Yes, it would feel good to get an opinion on it all. But, I'm not ready yet.... Look, let's leave it there for now.'

'Okay, but don't let us down on Friday and in the meantime, think about answering Tariq's calls, he really is suffering and doesn't care a jot about your deception now.'

'Just leave it, Hani. See you Friday.'

Feeling down in the dumps by Hamdi dismissing her in such a way, Hani's thoughts turned to Zuleka. When she'd last seen her she raved about a new boyfriend and how everything had turned a corner for her. She'd give no further information and a worry had set up in Hani's mind as to just what she was up to.

'Z, its Hani...'

'I know, girl, your name flashed, and your tune played... What's with the introduction?'

'Nothing, sorry. Look this is a summons – Friday night at AA.'

'No-can-do, hun. I have me a hot date.'

'Cancel it. We have to get together, it's been ages. I have Hamdi coming and I'm about to work on Ayan.'

'Oh, okay, I'll get back to you.'

'Before you go, lady, who is this hot date and when do we get to meet him?'

'Bye... See you Friday.'

Zuleka was being infuriating, but at the same time very worrying. How had she cleared her debts? She hadn't got a job, and who is this mystery guy? All she could hope was that she wasn't doing anything stupid.

'Ayan, remember me? Yes, I am still alive, you know! You have dropped off the radar lately, girl, no meeting up, no text and not answering mine. What's happening?'

'Quite a lot actually, but nothing you and the girls would approve of.'

'Try us on Friday night, AA, and don't even try to say no as I won't listen. We four are in danger of disintegrating as a group. We have to reconvene and get our gossip tuned up.'

To her surprise, Ayan agreed. Hani hoped, *the quiet a lot,* did not mean Siddiq had finally gotten his claws into Ayan's brain and that was why she hadn't been in contact. But consoled herself with the thought that if he was now making decisions for her, she still kicked against him because she sounded really sure about the AA date.

Friday night started like a funeral wake. Hamdi couldn't raise a smile and Zuleka looked and acted like the one who thought she would come in for the inheritance. Ayan had yet to arrive.

'Z, what are you up to? That's new isn't it?'

'This? No, I bought it ages ago on one of my shopping binges. I just haven't worn it that's all. And, I'm not up to anything. I have this great guy, but he's married so we have to go out in secret...'

'Married!'

'Oh, you needn't chorus like that, either of you. None of you are angels. My man is in an arranged alliance and his wife can't stand what we find delicious. And boy does she not know what she is missing with her guy. He's hot!'

'Z, be careful. I've been down that road and a lot of people get hurt.'

'I know, Hamdi, but you were only a kid. Your boss took advantage of you. Me, I'm all grown up, and so is he. It's good. And, he keeps me in rent and stuff.'

'You mean you prostitute yourself...'

'I do not, Hamdi, how dare you. We respect each other. I guess you could say I am something of a mistress. There's nothing wrong in that seeing as though we can do nothing about our circumstances. It's not like am taking money for sex, honestly'

'Me thinks she protest too much...'

'Okay, let's cool it, bitches. Don't forget, we can tell each other anything, right? And no judgement goes down, right?'

'Yeah, I guess so. Sorry Z, it's just me, I'm not myself lately.'

Hani couldn't believe it when Hamdi wiped a tear away from her eye.

'Forget it, hun,' Zuleka told her. 'It's nothing. Hey, cheer up, here comes Ayan, now that is a surprise. Let's hope things are okay in her court. Oh, but, don't tell her about me. Not yet.'

They nodded and greeted Ayan.

'Are you okay, Ayan?' Hani couldn't believe how emaciated, tired and unhappy she looked.

'Anything, but ok. It's over.' she said as she slumped down on the sofa. She must have lost a couple of stones in weight and looked around the size 10 mark, but the loss hadn't brought her the happiness she'd hoped for by the looks of her and from what she'd just said.

'What happened?'

'Everything happened, Hani, and I can't take it anymore. He is just too controlling, and I feel like shit when I am around him. I tried to make it work but every day I felt like I was dying inside.'

'Losing so much weight so fast can't have helped. If I didn't know you'd been dieting so hard I would think you were sick or something.'

'I know. I can't even get that right.'

'Did you stop seeing us because of him?' asked Hamdi

'We were arguing everyday and I thought if I just let him have his way he would stop being such a pain. I am sorry guys, I've missed you all.'

'There is no need to apologies, hun. These things happen.'

'Oh, Hani…' Her phone started ringing. She looked at it and said, 'It's him!'

'What does he want?' Zuleka asked.

Ayan hit the red button on her phone, 'The usual. To apologize, to say he loves me and all that.'

'Did you just break up with him now?'

Ayan put her phone on silence but it kept flashing with Siddiq's calls, while she answered their questions, 'Yeah, we just had another argument and I'd had enough. I caught him looking at the messages on my phone and he had the nerve to get angry about some stuff he saw. I mean they were my messages and he had no right to be snooping on me like that.'

'Stuff ? What kind of stuff?' asked Hamdi. Hani caught her look and read the look of bewilderment. *This was Ayan they were talking about. There was nothing he could have seen to make him angry and prompt her to end their relationship. Could he??*

They all looked at Ayan. She looked confused and hesitant.

'So what did he see?' prodded Zuleka

'Nothing really,' she avoided eye contact with any of them, 'Just some texts from this guy I have been talking to. I mean there was nothing bad about it...'

'You mean you've been cheating on him?! Damn, I never saw that coming. I have to say, I like this new skinny you, girl!'

'No, no. It's not like that, Z. I would never do that. We were just talking and exchanging messages that's all.'

'Ha-ha, that's emotional infidelity, love.'

Even though the conversation seemed to cause Ayan a lot of grief, Hani was glad to see Hamdi joining in with the teasing. And she'd actually laughed at her own joke. Besides, opportunities to rag Ayan about her morality never came around. They all milked it and took turns to make fun of her about it before asking the next logical question, who was the new guy?

'Hassan!'

Hani didn't know how many of them had exclaimed his name. Silence fell, but only lasted a moment. Having absorbed the information she leant forward and asked, 'do you mean the same Hassan I had heard the CNN ladies make a mention of at the wedding?'

'Yes. They followed it up after and my aunt got involved. It is a connection through the family.'

'You mean it's serious then, if the family is involved? You are getting to know one another for the purpose of marriage! Wow, girl, your moving fast nowadays, when did you accelerate to life on the fast lane?'

Hani sat back. She had to absorb this: Ayan was actually talking marriage with somebody while she was still in a relationship with Siddiq. If she had not heard the words coming out of Ayan's own mouth she would not have believed that the whiter than white Ayan was capable of doing such thing.

It took a moment to process the information and it must have done for the others too as they sat with their eyes open as wide as their mouths.

'Have you met with him face to face?' Hamdi asked.

No teasing now, Hani noticed. But then, this was serious stuff. One of their numbers contemplating an arranged marriage! She never thought she would see the day. A mental image of Hassan, formed after overhearing the CNN ladies mention him, came back into her mind, 'Is he like fat and bald?' she had to ask.

'No, Hani, of course not. I've seen his pictures.'

At least she could see the funny side and, Hani imagined, enjoyed having gob- smacked them all, if the smile on her face was anything to go by.

'He's not fat or bald, in fact he's kinder cute, in a mature sort of way.'

'What do you mean by mature?' Alarm bells sounded in Hani's head. Mature, most definitely sounded like a euphemism for old in the same way that s/he has a good personality is a polite stand in for s/he is ugly.

'Well, he's much older than Siddiq. He's 35, over a decade older than me.'

'Well, I can vouch for the more mature man...' Zuleka blushed, 'I mean well, they say they make better lovers and things like that. So, are you like seriously considering getting married to him, Ayan?

'Like I said, we are just talking and getting to know each other at the moment. Look, I know you are all a bit surprised and shocked, but it's not that big a deal. Anyway, I have tried doing it the other way and it hasn't worked for me. I went into this with an open mind and he has turned out be very different from what I had expected.'

No one spoke, all eyes remained fixed on Ayan as she continued, 'I owe it to myself to pursue it further. What difference does it make if my family introduced him to me or if met him elsewhere? If something is there, it's there; it's as simple as that.'

Hani realised the silence didn't mean they disapproved, just that this had come as such a surprise. They had all agreed arranged marriages were regressive and so archaic, yet here one of them was announcing that she was seriously giving it some thought. It did not make sense. Not to her and not to the others judging by the weird curiosity Ayan had awoken as evidenced by the 1001 rapid questions they fired at her:

Did she have an epiphany moment or was she merely reacting out of frustration to yet another failed relationship? Were her mom and aunt pressuring her into this? Was she not scared of making such a major commitment to a virtual stranger?

With a surprising degree of calmness Ayan answered them all.

No, she did not have an epiphany moment and nor was she acting out of frustration. She was merely exploring the other options. Yes, her mom and aunt were pressuring her to get married, but what else was new? And she was not stupid enough to agree to marry him on the back of that alone. Yes, she was scared of committing to marriage to somebody she did not know and that was why her and Hassan were talking, to get to know each other and see if they were compatible; nobody was suggesting they walk down the aisle tomorrow.

Even with all the explanations Hani still could not pretend to understand her decision.

'But, Hassan lives in the Middle East and you have only seen his picture, and spoken to him on the phone and by text. Is that enough to get married? What if he isn't telling the truth about himself? After all, in new relationships people always lie or embellish the truth to make them look better in the eyes of the other person. If Hassan is lying about himself you may not find out until after you married him! Surely that's a recipe for disaster?'

Ayan laughed at Hani, 'Not really. Our families know each other. Anything he says is easily verifiable and there is no reason why he has to lie. It's in both of our interest to tell the truth to each other from the very beginning. It's not like dating where people play mind games. This is totally different, in fact, I think it's better.'

'Well, we shall see. In the meantime girls, there are four of us and we all need to catch up. I need to bitch and to get some comfort and we're using all the time on Ayan.'

'Oh, Hamdi, you take the cake. Come on, then. Let's have the latest in your love life.'

Not that Hani didn't already know it all, at least from Tariq's perspective, but she felt real relief and thankful to Hamdi to bring things back to normal. That's if they ever would be again.

***

As they said goodnight, Zuleka sighed a deep sigh of relief. With all the attention Ayan's antics commanded and which Hamdi took over, the conversation hadn't returned to her. Her story about being her landlord's mistress had given her the perfect cover for why she no longer worried about money. It hadn't all been a lie. They had something going in that he called her up now and then and they got together. Yes, he gave her grace on her rent, but then, so he should. She'd never tell them about that though. Sometimes the shame of it haunted her, but mostly the relief of her circumstances lifted any negative feelings she had about it and she shelved it, never dwelling on it too much.

She thought about the fabulous time she was having lately, not worrying about money. Other than Asif, she had hooked up with a couple of other people, richer people who lavished gifts on her and her bank account bulged. *Oh the joys of being debt free and of having money.*

Thinking these thoughts she had a longing to try her hand again. Not for one night stand, but maybe meet someone, someone like her ex Feisal, who could treat her to the kind of life she yearned for.

As she dialled a taxi Hani stood next to her so she asked for it to take her to her home address. Hugging Hani as they said goodbye felt good. It re-enforced her thoughts that all was well with the world, but when she closed the door of the taxi she changed that world, 'I've decided not to go where I said, driver. I'd like you to go in this direction until I am out of sight of my friend and then, double back and take me to Maymuna lounge in Mayfair, please.'

She knew he would need no more details, all the cab drivers knew it. It was a favourite haunt of the rich Arabs who came to town; it was located just opposite the Saudi Embassy.

Chapter Twenty Two
When is a prostitute not a prostitute?

Catering to a clientele that had plenty of disposable income, Maymuna was ridiculously expensive and its opulence decor striking. Royal-purple and rich burgundy cushions lay scattered on the low seating sofas that lined the room. Thin, see-through drapes of similar colours elegantly draped the arched doorways. Large green pot plants stood in every corner and the wall opposite the entrance had gold Arabic inscriptions done in beautiful calligraphy, boldly proclaiming: *'Ahlan Wa Sahlan'*; welcome.

Dim lighting enhanced the comfort and beauty. The whole place alluded to a Sultan's private harem rather than a place of business. To complete the fantasy the management threw lavish parties with sensual belly dancers to entertain on every Eid and New Year.

For those who enjoyed their liquor, the bar stocked an extensive range of expensive brands of alcohol. Champagne corks popped all night, and they served the most delicious of virgin cocktails at anything from £40 a glass.

Zuleka had met Feisal here last season. On that occasion she'd had the girls with her, but they hadn't liked it so she felt reluctant to ask them again, though she thought it would do Hamdi good, take her mind away from Tariq and other troubles.

Listening to her earlier she'd nearly asked her to come with her tonight, but she'd gone on and on until in the end she'd got on her nerves that much, she told her to get over Tariq; after all, he was just a man, not the Nobel Peace Prize. She laughed at that now, and could dismiss it as Hamdi had found it funny and it had stopped her tirade. As she looked around her she thought *if anything came up to winning a big prize this did.*

As she passed a mirror she did a quick check. The outfit she had on was new, but she'd felt compelled to lie to Hani earlier. The slinky short silver dress with a fitted black blazer nipped in at the waist and strappy sandals looked fabulous, and cost her every penny of her last tryst, plus some. The thought sent a tingle through her. But then, she was a woman with a game plan and the outfit formed part of that.

As she waltzed into Maymuna she dazzled every eye that happened to fall upon her. With the grace of a nubile model walking down the catwalk she slowly approached the bar and perched herself on the tall stool opposite the counter. As soon as she crossed her legs and leaned back on the bar counter the waiter bought her a margarita cocktail, courtesy of a gentleman sitting with another man on the nearby chaise longue. Zuleka accepted the drink and smiled at him. He rose and came across to join her.

'*Salaam. Mashallah,* you are a very beautiful woman, very beautiful *habiba.*' His eyes travelled the length of her body.

'*Shukran,* you are too kind.'

'My name is Khalid, my friend and I, we have a table over there; perhaps you can join us?' he said in a mixture or Arabic and English.

'I am comfortable here,' she replied in perfect Arabic, putting as much into her look as she could to tell him the rejection wasn't to do with his company. She always took her time with these things and she hadn't yet sized him up. Plus she wanted to know how far he would go to get her.

'You are welcome to join me,' she told him. There were no empty stools so joining her meant he would have to stand even though he had reserved a nice lounge sofa. *A real test of his intentions.*

He chose to stand. Soon his friend left his seat and came to join them. Like two faithful puppies they stood in front her and she lavished attention and charmed them both. Honey dripped from her tongue as she impressed them with her Arabic. She oozed sophistication and class as she complimented them on their taste and laughed at their not so witty jokes. She sizzled and she knew it.

'*Habiba*, why don't we go somewhere where we can relax and chat and have some good food, we are staying at a hotel not too far from here. We can get everything we need there,' Khalid asked her.

'And what kind of a girl would I be if I followed you to your hotel?'

They fell over themselves trying to persuade her they didn't think of her as anything other than a beautiful woman they wanted to spend more time with. She pretended to listen, but she was already bored of them. They both portrayed juvenile tendencies and a ménage a trios is not what she had in mind.

'You are a very hard woman to read.' Khalid said when he saw her attention drifting.

Zuleka decided to give him a little more encouragement. 'Have a little more faith in your powers of persuasion and try harder.'

As they continued in their quest, lavishing her with expensive drinks, saying how beautiful she would look in the some jewellery they had seen today, and what a pleasure it would be to buy it for her, she kept some of her attention on them—just in case, but discreetly scanned the room checking to see if there were more potential's at the same time.

Her eyes rested on the younger of the two men sitting in the far corner, engrossed in a conversation of a business nature, judging by the thick file and the A4 size documents sitting on the coffee table between them; they must have missed her grand entrance.

The table they occupied held a prime spot and only a minimum tab of £500 could get you seated there; this she knew because it was her and Feisal's favourite area to sit whenever they came here with friends. As she secretly weighed them up she wondered which of the two men would foot that bill.

She decided it must be the younger guy. In his early thirties and good looking, in that nerdy sort of way, his brow creased in concentration and he appeared more in charge and self assured than the older guy who constantly referred to the documents to support whatever he was saying.

Zuleka wanted their attention. She needed to make a loud noise. Only laughing out loud would be acceptable. She looked at her two new friends and let out a husky laugh as if they had just told her the most hilarious thing. Their expressions of astonishment made the laugh real. She looked past them to see if her trick had worked.

It had. The younger man lifted his head. His look held surprise as if he'd only looked up a few seconds ago and she hadn't been there. Zuleka held his gaze for a second before looking away.

She could feel the intensity of his stare. After a few more minutes of feigning attention to her current admirers she picked up her bag and excused herself from their company. They didn't protest. She knew her bizarre action had unnerved them.

Outside she refused the cab which drew up, as they did when anyone appeared from those doorways, telling the driver the lie that she just needed a cigarette. He looked annoyed. She knew he'd have to rejoin the queue of cabs parked a little way away and may not retrieve the first place slot he'd held.

She stood with her back to the waiting cabs until she heard the door open behind her. She didn't doubt who it would be.

'Are you leaving?' Then as if remembering his manners, he said, 'I am sorry, my name is Mohammed.'

'It's nice to meet you, Mohammed. I am Zuleka. And in answer to your question, yes, I am heading out now. It's late and I have exams this week so I have to go and hit the books. I only came out for a little break.' Inside, she giggled at how easily she lied these days.

'Oh, you are a student? What are you studying?'

'Medicine' she put her hand up in the direction of the cabs as she said this.

'Smart girl, and your excuse for leaving is one I cannot argue with, but I wish I could.'

'I'm sorry, I have to go.' The cab pulled over to the kerb. She was glad to notice it was the same guy who had pulled up a few minutes ago. She made a note to tip him well for his trouble.

'Can I at least have your number, Zuleka? I am in town for some business for a few weeks. Maybe I can call you sometimes?'

'Sure." He passed her his Blackberry and she typed her number into it, 'I should be free from school work in a few days and ready for some company." She joked.

A week had passed since she had met Mohammed. He'd called on several occasions, but she'd declined citing her studies, until he stopped calling.

She had to play it cool if what she had in mind for him was to work. Mohamed, if hooked, could give her more than her one offs usually did. She was tired of the game and ready for more, but only with the right man. Asif treated her like a mistress at times; he was coming to visit and hang around her more than she cared for. If she was going to be anybodies mistress, then it would have to be man who could keep her in style, not just give her a poxy rent free flat.

God, how had she turned in to such a calculating bitch? But then, was she? She decided that she wasn't and it was all down to needs must. *I have no choice. I starve or I survive. All I am doing is surviving.* With this justification she rang Mohammed. He only had a few days left of his stay. She had to act fast.

They went out for dinner twice before she agreed to go back to his hotel room. She wondered if this would be a one off, she hoped not he seemed to like her.

As he closed the door to his suite he asked her if she would like another drink. She said yes, not really wanting one, but she could use the time it took for him to get them. As he disappeared into the kitchen annex, she slipped off her jacket; she looked so much sexier in her dress.

He stood a moment in the archway looking at her. Then, putting down the bottle and two glasses, he crossed over to her discarding his jacket on the sofa and started kissing her passionately.

'Let's move to the bedroom.' he said softly.

Unlike before with others she didn't emerge an hour later but spent the whole night there, followed by another night, and another night.

In the next few days they went to clubs, dinner, movies and then back to his. To pass the afternoon hours they shopped. Mohammed happily picked up the bill, but he never offered her money. This thrilled Zuleka as she thought how neatly her plan was falling into place, Mohammed wanted the same thing as her; a relationship.

On the day he had to fly home, he dispelled all her plans. She woke up hours after he'd gone having made love to her before he'd left and telling her he would ring, to find an envelope full of cash sitting on the night stand. *Fuck it! How dare he!*

She had allowed herself to believe this was different. Her skin crawled with the dirt he'd smeared her with. How could she have been so naïve? She threw the envelope to the ground. £50 notes scattered over the thick white carpet like petals of a purple lily. She hadn't acquainted what they had shared with prostitution. But if that's what it was, no man would ever catch her out again or have the upper hand with her. From now on, she called the shots. She picked up the money, counting it as she put it in her purse. *My God - £2000.* And for what? Her mind went over the pleasure of the last few days and her eye caught sight of the beautiful bags waiting for her to take home with all her spoils in them. She smiled as she headed for the bathroom.

A lovely spa and a shower had given her time to analyse what had happened. Once again she'd been able to justify it all, but now she wondered if she needed to. She'd had a great time. No one had been hurt. Her coffers brimmed in the way she needed them to, so what the hell?

As she followed the porter she'd summoned, her composure was one of a woman in control. She was ready to conquer the world of men and have everything she wants out of life. *Bring it on.*

Chapter Twenty Three
We need a resolution

Hamdi woke. Sweat poured from her body, her head ached with the tight fear that gripped her. She flicked the switch next to her bed. The room lit up. The mosaic of disturbing dreams and images swam away from her. Her eyes scanned the room, the familiar surroundings soothed her. *It had just been a dream.* She was home, in her bed, and not in Somalia or the camps of Ethiopia; she exhaled in relief and settled back into her pillow.

Lying flat on her back she stared up at the ceiling, unable to close her eyes; afraid the images would push back into her consciousness and torment her. In the dreams she felt the hunger and her throat parched once more. She wandered alone in the desolate desert, not knowing where she was going. Her steps slow with fatigue.

She had first experienced such dreams when she came to England and they recurred with varying levels of intensity throughout her teenage years. Eventually they had stopped altogether, until tonight.

She switched off the light, but could not settle. She knew what she wanted to do but tried to resist. Finally, exasperated with herself she got off the bed and went to the kitchen to take out the tape from her mother.

She held it in her hand as if it was an alien object she wasn't sure what to do with. She rarely used her stereo since she had bought herself an iPod. She found it hard to imagine people still used CDs let alone tapes. She hesitated before pressing the 'play' button. What did she hope to hear? Did she really want to do this?

The stereo made a whirring, crackling sound, the tape looked well used. Just as she went to reject it, a voice, frail and distant came through:

"In the name of Allah, the Most Gracious, the Most Merciful. I pray this tape has reached you in good health, my darling Hamdi. I know you have many questions, and I am not sure I can answer all of them. I am sorry for the pain my absence may have caused you over the years, I had to leave you but know that it wasn't with a mean heart or ill intentions. I was younger than you when I got married, younger than you are now when I conceived you, and younger than you are now when I was divorced from your father. The divorce left me destitute, with no strong clan of my own to take me in, I did what I thought was best. Your father could give you the security and honour of his name, I could give nothing. After the war broke out, I tried to look for you......I refused to leave Somalia for a long time because I thought I would lose you forever If I did. My dear child, I know I have wounded you, and in a cruel world left you alone, but know that not a night has gone by that I haven't thought of you and prayed for your well being all these years....please forgive me.

The one side of the tape came to an end and Hamdi flipped it over to listen to the other side.

Time is running out, I have so much to say but I must make haste. I am now living in Garrisa. I moved here as a poor refuge with nothing but I met a man, a Somali Kenyan with modest means and we married. He was a kind man, generous to a fault, he passed away sometime back, may Allah bless his soul. We have a daughter, I named her Haweya and I often tell her that she has an older sister with a name similar to hers. Hamdi, I am sick, the drought here has taken everything we have and I fear I have little time left. I have no right to ask for your help, but please, if you can, look after Haweya....please.

She heard her mother stifling a cry before the tape come to an end. Her own tears flowed freely; she used the sleeve of her pyjamas to wipe them. *What should she do? Oh god, it was all a mess...* a knock of the door shocked her thoughts away.

'Hamdi! Open the door I know you are in there.' Tariq shouted.

She looked at the time - 3am. Not wanting to, but afraid he would disturb the neighbours she opened the door. 'What are you doing here? God, do you know what time it is?' He barged in past her. She could smell alcohol on his breath and see anger in his face.

'Have you been crying? Baby, are you ok? What's going on?'

'None of your business, what do you want? I don't need your drama, Tariq; I have enough going on in my life. And I am not your baby. Don't call me that!'

'What happened? Has somebody done something to you?'

'I told you, it's none of your business! Why are you harassing me? It's over between us, now get lost!'

Tariq took no notice of her. Taking off his jacket he threw it on the sofa. 'I came to sort all this out. I am so angry with you, Hamdi, and I am not letting you run away from this one, but I can see that now is not a good time. So first we can talk about what's making you cry alone in god forsaken hours, I am not leaving until you tell me.'

'You can sit there by yourself then, I am going back to bed.' She turned around and went to her room, slamming the door behind her. Why must he interfere in her life? Couldn't he see that she just wanted to be alone? She pulled the sheets up and cuddled her pillow. Stifling a sob, she listened, *had he left?* No sound penetrated the wall. *Oh, fuck him. I've other things on my mind.*

In a spider-web haze Hamdi, imagined herself curling around Tariq's body. For some reason he still had his clothes on, but it felt good. She snuggled her head into his arm and could smell his after-shave and body spray.

Happiness settled around her and dispelled the deep heartache that had become her constant companion since she'd seen the photo on facebook of one of his 'friends'.

Something disturbed her dream and woke her. She opened her eyes. Light streamed in through the curtains. Her senses took on the reality of the dream.

Tariq! *What the fuck was he doing! What was SHE doing entwined around him!* She sat up.

'Ready to go back to your side now, huh?'

'It's my bed, so all sides are mine.' She moved away from him. 'What do you want from me, Tariq? I don't understand you. I told you I am not the girl for you.'

'I wanted to say I am sorry,' he said softly, 'I am sorry for everything. I've been such an idiot. I never intended to push a different identity on to you. Honestly, I don't even know how we ended up in this maze.'

'I do. It's because that's what you wanted me to be. Clearly that's what you'd been looking for in a woman and I was stupid enough to try and pretend I fitted the bill.'

'I don't care about any of that... Look, just let me explain without you scratching my eyes out. You've never listened to my side.'

'I know your side…'

'No you don't, Hamdi, but I will try to explain, it's up to you if you listen or not… I didn't know what to think at first, your whole attitude and your fun loving ways spoke a different language to what you gave off when I tried to take things further. For over a month you found excuses not to go the whole way with me. So, I began to think you held values that prevented you. I analyzed how I felt about that and decided you deserved respect.

'But it was a charade and one that brought us to where we are now. The lie you told was a deal breaker and yet you piled the guilt onto me. I've been nothing but straight with you, Hamdi. I didn't cheat on you, though

God knows I had plenty of opportunities. I know now that my suggestion was so far off the mark and a crazy thing to come up with, but at least it forced you to be open with me. That, followed by you dumping me left me stunned. I was furious to discover you had taken me for a ride and thought I'd just be able to move on and get on with it, but the separation from you has been sheer hell...'

Listening to him made her feel guilty for lying to him for so long, she had to explain: 'I'm sorry, Tariq, I was just trying to make you like me. You kept pulling stupid stunts and disappearing on me. I didn't know where I stood with you from one minute to the next, and the moment you thought I was this virginal girl, you started to act straight.'

'What? You got this all wrong. Yes, I had a lot of out of town stuff to tie up, I was involved in a lot of clubs at the time, that's my business and how it operates. I didn't want to look too full on. You were something different, besides, you played up that much I was scared you were going to have me down the aisle before I could blink. I'd never felt like I did and I thought I'd be trapped, Oh I don't know, but that's gone, I am telling you now; I stayed in this relationship with no sex all this time because I cared about you. Not because I thought you were a virgin! I mean what good is that to me? If anything I hated it, but when you love someone you accept them and their values, even if you don't understand them yourself. I thought that's what I was doing, but I managed to make a huge mess of things.'

'You love me?'

'It would be better for my peace of mind if I didn't, but I do.' He smiled. 'You're crazy as hell, but I love you. I want you back, babe.'

'Oh, Tariq, if only I'd not...'

'Let's forget it, eh? We can start fresh from now. And anyway, maybe it was all for the best. Perhaps we had to go through that, given the type of people we are, to get to a real understanding of each other. I love you, Hamdi, and I want and need you...'

His voice told her of his desire. Her heart swelled with his love for her. She wanted to pour out all her feelings for him as they manifested into a truth inside her; she loved him.

'I guess you're right, now we can start to explore the real 'us'.'

His kiss cemented her feelings and she relaxed into his arms. She still had the tape to deal with, but she felt stronger now. She'd leave it a while. Take a little time to come to terms with it all, she needed to weigh up how she felt. At this moment she still held mistrust and the damaged part of her warned of her mother's cunning ways. Maybe she'd heard on the grapevine that her daughter was doing well and she wanted some of it. Yes, that would be it. This thought brought renewed pain, but she brushed it back into the part of her that held all the bad things in a place like a steel vault in the corner of her heart. She had all she needed now. She didn't care if she never reconciled with her mother. She had Tariq and he loved her. His kisses burned away any doubt. Hurt melted into passion.

Chapter Twenty Four
Falling in love with the Boy

Izzy spent most of his time in the studio recording tracks or writing new material for his debut album. Hani found this difficult as it meant they had little time together, but she admired his work ethic and meticulous attention to detail. She thought, if he could, he would have taken a mattress and slept in the studio. Not wanting to, but thinking she might help the situation, she offered to step back and let him get on with it.

'We, *us*, are also important,' he said to this, 'So no talk of bailing out, okay?'

To maximize the little time they had she would drop by his place, even though it meant they spent their time in his room while he stared at his notebook. Not that it was a penance, she enjoyed fixing him something to eat, and helping him with a lyric if he had writers block. She noticed he changed when he was in his writing mode. The macho bravado went and he became a philosopher, if not quite sensitive, then at least more aware of worldly things than his peers.

The more she saw the many different sides to him the more he wriggled into her heart. She found him charming, inquisitive, and spontaneous and knew she sat on a slippery slope, compelling her, despite her efforts to stay aloof and in control, to slide towards falling in love. Though the intensity of her feelings frightened her and felt more like a tumble than a glide.

Hints came in the way she filled her thoughts with his smile, the cute dimples that formed on his face when he grinned, and those piercing green eyes, making her daydream like a sixteen year old school girl whenever she wasn't with him.

These feelings overwhelmed her and doubts crept in the form of questions: What if he didn't feel the same? He had talked about them moving in together, but what did that even mean? She found it difficult to imagine that he felt half of what she felt. Was she setting herself up for a major heartbreak? Common sense, caution and prudence all told her to pull back, to slow down, but she didn't listen.

The magazine she had been trying to concentrate on whilst these thoughts assailed suddenly felt heavy and its contents boring. She looked over at Izzy. He sat perched up on pillows on the other side of the bed, flicking through his notepad.

'The way you dropped that mag, you seem pretty fed up, babe. Here, see what you think to this, I wrote it for you when I was at the studio today.'

'For me?' Hani took the scrap of paper he passed to her.

'It's silly stuff really…'

> *Throwing the dice, playing the game you could say I was successful- but being a player was becoming kind of stressful. Until caramel-honey come to my rescue. My boy's think I am slipping, but am chilling, real feelings, y'all need to stop tripping.*
> *I am out the game, but right now, it's me that's winning*

'Your boy's think you're slipping because you are dating one woman? They must be tripping…'

'They think I am slipping because I am in love.' He turned to face her.

'You're in love?'

'Yeah ... I am, with this east African girl,' His low, husky voice caressed her skin and sent shivers down her spine.

'Well, I think I am in love with a green-eyed, mixed-race boy.' She allowed a moment of silence to pass before throwing a pillow at him, 'But I am not saying it's you.'

'Oh totally! I mean, this east African girl who's troubling me isn't you either, we should just be clear on that.'

'So clear,' Hani kissed him. A light kiss, but it didn't stay that way. Izzy took hold of her and pulled her to him deepening the kiss until their bodies entwined and the feelings that took her sank any resolve she may have had about keeping things real. Nothing was more real than this.

As she waited for the tube home, she re-visited the wonderful sensation his word of love had stirred in her. She had to fight with herself from jumping up and down with happiness. Izzy wasn't the first non- Somali or non Muslim boy she had dated, but he was the first she had serious feelings for. But where would it lead her? She couldn't discount the impact the differences in their religion and background would have on them.

The worries stayed with her throughout the next few days, niggling under the surface, disturbing her sleep, making her jump every time she passed Salim as if he could somehow detect her sins.

Trying to keep her attention on the project in hand at work, her phone interrupted her. She read Izzy's text:

Have a business meeting – could get out at lunch time, can we meet for a bite to eat?

She had noticed he spent less time in the studio and more time having business meetings with executives from his label company lately. Technically, the album was finished, but there was still a long way to go. The best ten or so tracks that will feature on the album had to be selected: it should have been an easy task but everybody involved in the production had different ideas on what should go and what should stay.

Just as she left work her phone buzzed. *Right on time, babe,* she thought. And then, her heart skipped a beat as his text said he sat in the Prêt a Mangier not far up the road. *I'm going nuts! Feeling like this just because he is so near!*

When she arrived he surprised her by already having his sandwich in front of him. 'Sorry, babe, I was starving, and couldn't wait.' He kissed her on her his lips and she tasted a bit of his sandwich.

'What did you order? It tastes kinder strange.'

'A bacon sandwich, I've been dreaming of it all….'

'Are you taking the bloody piss? I am a Muslim, I don't eat pork! You know that, how can you kiss me when you're eating that and put it in my mouth?!'

'Oh c'mon, it's not like I forced it down your throat. Plus, you drink alcohol, but you're not allowed to, so what's the big deal?'

'I don't eat pork. And I don't kiss those that do, that's a big deal!'

Hani stormed to the ladies. Once there she rinsed her mouth. Disgust made her retch. She could still taste the forbidden meat. She may not be a practicing Muslim or even a good Muslim, some may even argue that she stopped being a Muslim long ago, but pork was something she'd never, ever eaten, and probably never would - just the thought of it made her nauseous.

Izzy half laughed as he apologised when she went back out, 'I am sorry, I didn't think it was such a big deal.'

'It is a big deal, and it's made me lose my appetite.' She thought better of trying to explain knowing his feelings on such things. Besides, she didn't really understand her aversion. It was just that from a young age she'd had it ingrained into her that pork wasn't something they ate and ever since then she had been repelled by it. Oh, she knew she broke many of the rules drummed into her, but that was one she could never get past.

'So, I guess if we were to get married there would be no full English breakfast in the house, huh?'

'We, Izzy, could never get married. For one, I would like to raise the kids as Muslims and I can't do that if the father isn't one, plus my family would never accept you.'

'Really? Even if I converted to Islam they would still not be cool with me?'

'Well, you converting might shame them into reluctantly accepting you, but in all honesty they would prefer that I take home a Somali boy. Would you really consider converting for me, though?'

'On principal, probably not,' he admitted, 'but if that was the only way for your family to agree to us marrying or something, I'd probably fake it, after all the Islam you practice isn't exactly difficult, I could cope with that.'

Hani felt shamed at his words. She knew she was a poor excuse for a Muslim, but to hear someone else say it, hurt.

***

More troubled than ever she laid awake most of the night pondering over the differences between them.

Izzy failed to identify with any aspect of her religion or culture. There wasn't a lot to bind them whilst plenty threatened to separate them. She knew enough about Islam to like being a Muslim, even if she didn't follow the teachings down to a 'T'. The Muslim identity she had, had shaped her world view and perspective on many things. Could she really make a commitment to spend her life with someone who wasn't a Muslim? The answer surprised her:

If Ayan could even contemplate making a similar commitment to someone she had never even met then why couldn't she do the same to someone whose character she did know and whose dimpled laugh always made her smile? If push came to shove then she had to admit that she didn't care what God, if any, Izzy worshipped or about the fact that he wasn't a Somali, as long as he loved her.

She liked how he made her feel when she was with him; everything else was just details, *wasn't it?*

Chapter Twenty Five
Working girl

'You did what?! How could you do that?'

Zuleka knew this would be the reaction of Hani and Hamdi when she told them about her new life, but she could no longer keep it a secret. She had to tell them. She was convinced that as her closest friends, they wouldn't judge her, but seeing the stunned looks on their faces made her worry.

'Listen, Z, everybody already thinks you are trash, your name is still like mud in the community, and this is just going to prove them right! Don't you see that?'

'I see it, so what difference can it make? Why should they find out anyway?' She asked defensively.

'Jeez, how the hell did this even start, Z?'

'I was really broke, and in a bad way, Hamdi. My landlord... Well, he came round giving deadlines, then he sorted of hinted. It just happened, ok?" she snapped, getting angry and feeling ashamed by the way they stared at her. 'It took the weight off my shoulders... Look, you guys, I was seriously considering suicide that afternoon. I had prepared everything. I had nowhere to turn. My only alternative would have been to go home and be married off, I just...'

'Couldn't you have got a job?'

'Everything is black or white with you, Hani. Sometimes you just don't see what is happening. A job would have taken at least a month to find, then another month to wait for a salary cheque. Anyway, I only meant to do it the once... I thought Mohammed would be different...'

Zuleka told them about Mohammed and how he had treated her and how she'd felt afterwards.

'I guess it's just sex,' said Hamdi, coming to her defence, 'No judgments, right, Hani?'

Hani couldn't help but disagree: 'I'm sorry, Z, I'm trying not to judge, but having sex is one thing and selling it quite another. That is some next level shit that I can't relate to. As for being broke - plenty of students struggle with bills, but they all manage to cope without resorting to prostitution – and you can spin it how you want, but when it comes down to it, that's what it really is.'

'Don't get on your high horse with me, Hani, you're the same person who didn't want anything to do with Izzy until he got a record deal then you were all over him. How is that different from what I am doing? You stand to profit from that relationship, too.'

 'You think I am with Izzy because he's got a deal?!' Hani gasped

'That's how it looks. Izzy had been dismissed as a no good player, the night he get's signed, look who is interested in him again?'

'Guys, calm down, Z, Hani…'

'Newsflash, in case you missed the facts, I happen to be in a relationship with Izzy because I care about him. You might not like it, but it is what it is. Don't you dare bring it down to your sordid level!' Hani jumped up and grabbed her bag.

Zuleka didn't care. Her anger boiled over. 'Go ahead, walk away, you self righteous bitch!'

'Don't call me the bitch, you stupid tramp! I can't believe you have stooped so low, it's disgusting.'

Zuleka lowered her head.

'Hey, girl, she'll come round. I am sure she didn't mean what she said.' Hamdi quashed her own reservations about the path Zuleka chose and tried consoling her, 'but be careful, Z, this could lead to sticky situations. Promise me you'll be careful'

'I will, Hamdi. Oh fuck! Look, give me some of that double apple, will you. I need it.'

Hamdi met up with Hani the next day. 'Hun, you've got to cut her some slack here. Not everyone is like you.'

'I know I was a little bit harsh on her, I texted and apologized, but she hasn't replied. I shouldn't have said those things to her. I know she has it rough and I feel like I bailed out on her when she needed me most.'

'Keep trying, she has hurt pride in more areas than one.'

'But why must she do this? I understand if she needs the money, but there are other ways. She has cleared her debts, she told us that, so why? She doesn't seem to even see anything wrong in it. And what about her safety?'

'We've talked about that and she is in control of the situation. She has no-go areas and a line she will not cross.'

'She *has* crossed the line. Hamdi, you need to be with me on this. These Arabs she is taking up with don't even live here. If anything did happen they can disappear as fast as they appeared.'

'You need to reign in your imagination, girl. They are just wealthy business men looking for a bit of entertainment. They are not some losers or criminals hanging around street corners. Relax; your fears have no foundation. And, anyway, she's a grown woman; let her make her own choices for god sake; as her friend just be there for her.'

'I don't know how you can view it all like you do. You should be with me, Hamdi. Together we should be helping her to stop this.'

'You're not blaming me, are you, Hani? I know I talk the talk, but I didn't think what started out as a bit of harmless fun would lead to one of us selling sex to rich Arabs. Anyways, it's her family's fault, if they had just given her some breathing space, none of this would have happened. She is tearing down and discarding all of the rules because they wouldn't let her break even one.'

Hani looked despondent as she said: 'I remember the time Zuleka found it difficult to even tell her parents that she did not want to wear a headscarf, and now this?' she shrugged with sadness. 'But you're right, it's her decision. I'll keep trying to call her. Perhaps it will help if I say I am sorry, even if I still don't understand'

Chapter Twenty Six
Ayan's wedding

'**O**h my god! You're engaged!'

Ayan flashed her princess cut diamond ring. Hamdi grabbed her and gave her a big hug, 'Congratulations, hun. I really hope this works out for you, when will the wedding be?'

A Muslim lady walked by and looked amazed as she saw Hamdi and Ayan together. The one in an Abaya, the other dressed immodestly. Hamdi laughed, 'Hey, you'll be the talk of the town having coffee with me.'

'Oh, I don't care. Hassan knows I have some friends who are less than conventional. He knows it's up to me to choose my friends and I am positive he will like you all, he trusts me, and if I like you, he will.'

'Wow, that's sounds like a good start. What's he like and when is the wedding and do the others know?

'Fabulous, very soon, and yes, I have told you all now. I didn't want to do it in a group. That way, if one dissents you all seem to.'

'Oh, yeah, I suppose we do. On some things anyway. What did they say?'

'Zuleka grabbed my hand and demanded to know if the diamond was real. What is it with her? She paid me back in full, when she said she couldn't do so until she started her doctor training and well... I have heard rumours...'

Hamdi didn't know what to say to this. If she told Ayan, there is no way Zuleka could attend her wedding, it would tar Ayan with the same brush. Ayan saved her by voicing her fears, 'Hamdi, I am in a predicament. I don't know how to put this, but Z... Well, I don't know if I can ask her to my wedding. I haven't discussed this with Hani. I thought you would be the best one to help me.'

Fuck. This is where the cracks appear and it's our own actions that have caused it. 'Is it because of the way folk are talking? I know the jungle drums are beating like mad over Zuleka.'

'Yes, my mother and aunty would not agree to her coming if she is identified to them. I don't know what she is up to, but it doesn't take a master brain to work it out. Oh, Hamdi…'

'Look, I think she will understand. She has to. She cannot possibly do any other; after all, we all stood by her. You in particular helped her. She didn't deserve the gossip then, but this is different. It is something she has chosen to do. I think your best bet is to just ask Hani…'

'No, I want you all there. Oh, it's just a mess…'

Hamdi leant forward and wiped a tear that had escaped and run a silver line down Ayan's cheek, 'Girl, we know that. There is no question. But we are all Somalis and we know the score. We can have a private celebration with you. It can be at mine. Then, Hani who was the original friend you had from the three of us can go to the wedding and report it all to us. We can watch the DVD later on and we can spend a great night toasting you as if you were there as we watch it all back.'

Hamdi thought for a moment that Ayan would protest again, but another Muslim, a man this time, and known to Ayan, walked by where they sat at a pavement café. He acknowledged her and gave Hamdi a dirty look once he saw her short skirt.

Fighting all instinct to scratch his eyes out, Hamdi had a pang of pain hit the bottom of her heart. He thought her trash. He was one of her own – a Somali, and yet, he looked down on the fact that Ayan sat with her.

'I take it you know my counsellor and that is why you are staring at us?' Hamdi used aggression in her voice the way she imagined someone who needed help would.

Ayan, known for her charity work in the community, smiled. Hamdi knew she understood and her pain deepened that she thought it right to go along with it. Surely that meant, she too, thought she should not be dressed how she was? She bowed her head, but not before seeing the man give Ayan an encouraging smile and walk off.

'Ayan, we are not in your league. We never have been. I don't know how you put up with us.'

'Don't say that. I feel desperate that I had to carry out that little charade just then, but I have to take care. I have found someone I care for very much. I think it is a good basis for me, I think love will grow. He is a conventional man, hence my dress. We have all had fun together, Hamdi, but I am ready to settle down and be a 'good citizen" she joked. 'You know what has happened to Z, if I...'

'It's okay. I understand.'

As soon as she parted from Ayan, Hamdi rang Hani. She explained all that had gone on.

'Oh, Hamdi, it will seem like it is all because of our dispute.'

'No it won't. Anyway, you have made up haven't you? I thought you went out together the other evening.'

'We did and it all came out okay, but don't you think this will send it all back again?'

'No, I think Zuleka will understand. It's Ayan's day, it should be all about her'

'I know. I guess if people recognize her, it will be awkward, but...'

'It will be more than awkward. It could ruin things for Ayan. Besides, I can't go now anyway, I just passed myself off as a charity case.'

She laughed and explained everything to Hani about the incident outside the café.

Glad to hear Hani laugh, Hamdi allowed herself to lighten the moment. 'Look, let's leave things for a while; see what Ayan comes up with. I mean, there is nothing sorted. She says it will be very soon, but we know our Ayan. Who isn't to say this is another Bridget Jones moment?'

'No... Hamdi, don't say that! I couldn't bear it. We have enough on our plate as it is.'

The next week, showed just how prudent Hamdi had been in not making a move as Ayan met up with them all and gave them all invitations including Zuleka.

'I'm having a traditional Somali wedding, no white dress or evening gowns....I will wear a *Guntino* and you guys, as bridesmaids, will wear matching *diraacs*. It's going to be the real authentic thing.'

'You mean me too? I am invited? Ayan, are you crazy? You don't have to do this. I know what the gossips are saying, if they see me at the wedding and as a bridesmaid...'

Hamdi felt shocked at hearing Zuleka's protests, she had no idea she knew people were already talking and speculating about what she did.

'There will be no gossips there. No one will be there that knows you, Z, nor any of you. I am having a small wedding held at my home.'

'What... Why? You can't...'

'Hani, you sound just like my mother. I can and I am. It is what I want. I couldn't bear all that pretence, all that money wasted. And being on show... No, I couldn't do it. I just want the group of people I love to celebrate with me. Hassan's family cannot all travel over, only his parents, but they are organising a huge party over there for everyone they know. The thought of that is enough.'

'So, you really are going to live in Dubai?'

'Yes, I really am, Z. I'll miss you all, but you can come and visit.'

They all went quiet. Hamdi never thought the prospect of losing Ayan would affect her so deeply. God knows what Hani thought. But it was Zuleka that shocked her. Tears streamed down her face.

'I can't bear it. It's like we are no more. Where did it all go…?'

Hamdi, like the others comforted her and inside came to an understanding of her sadness, *Ayan's marriage meant even more changes. And the least one ready for them was Zuleka.*

'Oh, blow it. What's the matter with me?' Zuleka smiled through her tears, 'I'm very happy for you, Ayan. It is a great honour to attend you at your wedding and I'll wear whatever you want me to. I hope you will be happy, but I am going to miss you more than I can say.'

'I second that!'

'And I third it,' Hamdi said, 'which means, we are still all for one and one for all, yes?' They hi-fived each other and giggled like school girls.

'Thanks, guys. I'm sorry, but I have to go meet up with my cousins in Oxford Circus, wish I hadn't, we could have had one of our sessions. I will keep you all updated on everything that happens.'

Ayan waved from the doorway, now half of her previous body weight, super confident and beautifully dressed in a long loose summer dress with a pashmina scarf drifting like a cloud around her shoulders, she commanded the attention of every man in the room.

How things move along, Hamdi thought, then the sadness of the situation revisited her as the thought came to her: *this is probably the last time we will see Ayan in AA.* She had to swallow hard. Her feeling didn't last long. A sense of pride replaced it, *to think, such a nice, good person, thought of her as her friend.* This settled in her with a happiness that at least one of them had what she wanted.

Hamdi knew they'd all had their views turned upside down, otherwise why hadn't they argued against this arrangement? Why did they all feel so happy for Ayan? It must mean they now thought it actually possible that two good looking and successful people would want to have an arranged marriage? Like her, the other two would surely see that Hassan and Ayan were the proof against misconceptions and prejudices. She suspected there would be no more talk against arranged marriages.

Zuleka, as she was in the habit of doing today, surprised her by being the first to share these thoughts out loud. 'So, who knew Ayan would end up marrying a stock broker living in Dubai, eh? I am happy for her, but in a way, I feel like she's living my life, if only I could have been how my parents wanted me to be...'

***

'I can't believe she is getting married,' Hani said as they watched Ayan getting her henna done for the nikah ceremony that would take place the next day.

They were all at Ayan's mother's house where they would spend the night in preparation for the big day. The house bulged with people; aunties, cousins and close friends, most of who came from out of town, but those who didn't had no idea who the girls were.

An impromptu celebration had begun amongst the gathering as they waited for their turn to have their henna done. Everyone joined in, cooking, eating the spoils, and dancing to modern Somali music until the older women stepped in. They turned off the music and Ayan's grandmother started beating on a drum. They made a semi circle and clapped their hands in rhythm to the beat. Ayan's aunties started the *buranbuur*, the traditional dance, in front of the sofa where Ayan sat with her arms and legs stretched out while the two Indian ladies painted beautiful elaborate designs on her.

She had been sitting still for over an hour, turning to various sides as they worked, while this went on Hani and the five other bridesmaids, Zuleka, Hamdi and three of Ayan's cousins, catered to her; giving her something to drink and taking turns to feed her as the intricate patterns started to take effect; transforming her into a bride right before their eyes.

Hani thought Ayan looked beautiful and like her, the others felt emotional. They all held it in as best they could and gave comfort to each other whenever they were out of earshot of Ayan. None of them could say how she had got under their skin and claimed their love, but they knew she had and knew what a wrench it was going to be to say goodbye to her.

The next morning everyone woke up very early to get ready and compete for the shower. The nikah ceremony would take place in the house, and the Imam, the groom and the rest of the men would make their way there after the noon prayers. Around ten, the makeup artist and the hairstylist arrived and went upstairs to work on the bride.

Ayan looked a picture when she emerged. Cameras clicked and flash bulbs made the room look like a disco.

Her mother adorned her in the gold jewellery that tradition dictates she must wear. For Ayan, a chunky necklace and a set of bangles that her family had passed down through three generations, all would stay in her keeping.

'You must take good care of this gold set,' Ayan's mother told her, 'God willing you too will pass them on to your daughter even as I am now.' Hani smiled at Hamdi and Zuleka as she saw Ayan's mother take a tissue and wipe her eyes, only to receive the wrath of Ayan.

'*Hooyo,* stop it. Otherwise you are going to make me cry. Let's just get through this day with no tears, okay.'

'Mashallah, this is a good day! There will be no crying,' Ayan's aunty entered the room and went to kiss Ayan.

'Niece of mine, you look even better than Nura did on her wedding day,' she said, referring to her daughter, 'And you girls have to go and get ready,' she chased Hani, Hamdi, Zuleka and the other three bridesmaids from the room.

Once all the main players were ready they made their way into the garden for the reception. Ayan's parents had spent a small fortune and put a lot of thought and care into transforming their small garden. They had hired a professional and he had turned the ordinary space into a fairyland. Red and white roses were everywhere. Soft fabrics made a canopy and a stage for the bridal party at the back of the garden.

Hani gasped as she saw it and at the sight of her friends in *diraacs* matching her own in a deep maroon. The sun danced on the silky fabric as they moved. Ayan wore a jungle green for the nikah. Hani could see it was all she dreamed of; her happiness shone from her.

The Imam, the groom and other male relatives gathered in the living room for the reading of the al Fatiha, the opening sura from the holy Quran, invoking God's blessing on the auspicious occasion. Ayan's father, who was her representative, wrote on a piece of paper the dowry that Hassan was expected to give to her as a marriage gift and handed it to the sheikh who handed it to Hassan. He agreed. With a few more words from the sheikh they signed the marriage contract and dispatched one of the little boys to the garden to tell the women.

The sound of women ululating rose up into the sky.

'*Mabrouk! Mabrouk!*' They shouted as the music began to play and the dancing commenced.

After a time, Ayan went for an outfit change and rejoined them wearing a *Guntino,* which Hani thought was the sexiest of all the traditional outfits. It consisted of a full length piece of brightly coloured fabric wrapped around the body and nipped in at the waist. The way that it tied around the body it resembled the Indian sari in that the arms and shoulders were half bare. It looked very exotic! Surely, Hani thought, back in the days before religious fundamentalism kicked in, it must have helped the sisters in Somalia break a heart or two.

Shortly after Ayan had changed, the announcement came that the groom was coming to greet his bride. The sound of the ululation from the women following behind him let everyone know he was close. This was the first time Hani, and the others would see him in person and she knew, like her they were very curious. They pushed their way to the front to make sure they got a good look.

Tall with broad shoulders and not at all bad looking, he wore a *macawiis*, a long plaid kilt, with a crisp linen shirt. On his way to the stage someone handed him a cup full of milk for him and his bride to drink from. Hani knew their culture emerged from a pastoralists and nomadic society and milk was regarded as a sign of prosperity. If you drink it on your wedding day it is said it will invoke good luck, affluence, and success. She reflected that they might now live in urban cities and owned no livestock, but the tradition still continued. On reaching the stage, the bridegroom took a small sip first and then Ayan followed suit. As soon as they'd finished the cries of jubilation filled the air.

Wiil iyo caano! Gabar iyo caano!
'A son and a beaker full of milk!
A daughter and a beaker full of milk!

The older women shouted in unison, wishing them success and many children. Laughing out loud at the merry scene Hani, Hamdi and Zuleka joined in. They clapped and shouted as if from the rooftop:

Wiil iyo caano! Gabar iyo caano!
'A son and a beaker full of milk!
A girl and a beaker full of milk!

'I'm having a great time!'

'Me, too. It's fabulous. I wouldn't have missed it for the world.' Zuleka grinned in jubilation.

Hani listened to Zuleka and Hamdi and she couldn't help but think that this was the most traditional of all the weddings they had been to, and yet, it was the one where they were having the most fun. Ayan had taken them back to the heart of their culture and the result was amazing. Everybody there was having a ball.

Soon it was time for the bride and her groom to leave. Everyone followed them out of the house and to their car. They were going to spend the night at a hotel before flying out the next day for their honeymoon in Bahrain and from there on, Ayan would go to her new home in Dubai.

Before she got into the car she came over to them and gave them all a kiss and hugged them. Hani felt her tears on her face. She couldn't say anything for fear of crying even harder than Ayan did, and that would spoil things, besides it was expected of Ayan, 'You guys have to promise to visit me ASAP,' she said to them all.

'Of course we will,' Hamdi spoke for them all. 'Now don't spoil your make up, it's your wedding night, girl, and you have to look fly for that hubby of yours.'

Hani laughed - one last tease for Hamdi.

'Good luck with everything,' Zuleka hugged her once more, 'and take care of yourself, okay? I'll never forget you or what you did for me.'

Ayan hugged her close, 'Everything will be all right, Z. Think things through, hun. I'll write.'

With that, Ayan left them for her new life.

This signalled time to get the partying going and the women went back inside. They planned to carry on dancing and have a good time until late into the night, but for Hani, Hamdi and Zuleka the party was over. They went upstairs and changed into their ordinary, well chosen for their modesty, clothes and headed for AA. They wanted to have a shisha in honour of Ayan and the times they had shared with her there.

Chapter Twenty Seven
On the radio

Driving towards the supermarket, Hani felt tense but didn't know exactly why. Salim's treatment of her and her sister had changed these last couple of weeks. Yes, he'd preached, but in a pleading way not with the dictatorial, *I know better than you,* attitude he usually displayed. He only wanted for them, he had said, what he had found and believed to be the right way. And though she'd heard it a million times she knew a new depth to his sincerity. *"Have some fun my sister's, but retain your modesty. Wear western clothes, if you must, but choose wisely. Some fashions are not for my beautiful girls."*

Tears had come to her eyes at time; listening to him she had felt shame creep into her, opening up the pockets of doubt already sown by Ayan's wedding and what had happened to Zuleka, which had seen her question the way she led her life.

But, Salim's actions the morning he'd left to go to Egypt on holiday last week had really set her on edge. He'd looked like he'd wanted to hug her, but held back. His eyes had held something unfathomable then his smile had lit them with a light she had never seen before. And his clothes! Jeans, a hoodie top and trainers, she hadn't seen him dressed like that for at least eighteen months. He'd grinned at her expression of surprise and said, "I don't want funny looks, you know, people thinking I am going to blow up the plane." Then he'd laughed sending a shiver down her spine. Just before he'd left, he'd thrown his car keys at her, "Here, enjoy, and, Hani, remember when I got cross with you, it was because I love you."

Oh, stop being silly. She physically shook herself. She would not let in the thoughts that threatened to destroy their family.

Leaning back she tried to relax, taking in the last of the autumn colours of those leaves still clinging to the trees lining the road she drove down. She thought of her childhood when, on the way to school, her shoes would scrunch the crisp leaves and she would kick a pile of them into the air. Everything had been so simple in those days. She had felt safe. She'd had a happy upbringing. She and Salim had been very close and very naughty at times, but in an innocent way, where had that Salim gone? Leaning forward she turned the radio on.

The beat she'd heard numerous times blared out at her thumping its familiar sound through her body and lifting her mind out of the doldrums and into a zone filled with excitement. *Izzy! Izzy on the radio!*

The draught from the window as she wound it down whipped her face, 'Hey, that's my boyfriend on the radio!' Passersby looked at her bemused, she didn't care. Jigging up and down to the music her excitement mounted. The bend came out of the blue. She braked. 'Oh, My God! The car spun round. For a moment it teetered on two wheels, but then righted itself and mounted the pavement. Her screams mixed with the music. She fought with the wheel, and regained control. Sweat poured from her as she sat bolt upright, the car now on the road and parked against the kerb. Her breath came in short pants; her heart thudded in her chest. Looking around she saw no one had witnessed it. Those she'd passed walking along hadn't reached the bend yet and no one came out of the houses.

A nervous giggle fuelled by the adrenalin rushing around her body resisted her attempt to stop it. It took her over. She quickly changed direction and headed to Izzy's house.

The thirty-minute news update heralded the end of Izzy's breakthrough moment. The words spoken by the deep, serious voice of the news reader cut through her. Her excitement stopped in an instant as if a knife had sliced it from her body.

'Our headlines at 10am: Police have raided a flat in North London and have uncovered a terrorist cell of major significance. Among items taken from the property were: Instruction manuals on how to make incendiary devices. Equipments and chemicals used in the construction of bombs, suicide vests and computers. A category one security alert is in place for the next twenty four hours whilst investigations continue. There are a number of people held under the terrorist act. The Counter Terrorist Force, have issued a warning to everyone to pay attention to and report suspicious objects or activity in their area and to ring 999 immediately if they see anything untoward.'

Hani switched off the radio. Staring ahead she tried to make sense of why fear had gripped her body. The broadcast had made sense of so much. She rested her head on the steering wheel.

'Salim! God no! Please, Allah, don't let Salim be involved. Please let him have really gone on holiday.

Fumbling in her bag she took out her mobile and selected his number. *'This is Salim, leave me a message.'*

She turned the car round.

'Hooyo, what is it?'

Hani's mother's wailing had penetrated the walls of the house and greeted her the moment she'd stepped out of the car. Her heart, already heavy gave her the feeling of carrying the world inside her. Her dread increased.

Taking the sheets of paper her mother offered her, she recognised Salim's handwriting:

My dear family,
I should have found the courage to tell you myself, but I didn't so I am writing this letter. I have had to follow my heart and in doing that I am in danger of breaking yours, but I have no choice. Allah has called me. He has honoured me by having Al Shabaab, the group fighting for freedom in our beloved Somalia, accept me.

My leaving you was not to go on holiday, but I cannot give you my true destination. We may never meet up again here on earth, unless the cause triumphs whilst I am still alive, but before then, if those who wish it of me direct me to give my life; I will have no hesitation in doing so.
I have transferred the money left from fathers will and my own savings into a bank in your name, Hani. You will receive details of this very soon.
Live a good life, my sisters. I wish I could be there to help with your marriages, but it is impossible. You have to think of me as gone.

I could not go without explaining and as you, too are good Muslims you will understand. I must play my part in helping our country return to being under the guidance of good. The evil transitional government must go.

May Allah bless you and take care of you for me, my dear Hooyo, Hani, and Luul. You remain with me forever. All blessings and everything you wish for yourselves. Pray for me as I will for you, Salim.

Hani's emotions tumbled. Relief gave way to despair, and then to anger before settling in extreme horror. *Salim... Salim, you idiot... You bastard! How could you? Oh my god! I did not know you...* But as she thought this, she knew she had known. Deep down, she had known...

Her eyes glazed with un-shed tears. A hollow space opened up inside her, from it she wanted to scream and scream, but the noise of her mother's distress stopped her. Taking her mother into her arms they rocked together. She did not try to stop her mother's wails; only quieten them in case they alerted the neighbours to something amiss.

'*Hooyo*, hush, my poor, *hooyo*, it will be okay. One day we will see him again. He has to do what his heart tells him to.' As she said this she realised that was exactly what she was doing in her life and the consequences could bring just as much pain down on to her mother. *But, my god! Joining an extremists group! No. Oh god! How could he?*

The enormity of what it all meant smacked her in the chest. She held her mother closer and closed her eyes. A strength borne of her mother's vulnerability and that of Luul's came into her. She had to cope. She had to take care of them.

***

'I am so sorry, baby' Izzy held her close. For a good few minutes she stayed in his arms unable to speak. At home she had to put on a brave face and remained optimistic so as to reassure her mother and sister, but it felt good to have someone to listen to her own deep concerns.

'I just don't know how he could do such thing... I really don't. I feel like someone brainwashed him. I should have talked to him when I saw the changes in his attitude instead of just arguing with him.' Her emotions still swung like a pendulum, from anger at Salim, to blaming herself, to confusion.

'From what you have said about your brother in the past, he sounded like an intelligent guy so I am sure no one got at him. These decisions were his own based on what he had come to believe. You could have done nothing about it so don't blame yourself, okay?'

'I guess....'

'This is exactly why I have beef with religion. It controls and messes people up. The amounts of crazy shit people do in the name of it boggles the mind.'

'Stop making random generalizations!' she shouted, 'you don't know anything about religion or what motivates people to act to defend their views, so stop talking as if you're an expert.' His words had provoked what she hadn't wanted to think about: She didn't want Salim thought of as one of those religious loonies that beheaded people and posted the video clip on YouTube.

'I know it causes more problems than it solves.' Izzy replied, 'look at how many people are ready to kill in the name of God. Total bullshit if you ask me.'

'Well, I'm not asking you. Anyway, I have to go back home. I'll talk to you later.'

He pulled her closer. 'No, stay a little bit longer, I haven't seen you for over a week with all this shit going down. Look, I'm sorry. I should have learned from last time how mad you get when I express my views on these things, now wasn't the right time.'

'I'm not cross with you. Of course you have your own opinion. And one I don't think we will ever agree on, more so at the moment as it is such a sensitive subject. But I can't stay. My mother might need me.'

Izzy walked her to the car and kissed her again. Inside a battle of wills raged as she fought not to turn back and lose herself in his arms. She clicked the fob to release the lock. Her phone buzzing Hamdi's tune saved the day. Izzy went back inside as she answered it.

'Hey Hamdi...'

'Hani, I've been out of my mind with worry, why haven't you returned any of my calls? What is going on?'

'I am sorry. Family problems, I needed to be at home.'

'Are you in some kind of shit?'

'No...' She told Hamdi what had gone on.

'Al Shabaab? Fuck no?!'

'I know. I could kill him for what he is putting my mother through. And, Luul, of course, bless her.'

'I am really sorry to hear that, hun. Anything I can do?'

'Not really. There's nothing any of us can do. He's gone and we can't contact him, and that's that. I just need to spend time at home to help hooyo and Luul over the shock and to adjust to things. I'll call soon.'

'Hey, hun, I know it's bad, but think of the upside. No more creeping round him and worrying about what he might do if he found out what you'd been up to. That's got to be a bonus.'

As she said goodbye to Hamdi she thought, *Yes, I suppose she's right, but somehow that didn't compensate for all the tears and worries.* 'Oh, *fuck you, Salim!*' Her phone slammed down onto the passenger seat along with her bag. *'You've messed my life up, you bastard!'*

Chapter Twenty Eight
The Mercury Prize nomination

The telephone rang out filling the quiet house with intrusive noise. Hani took a deep breath, anticipation the usual rush from hooyo and Luul racing to pick up the phone and their subsequent disappointment when it wasn't Salim on the line. The sound persisted a few moments and then stopped. Putting her head around the living room door she looked into her mother's soft brown eyes. '*Hooyo*, did you answer the phone?'

'No, dear, I have accepted he is gone.'

'Oh, *hooyo*. Listen, it is the best thing for you to do. I'm so glad. Has Luul done the same?'

'Yes, we talked. Getting our hopes up that Salim has changed his mind and is ringing to say he is coming home and dashing to answer every ring sure it is him, only to have bitter disappointment when it isn't, is not helping. We have decided to get on with things and to let you move on, too. You have been a tower of strength to us, daughter. Life has to get back to some kind of normality now.'

Her mother's body felt frail as she hugged her. 'And you will start to eat better, too?'

'Yes. Luul still needs me. I have to make her my priority.'

'We both need you, *hooyo*. It has broken my heart to see you suffering.'

'My daughter, you must remain strong. Your strength is what I can cling to; sometimes I doubt I have enough of my own to give to Luul. I love you very much; you'll have to take over Salim's role in many ways, but you are very strong, so *inshallah,* all will be ok'

The burden of this shackled her, and yet, released her at the same time. Yes, she could move forward once more and get back to something like her usual life, but her responsibility for her mother and sister weighed heavy.

'The first thing to do, *hooyo*, is to get Luul back to college. Then, as soon as you feel up to it, you take the reigns of the house back, with our help of course. Get back into your routine again. Though one thing is certain, you are not going back to complete drudgery as before. We'll have a rota for the cleaning and washing and ironing, but as of yet, neither me nor Luul can cook well. I don't know about you, but I am fed up with takeaways.'

Her mother smiled and nodded. 'I'll need some shopping. We have nothing in. And I'll teach you. We'll have a cooking session each week. On a Saturday, yes, that is a good day.'

'That's the spirit, *hooyo*. And another thing, with us all pulling together you should have more time for yourself. Why not look into joining the women's group and maybe a class to improve your English… Now don't dismiss it, you are a very clever lady, it will be easy for you once you put your mind to it. You're not just here to cook and clean for us, you have a life, too.'

The protests stopped and a little giggle told of the pleasure her words had given. They hugged. Some of the weight lifted, funny how they say that every cloud has a silver lining. Perhaps this will be the making of her mother.

Her thoughts went to Izzy as she came out of her mother's embrace. She had been neglecting him lately as she'd not been with him as often as he'd have liked her to. As if her thinking of him had conjured him up her phone rang out his tone. She ran upstairs to answer it in private.

'Hi, babe, am I all fired up!' His voice lifted her further as it bubbled down the line.

'What is it, you sound happy?'

'I'm cooking on gas, well at least my music is. I just got news I've been nominated for the Mercury prize!'

'Oh, Izzy, that's amazing!' she exclaimed in joy.

'Where are you? Let's meet at mine, I'll be there in an hour.'

Without waiting for her to answer, her phone went dead.

Izzy's hug lifted her feet off the ground. Her body swung around in the air. She could almost hear the adrenalin pumping around him. Izzy rocked.

'Wow, babe, I can't believe it...' His hand punched the air and he hopped around in a circle in an imitation of a Native American.

'Calm down, Izzy, you'll have a heart attack.'

'I can't, I never felt so full of energy, I could run a marathon.'

'Perhaps you had better go for a jog...'

His arms reached out for her. She sank into him. His kisses tingled her neck. Her whole self wanted to surrender to him in a way she hadn't been able to for weeks.

Warm breath brushed her skin as he whispered, 'I know of a better way to burn this energy...'

A knock on the door demanding attention shocked them. Like two kids who had been up to something they shouldn't they scrambled to right their clothes. A fit of giggles took Hani as Izzy, his trousers harnessing his legs around his ankles shuffled to the bathroom. 'Get that, babe; I need me a cold shower.'

Blushing, the colour of a post box, Hani made it to the door just as another banging, made with the palm of a hand started up.

'Hey, man, let us in... Oh, sorry, I guess the timing is bad.'

'No, don't be daft. Izzy will be down in a mo. He just went up to shower.'

'Yeah, right. And I'll bet it will be a cooling one. I feel a right chump. Come here, let's give you a hug.'

'Pack it in, Dwaine, you're making it worse.' Mortified she looked at the crowd of friends he had with him, all grinning like they had shared one big joke.

Izzy saved the day, hopping and skipping down the stairs he entered into a high five ritual, played out to some stupid words. *Men!*

'What's going down, man? Tariq rang us. He'll be here soon with the rest of the gang. *The Mercury!* Are you kidding me? Congrats my man!'

'We always knew it would, right?' said Izzy, giving his friends a hug.

The atmosphere took on a party to end all parties; within minutes Tariq and Hamdi and a host of others turned up. Music blared and beer can rings fizzed their release. The air filled with the sweet smell of good weed.

Hani wanted the moment to last and last. The joy in the room and all for her Izzy took her the final step away from all the agony of the last few weeks. She popped into the kitchen, checked the cupboards for ingredients, and then rang her mother. She crossed her fingers as she said she was at Hamdi's, lying had become part of her life.

With what she had her mother talk her through how to make a biryani; oh, she'd cooked many times for Izzy before, but usually a mixture of meat or fish with a cook-in sauce bought from Tesco. This she wanted to be special, something she had created for him and his friends to mark his success.

Tears pricked her eyes as Hamdi walked in.

'What's this, crying while you're trying to be a domestic goddess? Not a good start.'

'It's the onions, silly.'

'Smells good, I'm starving. Can I give you a hand?'

'No, I want to do this for Izzy, all on my own. I want to make him proud.'

'He will be, even if you burn it to a cinder he'll eat it and extol its virtues. The man's crazy over you. Tariq says he's never seen him this way with a girl before. Anyway, talk of him being proud, you must be so proud of him as well.'

'I am. He works very hard and this success is totally deserved, I know it's only a nomination and he has a way to go before he knows if he has won or not, but it is still a massive recognition of his talent.

'You need any help with that?' Izzy came into the kitchen. Knowing the effect it had on her, he kissed her neck then grinned as she wriggled away from him. 'Top everyone's glass up for me, and behave.' She told him whilst savouring the look he gave her.

'You are famous now, are you sure you should be serving drinks?'

'Don't put any ideas into his head, Hamdi, God knows it's big enough already, if it gets any bigger it won't fit through the door.'

'My own girl hating on me,' he laughed, 'is there a worse tragedy to befall a brother?'

'Not hating baby, just keeping your feet firmly on the ground. Now, I know this party is in your honour, but play the host before I set about you.'

'Yes ma'am,' he gave a mock salute and flashed a dimpled smile. Hani's throat dried. She swallowed hard. 'He is so hot, Hamdi and he is all mine, how do you like that?'

'And you are worried his head might get bigger?'

They giggled as they joined the others.

The meal turned out just as she wanted it too. She could feel Izzy's pride in her. The drinks flowed and the atmosphere sizzled.

Tariq scored some joints of weed and passed them around. When one came to Hani, her mood was such that she didn't refuse. As she inhaled, she thought of Barack Obama, he'd admitted to smoking the stuff. As she inhaled it, she thought: if it was okay for the President of the United States to try it, she could too. At that moment everything seemed okay with her world and with Zuleka's and Hamdi's and Tariq's and without doubt it did for Izzy.

In her haze of everything turning to peace and with laughter taking the space around her she knew, though she would never forgive Salim, she understood his motive. He had a dream, a massive and misguided dream, but he had followed it. He'd given up everything, his family, his job, his friends to commit to it. She wondered if, when the time came, she could do the same. Something in her told her she couldn't. The thought didn't sadden her. After all, Izzy had said he wouldn't ask her to. He'd said he would even convert to Islam for her. Knowing his opinions on the subject, she knew this would be every bit as life changing for him as Salim's choice had been. Something in her admired that strength in a man. Yes, she could find forgiveness for Salim's principles, but never for the way he executed them. That was abhorrent to her.

Chapter Twenty Nine
The Sheikh

Zuleka hugged herself. Her body sank into her new sofa. She wriggled her bottom and the soft material caressed the tops of her bare legs. Explaining all the changes in her flat to Asif had been easy. He believed her when she said she had a job, working as a waitress in the evenings. Seeing her coming and going at late hours had fitted in with that. He visited in the day time and often said how pleased he was to help her back on to her feet. His one hundred pounds each visit and the free rent did little to enhance her income to anything like the level she needed, but he didn't know that.

She looked at his *gift* on the table, always grubby old notes, not like the crisp new ones her other clients gave her. The thought of the residents of some of his run-down properties handling this money before giving it to him almost made her refuse it, but she had to keep her cover. She wasn't in a position as yet to take on another place. But that would come. She knew it. And when it did: *no more Mr Landlord.*

She rose and made her way to the bathroom. No more money earning for her today. She'd shower and go out on a shopping trip before meeting up with the girls and Tariq. She didn't relish this last thought. Tariq had been a bit off with her lately. He made her feel uncomfortable as if he looked down on her.

'You went shopping without us?' Hamdi took her bags and looked inside, 'It looks as if you cleared out a number of shops and burned a serious amount of money, girl,' Hamdi pulled out the various purchases Zuleka had made and picked out the stuff she liked, 'I am going to borrow these shoes and these jeans they go so well with this top.'

'Sure, feel free, take one of the bags, and put the rest of the stuff all into two. Anyway, I didn't go without you intentionally, but Bond Street is on my way here.'

Tariq leant forward. Zuleka couldn't read the look on his face, but saw Hamdi shoot a warning at him. He ignored her, took the items from Hamdi's hand, and threw them back towards Zuleka, 'Nice did one of your Arabs pay for them?'

'No, *I* did, not that it's any of your business!' *How dare he! He could think what he wanted, but she did not appreciate him quizzing her like he was her father.* 'What's your problem anyway? Is it illegal for me to date Arab men?'

'You can date whom you want, if that's what it's called'

'Get lost.' Her cheeks burned. She busied herself with re-packing her bags to hide her confusion. The kick she saw Hamdi giving him under the table made things worse for her. It made it even more obvious they had discussed her. She looked at Hani. Hani avoided her eyes.

Tariq, she knew, had formed his opinion when she had visited a club he worked. She should have known better than to go there, but the date she had, one of her regulars, had wanted to go somewhere different before he took her back to his. *Oh well, who cared, she'd blank him for the rest of the evening. She was living it large and she didn't give a damn what Tariq or anybody else thought.*

'I have to head out. Catch you later,' Hamdi didn't try to stop Tariq. Zuleka felt no guilt at him leaving earlier than he'd planned. She realised she'd made things uncomfortable, but he deserved it. And even though she'd achieved what she wanted she couldn't help capitalising on it by muttering, 'Good riddance…'

'Z, don't say that. I know you have cause, he bloody well knew not to say anything. He's a prick sometimes.

He quizzed me, but I said you had a boyfriend, who happened to be Arab and liked buying things for you...'

'You needn't defend me, Hamdi...'

'We do need to, girl.'

'Not you as well, Hani?'

'We wouldn't do right by you if we didn't and besides, we're worried, a lot more people than Tariq are talking. They see your Gucci wallet lined with twenty and fifty pound notes. And, you haven't been exactly discreet. Riding around with Arabs in Lamborghinis and BMW X 5 was bound to lead to talk.'

'Ok, I'll be more careful, alright? Anyway, I look after you girls don't I? I never let you pick the tab up and you like the stuff I buy for you when we hit the stores. You don't seem to mind then and you know where the money comes from.'

'Z, to us you are you. We have no hang ups, you know that it's just, well, what if your family get to hear of it?'

'I can't damage them anymore than I have done. Anyway, I am not what you think. Not anymore. Things have changed. I have a client base of four or five men who visit the capital on a regular basis. They pay me for my company and to attend business and social occasions with them. I am free of looking for clients. I just wait for my phone to ring. Then when my 'friends' go home, they leave me well heeled. But, even that is stopping...'

'What, you mean you are giving it all up?'

'Don't sound so eager, Hani. No, not all, one of my friends is a Saudi oil tycoon. Let's call him the 'Sheikh'; he wants to set me up as his mistress, which would mean I see just him. It's a good deal, I am thinking about it.'

Thinking was all she was doing at the moment. Thinking and worrying. The Sheikh was much older than her – and with his beard and rounded fat belly and his conservative attitude he wasn't much fun to be with either.

'What's holding you back?'

'Well, I think he's got a nerve. He has a wife and kids out there and he expects me to tie myself down to him?' The smoke from her shisha pipe soothed her thoughts and blotted the others out for a moment as it curled around her.

'What is he like in bed?'

'Hamdi!'

'Well, I'm curious, Hani. And don't tell me you're not. We both have an unhealthy fascination for what happens in Zuleka's new life.'

'Speak for yourself'

'He's a one minute man,' said Zuleka and they all laughed with her at this and that settled some of her misgivings, but not all; 'but the worst thing is, he thinks he owns me.'

'Since he is paying you he probably feels entitled to think that.'

Annoyance entered her at Hani's flippancy in saying this. She knew it was a throw away remark but she didn't want to feel anyone owned her, but then, letting the Sheikh think it and playing the game his way could take her to where she wanted to be....

Taking the decision to do just that and give the sheikh exclusive rights to her, Zuleka couldn't believe the wealth it opened up for her. But, she knew she had to be ahead of her game at all times if she meant to enjoy the time he was away.

She luxuriated in the apartment rented for her in Sloane Square. The palest of blue and gold furnishings on white, thick carpets, chandeliers like thousands of delicate rain drops on a weeping willow tree and a view to die for had replaced the pokey little flat and Asif, with his paltry one hundred a time.

A platinum visa allowed her to drip feed the shopaholic in her to satiation and meant shop assistants catered to her every need. In the exclusive clubs she frequented, she went head to head with the premier league footballers and celebs in buying out the bar – Cristal, Dom Perignon, Krug, nothing less, flowed like water. She hugged herself. *This is how life should be lived.*

Crossing over to the window she felt an overwhelming urge to take advantage of the Sheikh's absence and enjoy one of the most exciting things that had happened for her. She squashed the moment of doubt. She'd call up the girls.

'You up for a night out, Hamdi, Hani is good to go. Izzy is out of town for a couple of days.'

'Yep, I know, Tariq has gone with him.'

'Couldn't be better then as the Sheikh is away, though he didn't say for how long, but it won't be tonight he returns as he always calls and he hasn't done so. So, I'm free to share a dream come true with you and Hani.'

'You sound excited, it must be one of your good ones.'

'It is. You know how often I've tried to get into Maddox, the private members club in Mayfair? Well, I'm in, hun. *And* by private invitation! How exciting is that?

'You're kidding me!'

'No, get your designer freak on. No club in London has a concentrate of international wealth than Maddox, it's the watering hole of young money, slick city bankers, and celebrities, and tonight we rub shoulders with them…'

The club oozed expensive charm. They paused briefly at the top of the grand stairwell and absorbed their surroundings. Zuleka looked at the comfortable leather booths that framed the dance floor and how the tables changed colour in time to the music. Everything dazzled her senses.

A quiet exclamation from Hamdi told of her feelings, 'It's stunningly beautiful…'

'Damn, beautiful is right'

'Okay, you two, act like we belong.' Zuleka told them as the host came up to them and took them to her booth. She ordered champagne, knowing it would set her back around £600 a bottle.

When they were on their own Hamdi whispered, 'it's like Mecca for the rich. I spy with my little eye Arab moneybags, Indians of high net wealth, flashy Nigerians, and old money Jewish kids. Z, this must be heaven for you,' she said with playful sarcasm.

'I absolutely love it.' Zuleka missed the sarcasm; she was enthralled as she lost count of the Chanel, Cavalli and Gucci floating before her on the dance floor. To her, all the women wearing them had something special and the designer clothes only served to enhance it. *This is me. That on the dance floor – that dripping wealth – is me.*

The music cut out as the waiter crossed the floor. From a glass encased booth near the staircase a celebrity DJ played the theme song of the 'bottle show'. Everyone watched the drinks carried on the tray, spluttering with sparklers, and taken to a group not far from them, knowing the expensive round had prompted the fanfare.

'I can never get used to the lameness of that,' Hani said, 'Why do clubs do that, just to pamper to the rich kids ego's and give them their few minutes of fame, it's pathetic.'

'I know, it lowers the tone and I didn't expect it here. I thought everyone in a place like this bought expensive drinks without even thinking about it let alone wanting the whole room to know, it cheapens it somehow.' Zuleka signalled the waiter as he turned to go back to the bar. 'Please don't do that for me. I find it vulgar. Just deliver and pour it for us, thank you.' The man bowed. A trace of a smile showed he appreciated the class she had shown.

After he had left Hamdi gave a low whistle, 'Check out the gorgeous looking Hispanic standing at the bar, girls.'

Zuleka looked over.

'You should make a move on that, Z.'

'Mmm, might just do that...'

Not one to let a challenge go Zuleka walked over to the bar. She'd admonish the barman, in a kind way, but do it from standing right next to the man in question.

'Excuse me, I'm not blaming you or wanting to cause a fuss as I can see you are busy, but no one has been to my table for a while now.'

She felt a pang of guilt at the devastation on the waiter's face as he glanced from side to side. She did the same and felt relief none of his superiors had heard her, her mission was not to get him into trouble, but to use him as a means to an end.

'I'll be right over, ma-am.'

'Okay, thanks, we need some nibbles and another bottle.' She turned to the Hispanic. 'On holiday? Oh, I hope you speak English I only have a little Spanish, '¿Estás de vacaciones en Inglaterra?'

He laughed, 'But no, I think you speak the Spanish perfecto. Si, I come to England for a holiday and for business, also.'

'Sounds good, but don't be fooled by my poor offerings I only have a few phrases remembered from school.'

'What is this, school, ¿escuela?'

'Yes, where did you learn to speak English?'

'I also learn at escuela, but I come here often and aim for perfecto.'

'Perfection... Anyway, I have to get back to my friends, enjoy your stay.'

'But, no. I would like it very much if you dance with me, no?'

'Si, senor, me amor bailando...'

His face lit with laughter. 'I also love to dance. Senorita, you honour me.'

Zuleka put out her hand, 'I suppose we had better introduce ourselves first: Zuleka, Me alegra encontrarme con vosotros.'

'And I am pleased to meet you, also. A pretty girl with a pretty name, si?' He held on to her hand, 'Alejandro, y feliz de estar aquí.'

Not half as happy as I am that you're here, love. Zuleka thought, but she just smiled one of her dazzling smiles at him.

His grey-blue eyes danced an appreciation of her. He led her to the floor with the grace and charm of a real gentleman. An excitement clutched her. With no intention of picking him up for business, this felt wonderful. Flirting for real and having someone flirting with her, something she'd almost forgotten how to do. For a moment she wished things could be different. How would it be to meet such a man and not be this *soiled* woman? But she banished those thoughts and enjoyed his fantastic dancing as he swayed her backwards and forward in moves that would rival dirty-dancing.

When the music changed she took him back to her booth, 'Guys, this is Alejandro. How exotic is the name? He's over on holiday.'

'Holas, Senoritas, it is good to meet you, up until now I have had a lonely holiday except for a colleague, but male company is not the same, no?'

'He's hot. I want me a Spaniard too,' Hamdi never failed to shock, but Zuleka wished she wouldn't at a time like this; it made her sound course and common, which tainted them all. *Ha, that's rich coming from me!* But then, she had wanted this to go in a different way, she wanted... *Oh, bugger, I don't know what I want anymore!*

'But, I can perhaps arrange that. My colleague will be here soon.'

'Great, but he has to look like you.'

'What is this? Like me?'

'Similar a la suya - guapo,' Zuleka translated.

'Guapo, me? Por favor, senorita. Si, my friend is also handsome.'

'Zuleka, I do envy how good you are with languages. You amaze me.'

'Oh, I'm not really, Hani, I think when you have mastered one, you just seem to obtain a knack. I haven't used Spanish since I did my GCSE's. I think I got a 'C'; not exactly good.'

Alejandro whisked her back to the dance floor. A slow number caressed them as they glided together. He snuggled his head into her neck and planted a kiss.

She pulled away, 'travieso, Senor, behave! You don't know me like that.' It felt good to play games, instead of connive to get him into her bed.

'But, Senorita, you are beautiful.'

They both laughed, Zuleka couldn't remember when she'd had so much fun.

When they went to sit down, Hamdi and Hani had gathered their things, Hani told her they fancied going to smoke some shisha at Maymuna lounge, which was only just around the corner from Maddox, before calling it a night.

'I will join you. I like to smoke and my friend is not coming, I think...'

The smoke filled haze of the Maymuna blocked out the groups sitting around, lounging on soft sofas. Alejandro pulled her closer to him. She liked the feel of his protective arm.

'There's a sofa free in that corner over there.'

Zuleka looked over to where Hamdi pointed, 'Fuck. I didn't know he was in town!' She shrugged out of Alejandro's hold. 'I'll have to go. Sorry.'

'Z, where are you going? Is that him, the Sheikh?'

'Yes, I'm sorry, I'll have to go and speak to him. I'll come over to you in a minute.'

As she left them she heard Alejandro ask: 'What is it? Why does she have to go? Is that... Is she with him or something?'

'It's just someone she knows,' Hamdi answered him.

His answer dropped her spirits even lower, 'I think not. I will say goodnight to you.' She turned as she heard this to see him push his way towards the door. Disappointment lodged in her breast nudging the fear of what the Sheikh would think.

'Zuleka, you look surprised to see me. What game are you playing? I do not expect to see you out when I have not brought you. And who was that you were with, are you taking me for an idiot?'

His words, spoken in Arabic had a cutting edge to them.

'I haven't agreed not to go out with my friends. I am not your prisoner. What do you expect? That I sit around and wait in my apartment until you call? Well that isn't going to happen. I have a life.'

'Friends! His voice rose. Some people close by hushed their chatter. None of them looked of the nationality that would speak Arabic so she knew they could only guess at what transpired.

'You are not what I thought. You mock me. You are meant to be mine and mine alone and yet you flaunt yourself like this when I am away!'

'I do not! These are my friends. Alejandro was going anyway, he only saw us safely in here as we walked from Maddox. He did not want to smoke and knew we would get a taxi from here. He is here on a visit and happy to see me.'

'I do not believe you. I want you to send your friends away and come back with me. We have to discuss this in a private place.'

'And if I say no?'

'You will do as I say. I have my men outside. They will see that you do.'

'Don't think for one moment you can use those tactics. This is England, not the Middle East! You can fuck off!'

'Zuleka!'

Something in his voice made her stay.

'I meant what I said. YOU WILL DO WHAT I SAY!'

Hamdi came over, 'You getting shit from this guy, Z? Listen, Sheikh...

'No... No, Hamdi. Don't... I'm okay. He expresses himself loudly. He is cross seeing me with Alejandro, but its okay, really.' Terrified of what might happen Zuleka turned back to the Sheikh and spoke quietly to him in Arabic, 'Stop shouting now. My friends are afraid for me, they may call the police. I don't want that. I am angry at you for not trusting me. But I will come with you, if you are nice to my friends and calm down.'

The threat of the police did the trick. The Sheikh turned on his charm. He stood up and greeted Hamdi. He spoke eloquently in fluent English, complimenting her and saying how nice it was to meet Zuleka's friends. Hani joined them and he turned his attention to her. 'You both must allow me to treat you to dinner one evening to apologise for my rudeness. I am a jealous lover. I love my Zuleka and thought the worse of her when I saw her with that man.'

'You have no need to worry,' Hani told him. Zuleka was just having harmless fun...'

'Yes, with our old friend, Alejandro. We were so happy to have him over again to see us, we met him in university, didn't we, Hani?'

Feeling a tension once more in the Sheikh, Zuleka made an excuse about why the girls needed to leave, this brought back his charm and once more he told them he would take them out and treat them the next time he was in town. Zuleka had to smile to herself: *Little did he know he had treated them, and to quite a lot. In fact, well over a thousand pounds worth on this evening alone.* This thought pleased her. It was like she had one up on him.

'I will just see my friends into a taxi and I'll come back to join you,' Zuleka told him while she ushered them away.

'Z, I'm worried about you.' Hani's concerned eyes searched her own. 'He is really angry. I could see it simmering underneath what he was saying. What did he mean when he said the word magic? My Arabic isn't all that, but I picked up a few insults and some phrases about witchery.'

'He called me a loose woman and that he shouldn't be with me. Apparently I compel him to do haram and he's unable to resist. His angry conclusion is that I have bewitched him.' She snorted in derision, 'He really does give me too much credit; if I had the power to bewitch I would be with Orlando Bloom, not him.'

'Is he really a sheikh? I find that hard to believe' Hamdi asked, 'I didn't count on him being bearded up and all but...'

'Of course not. Anyway, I really have to go. I don't want him to get even angrier.'

Something in her didn't want to say goodbye to them. A strange feeling like a heavy lump of lead in the bottom of her stomach urged her to say, *don't go, I've changed my mind, help me to get away from him.* But she thought they would think her mad so she hugged them both and turned back towards the Sheikh.

Chapter Thirty
Chocolate comfort

Hamdi didn't voice her fears as they sat in the taxi. She knew Hani had the same misgivings, but somehow, putting them into words would make them real. She just prayed Zuleka knew what she was doing and that she would be alright. Hani broke into her thoughts and surprised her by asking, 'Are you okay, Hamdi? Not about what just happened. I know neither of us is okay with that. I mean generally.'

'No, not really, Oh, I don't know, I have stuff on my mind that's all.'

'I thought you had. I've known for a while. I know you try to be the same, sometimes too hard, but you've lost that spark and to get it, you have to drink more and more alcohol. Whatever it is that's on your mind, talk about it. We've been shielding each other too much lately, like we are walking on thin ice, whereas we used to dish the dosh on everything. I liked it better then. Come on, share it.'

'You're the last one to talk. I thought you'd fell off the end of the world when... Well, you know.'

'I know. I wanted to contact you. I just had a lot on my plate, what with taking over the position of head of the household and trying to balance that with keeping Izzy happy. '

'I know, girl. I know more about what you are going through than you give me credit for. After all, I have had to fend for myself for a long time, remember.'

'Yes, of course, anyway, this isn't about me. What's troubling you?'

'Oh, it's my mother, the cow. You know I told you she contacted...'

'You mean your *real* mother? Though, that's a daft question, of course it must be, you would never call Nimo a bad name and you did say something once about her contacting you, when you came back from Leicester. I'm sorry, love, I meant to pursue it with you, but with all that went on. Do you want to talk about it?'

Hamdi explained a bit about her background and told Hani about the tape.

'But, if she's in trouble…'

'Trouble, my ass! Have you heard of a drought going down in our part of Africa? I've looked it up on the net and, yes it says there is some shit happening, but I don't think it's that big a deal. I know my mother. She'd think to use it to get something from me. You know how it is, news travels amongst communities everywhere. She knew where I was, some guy told her who had happened upon Nimo. So she thinks: *England, land of plenty.* She finds out more and that's all she needs to suddenly realise she loved this first born of hers after all. Neat ain't it. I hate her!'

'But despite that, it has unsettled you…'

'I suppose. She said she was sick. Oh, I don't know, what if…'

'Maybe you should get in touch with her…'

'NO! I… I can't, Hani. And yet, I can't dismiss her from my mind. She has another child. A girl. She sent me her picture. Something in her eyes…'

'That's cruel. What kind of woman is this that gave birth to you? Oh, Hamdi, don't cry, love.'

'It's just sometimes I can understand her actions. I mean look what happened to Zuleka, it makes me think how it could have happened that my mother is like she is. People judge on what they see. None of them know what led Zuleka to her way of life, or even know the real Z. It all makes me wonder if I have put myself up as judge and jury on what my mother did and never gave myself a chance to think it all through… I mean, a young girl cast out with no clan to help her, what else could she do?'

'Oh, Hamdi, maybe that is the way to look at it. The parallels in your mother's and Z's situation have opened up your mind to how these things come about and how helpless the person is in the situation. Perhaps you should do something about it all. You'll never be able to move forward until you deal with it, love.'

A stupid tear crept out and trickled a cold path down her cheek. She brushed it away. Hani's arm came around her. Like a child she leant on Hani's shoulder. Sobs racked her body.

'How about you stay at mine tonight, love? Hooyo and Luul will be fast asleep by now. I've got some lovely hot chocolate and loads of choci biscuits, we can have a midnight feast – well, a three in the morning feast. Are you up for that, eh?'

A smile seeped through her tears. 'Thanks, Hani. You're one good friend.'

But she knew that not even hot chocolate and Hani's love, comfort and wise words could melt the steel barrier to her mother. Yes, cracks had begun to erode it, but her mother's deceitful action in trying to worm money out of her stuck in her craw. *If she'd have wanted to, she could have found me years ago.*

The cracks repaired at the thought. *Fuck it. When she got home she'd burn the tape and that would be the end of it.*

***

Feeling better the next day, Hamdi left Hani's after breakfast. They had chatted till five am, sometimes crying, sometimes laughing until they'd fallen asleep, her in a chair and Hani on the sofa. They missed Ayan and felt afraid for Zuleka, they rued Salim's actions and wondered what the future held for them both, and Hamdi had poured her heart out about her family. Hani knew some of it already, but what she hadn't known shocked her and she had agreed that for now perhaps it was best to leave things to lie. Having someone to talk to about it all – helped. Hani didn't feel so ready to persuade her to open up old wounds now she knew everything.

Refusing Hani's offer of a lift, but accepting a loan of some jeans and a jumper, Hamdi walked back to her flat. The winter sun warmed her and the fresh air, the sights and the smells of London and the urgency of the crowds of people, who all seemed to have somewhere they should be, lifted her. She loved the buzz all of that generated. Not far from her flat a cat, big and ginger, stretched out his limbs in a patch of sunlight. His gesture told of a satisfying nights work. Hamdi laughed. She too was free just like him. She could do just as she pleased, couldn't she?

As soon as she got inside she rang Tariq.

'You sound brighter; babe did your night out do you good?'

She couldn't tell him about her worries concerning Zuleka, nor had she yet, told him about her family, but she didn't lie when she said, 'Yes and no. I miss you. When will you be back?'

'Earlier than you think, in fact I'm on my way. I tell you what. It's a lovely day, how about you pack a picnic and we jump on a train and head out to Henley. We could be by the river in no time and have us a real chill out afternoon.'

'Wow that sounds fantastic! Even if we will have to sit in our coats! I've nothing for a picnic in, but I'll ring Fortnams and have one ready for me to pick up, it's only a ten minute underground journey…'

'Bloody hell, Hamdi, that's living it big. Yea, let's do it, babe.'

Excitement banished all thoughts of her mother and Zuleka and the tangle of change that seemed to have entered all of their lives. Today she was going to have her some good fun. And with the man she loved.

***

Zuleka couldn't move when she woke. Every part of her hurt. The sheikh was no longer in her bed. She listened for signs of him being in the apartment, but no sound indicated that he was. Knowing him he would have sneaked back to his hotel room.

The scene of the night before played in flashes through her mind. The slaps, the vile name calling and... Oh, God! He'd defiled her. *The fucking bastard.* Stinging pain borne of memory and reality made her bite her lips until they bled. She winced in pain as she remembered the violent way he had taken her. *How would he justify doing that to her? How would he turn on to her when she'd screamed and begged him not to?* After that was over he'd hit her the hardest. He'd actually clenched his fist. She wished she'd never gone to that club and met up with Alejandro.

Blood caked her legs its colour matching the deep rose woven into the Persian rug next to the bed, the feel of which had been a source of pleasure for her on a normal day as it accepted her feet into its deep pile, but now it mocked her senses as she thought: *Today what everyone said about her had become true. The acts forced upon her had made her a whore.*

The water scolded her skin. It mixed with her tears. The nail brush she used to scrub herself punished and scratched her, but it couldn't remove the stains from her soul. Her legs buckled. The tiles of the shower room scraped her back as she folded. Thoughts of the aspirin in her cupboard seemed like nectar to her. How would she get out of all of this?

Easing herself up, she turned the tap off. Donning a huge comfy robe she walked back to her bedroom not even stopping at the medicine cabinet to get some soothing cream, she didn't trust herself. She had to think this through. There must be a way. One thing she would tell the sheikh, *never would he take her that way again.* Then she'd try to convince him that she would be good from now on. She wouldn't go to any clubs unless he was with her and she'd curb her spending. That way she could use him as a means to her own end, as a meal ticket until she could start to earn her own money in her chosen profession.

Chapter Thirty One
Changes

'I can't believe you didn't turn up. Oh, Hani, when they called his name...'

'Hamdi, I know, okay! And I have had enough earache about it from Izzy. I thought you would understand.'

'I don't. You have no worries now, girl, so why?'

'No worries? What about my mother? How do you think my picture splashed across the newspaper, attending an award ceremony, and revealed as the girlfriend of one of the winners, would affect them? Nothing has changed on that front, Salim or no Salim, the disgrace would kill them.'

'I suppose. But Izzy was devastated. He kept looking at his phone and glancing at the entrance...'

'He just can't or won't try to see how it is for me. But apart from all of that, I am so thrilled he won. Imagine – the Mercury prize for newest, most promising musician and Izzy won it! He has really made it, hasn't he, Hamdi? Things can never be the same again.'

'You need to sort out where all this is going, Hani. There has to be a solution.'

'I know, but not today. That was some party, girl, and my head still rocks. Anyway, are you going to eat that or keep shoving it around your plate? Cos I think we should get back, see if the boys have surfaced, yet.'

Hani paid the tab for their breakfasts and shrugged her body into her coat ready to face the keen wind outside. 'Come on, ugh, let's hope a magic fairy has flown in whilst we've been gone, I can't face all the clearing up. One thing though, if Izzy does get rich he'd have a maid, at least.'

'Not, 'we', then? You never talk like you and he have a future, Hani. Don't you realise how he feels about you?'

'Give it a rest, Hamdi. I just don't know where this is going, and Izzy isn't the only one to think about, you know.'

***

Winning the prize and her not attending seemed to trigger a period of strain in their relationship, Hani felt she would buckle under the pressure they had been under over the last few weeks and knew she hadn't averted another row as she sat in front of the mirror getting ready to go out with Zuleka. She could feel it simmering under the surface.

Izzy's success meant he had some event, interview, or gig to attend every day. And him wanting her to go to everything with him meant arguments became the norm as she tried to explain that even going to a gig now he was well known wasn't a good idea to her.

The sound of him mooching around getting dressed put her on edge. She knew he was nervous, but then who wouldn't be? Tonight was one of his most important dates so far and arranged at the last minute, hardly giving him time to rehearse. A supporting artist of Bizz Man, one of America's most successful grunge stars had cried off through ill health and Izzy was booked to take his place. And, to a sell out audience at the O2 arena. *God, thinking about it, had it really sunk in? The O2 arena for fuck sake!* And she couldn't attend...

Guilt visited her once more. She had papered over the differences in their culture and as Hamdi and Zuleka pointed out, had done so for her own gain. She had known how far she could go and knowing that, she should have reigned in a long time ago and not subject Izzy to this just when he least needed it.

She understood that to him, not having her share his glory dampened the whole experience. He felt he came way down on her list of priorities as he watched her cater to her family and friends. She knew the return of his arrogance was down to her. But knowing it all changed nothing. Her mother and Luul had suffered enough. Izzy *had* to be big enough to accommodate that.

Hani winced as for the second time in as many minutes Izzy cursed. *The talk they'd had had meant nothing, then? He really wasn't going to accept things as they are, his temper told her that.*

'Where the fuck are those shoes I wanted to wear? I can't find anything around this fucking place anymore!'

'They are already on their way, Izzy, everything is. Just get yourself ready and stop worrying about your gear for the show, I've seen to everything and the roadies picked it all up. You have nothing to worry about, apart from being late, that is.'

'Nothing to worry about! Ha, that's a good one. Nothing except…'

'Don't work yourself up, love. It won't help anything, you said you understood…'

'Understand… understand why you won't support me, you mean? Well, I don't. But don't let that worry you. You enjoy your night out with that tramp. I can amuse myself with the chicks who throw themselves at me, ready to demonstrate they appreciate me. Maybe I ought to tap into some of that adoration and have me some fun.'

'Zuleka isn't a tramp. You are so arrogant sometimes, Izzy, judging people, thinking everyone should conform to your ways and wishes…'

'Conform to *my* ways? That's rich coming…'

'Look, don't start. What's the point? Why can't we agree to disagree? Once the press stop following you and the awards are yesterday's news things will be different…'

'Oh, so you don't even believe in me, eh? You think it will all come to an end? Nice, at least I know what you think of my career'

'I didn't say that. I meant the press won't be at every gig once the furore of winning the prize dies down, and they certainly won't be digging into your private life like they are now. And, from what I have heard, the last thing they will want is for you to have a regular girlfriend so let's just keep me out of the picture. Everything will be alright, then.'

'Hani, I don't care how you wrap this up, it stinks. I don't care what the promoters, the press or anyone else wants. I need you by my side but as I come way down in your pecking order, I've no chance of that, have I?'

'Izzy, you've always known...'

'Known what? That I have a sanctimonious hypocrite for a girlfriend? No, I haven't always known that. It came as a shock to me. I thought I had a normal fun loving girl. Oh yes, I knew you had one or two hang-ups, but I never saw you bowing to the rules of your so called religion or behaving according to the ways of your culture. You're not supposed to drink, or...?

'Oh, here we go! Fuck off, will you...'

The door slammed with so much ferocity everything in the room shook. Hani put her head down. *Damn him... And damn his fucking career!*

She brushed away the tears and repaired her make-up like a plaster fixing a deep hole, slapping the cream on in lardy lumps. The ridiculous picture she presented made her laugh. As she passed Izzy's bed on her way to the bathroom to wash her face the crumpled sheets reminded her of what had taken place just an hour ago. *How could all that passion and love dissolve into blind hate in such a short time?*

The cooling water stopped the prickle of her tears. Using a wipe she cleansed the last of the stupid slap off her face and creamed it to a sensible level ready to re-start her make-up.

A night out with Zuleka would put her right. They hadn't been out together since that horrid night when they'd met the Sheikh and he'd shouted at her. That seemed yonks ago, now. And as for a night with all three of them, it just didn't seem to happen often anymore. One or the other always had a commitment. She wished they were all together tonight, raising the roof for Izzy. She'd tried to get Zuleka to go with Hamdi, but she still didn't feel comfortable around Tariq, so they had decided to have a girl's night out, just the three of them. She hadn't had to persuade Hamdi of course. *Lucky Hamdi.* She thought about Hamdi and retracted that thought. For all her bravado, Hani knew Hamdi still had a troubled conscience. She just wished she could put everything right for them all. *How did they all get into this mess?* Still, one good thing, Hamdi and Tariq were getting on to an even keel. Hamdi had talked of taking him down to meet Nimo, which was a massive step for her. Theirs was now a harmonious relationship and it was easy to predict where it would end. How she wished she could say the same for herself and Izzy.

***

There weren't many people in AA, a couple of Arab locals sat at a table by the door and a party of young people of various races lifted the atmosphere with their laughter and gay chit chat across the other side of the room. As always Hani relaxed as she absorbed the familiar smells and sound of the place. She wished she hadn't parted in anger with Izzy. But more than that they needed a solution to their problems so they could move forward, but even thinking about it hurt. *Oh, why was he so fucking arrogant? Everything has to revolve around him!*

No one sat in 'their seat' she slid into the bench and ordered mint and grapefruit shisha. Zuleka arrived at the same time as the pipe with a face on her like someone about to explode, 'I hate him!'

'No surprises there, then, but that pretty much sums up how I feel about Izzy at the moment.'

'You... You and Izzy? No, that's a match made in heaven, girl.'

'Maybe so, but in different parts of heaven... Anyway, what's with your hate and what has the Sheikh done to deserve it?'

Not that Hani needed to know, but hearing someone else's trouble released her from her own.

'He's suffocating me. He is spending so much time in London these days; I didn't think it would be like this. I *have* to work at my studies this year, Hani, I can't skip uni. He just doesn't seem to understand. He says I needn't study anymore, or get a job because he will support me financially forever, ugh, god forbid I am with him that long,' she shuddered at the thought. 'To make matters worse, when he isn't in town, he insist on talking for hours on the phone'

'What does he want to talk about? It isn't like you have mutual friends or anything. Is it just to check up on you?'

'Phone sex.' She blurted out, 'I didn't realise at first, but he admitted it. Fucking wasting my time keeping me on the phone so he can... Ugh, it's disgusting.'

'You mean he didn't ask you, he just...?'

'What, ask? *Him?* With being the pious and noble man that he is? Oh no, it's far too vulgar and beneath him to do that. He wangled things so that I initiated the talk along the lines that turned him on. That way his conscience is eased and he can think of himself as seduced and led astray by a young Jezebel.'

'Clever bastard. I mean he thinks you *bewitched* him, clearly he thinks he can abdicate responsibility for his actions. He should be studied, I am sure he would make a fascinating case for psychology students.'

'I am sure he would. His logic can be so weird sometimes. God, how I hate him.'

'Well, just stop seeing him, then. Nobody is making you do this.'

'Don't you think I know that?! I don't need the obvious stating, Hani. I will get out. I am so tired, so tired of him. He is such a creep, and you know what the worst thing about it all, is? He makes his wife wear the burka with only her eyes visible to the world and all the while he is lusting after me, a woman young enough to be his daughter. And then, he has the audacity to admit, the fact that I don't cover up turns him on.'

'He's creepier than creep...'

'I know. The only saving grace of the calls is they do at least serve a purpose; they keep him away for longer. I'd talk sex with him all day long if it meant I didn't have to be with him. He's repulsive.'

'I agree.' Hani said, 'I only saw him the once and I have to admit I don't know how you do it. I know I wouldn't be able too.'

'Believe me it's no easy feat. I should win an Oscar for my performances: *Habibi* would you like this, or would you like that? And then, when he collapses on top of me I have to feign pleasure that isn't there.'

'Do you want to talk about it?'

'We are talking about it, dummy.'

'No, I mean really talk about it? Has he done something to you, you sounds really mad?'

'Uh, uh, don't try and psychoanalyze me, girlfriend.'

She laughed. 'I am not qualified to. I am just trying to understand. It sounds like hell, that's all.'

'I just... He's just so dirty and pervy, Hani. And that makes me feel the same way about myself and I loathe it. Every time I sleep with him I have to shower with scolding hot water and scrub my skin to remove the feeling of filth. And things have changed since that night he caught me with you and Hamdi and Alejandro. Well… His punishment of me was physical… '

'God, Z, you mean he hit you!'

'Yes, he was very angry and I thought it would be the last time if I behaved. But though none of it has been as bad as that night, he does slap me around. It hurts, but I wouldn't call it violent. In a strange way I understand why. He is so conflicted about what he does; his anger has to find a target.'

As she listened to Zuleka, Hani's fears for her deepened. It seemed clear to her that what Zuleka thought was right. He assuaged his guilt of his own vile actions of sinning and lusting after Zuleka away from himself and directed it at her.

'Zuleka, you must leave him – and now!'

'How? Where to? How do I live? I can't get a job, my studies are too intense so my only option, which would enable me to manage on my grant, would be to live on campus, but they turned down my application as most of that accommodation is for first year students. Staying with him is a solution. I just have to think of it as coming to an end when I want it to.'

'But, suppose he doesn't want it to?'

'There's not much he can do about it, is there?'

Hani didn't feel so sure, but the conversation had become too uncomfortable, she just didn't want to think about what the Sheikh would do. He sounded very controlling and those kinds of men did not let go easily. 'Oh, it's all a mess. Come on, let us have us a good smoke and forget it all. I had an email from Ayan the other day. Let's talk about her and her good fortune and stuff we used to do before all of this happened. I need me a diversion.'

Relaxed and feeling better an hour later they kissed goodbye. Hani looked at her mobile for the umpteenth time as she waved Zuleka off in her cab. Nothing. Pressing Izzy's number she entered a message. Three simple words: *I love you.*

Chapter Thirty Two
A reunion too late

The winter snow disrupting the country took up a lot of the news beaming from the television screen, but still it left room for what happened in the big wide world and in particular the human disaster of the droughts in the region where her mother lived. Hamdi watched the pictures projected into her living room through the shimmer of her tears: The stick thin bodies with ribs protruding and huge sunken eyes and babies, emaciated, sucking on empty, long breasts while flies and midges crawl over their skin, allowed by hands too weak to waft them away, and yet, holding a strength to reach across the oceans to crack the hard veneer she'd put up against such things happening to her mother and sister.

Some of her anxiety stemmed from guilt. Seven months had passed since she'd been to Nimo's and already they were in February of a new year. In all that time she had sat on the fence, angry and not accepting of her mother's plight. She'd paid for her decision not to believe the contents of her mother's message in many ways, not least the crippling nightmare that had become a regular sleep visitor. Always the dessert swallowed her up and parched her throat whilst the sun baked her. Images shimmered in the heat. Horror sat her body upright bringing her to wakefulness with the impact of a bullet shot from a gun.

She couldn't escape it any longer. Hani was right. She needed to deal with it.

Frantic to find the tape and the paper wrapped around it which held her mother's number she pulled her bits and bobs drawer out and scattered the contents on the floor.

Thank God, she'd not carried through with her intention to throw it away.

A smiling face looked up at her. The photo brought the image of Zuleka to mind and an understanding of how it all could have happened that her mother had become who she was, further melted her hate. Then a different pair of eyes, her sister's, in their depth they held a pain which mirrored her own. Life is tough out there; she had firsthand knowledge of that. Why hadn't that alone persuaded her to make the call long ago? She grabbed the crumpled brown paper, smoothed out the creases and there it was: a link to her mother.

The tone, similar to an engaged tone, beeped a monotonous drone in her ear. Her heart thudded against her chest. A voice answered in Somali. Hamdi didn't catch what he said to accept the call, but it sounded official. Her throat constricted, 'I wish to speak to Cawa ...' God *she'd expected her mother to answer, but then, why would she? How did she expect she'd be able to afford a phone?*

The silence unnerved her... 'Hello, can you hear me?'

'Please wait. This is the office of the co-ordination of the aid. The villagers do receive messages here, I will fetch someone.

Five minutes went by. In that time feelings of longing took over her, *Please, please find her...*

'Hello.' *A woman's voice...*

'*Hooyo?*'

'Who is this, I am not your *hooyo*, girl, I am nobodies, *hooyo*.'

'I'm sorry, I thought this was Cawa, I am her daughter, Hamdi.'

'*Subhnallah! Ina Lilahi, wa ina Ilahi rajuun.*'

'The words she'd uttered, *from Allah we come, and to him we return* could only mean one thing! 'My...my mother is dead?'

'Yes, I am sorry, Cawa passed away two weeks ago, walalo. May Allah give you strength! She waited a long time for your call... Hello, are you there?'

She's dead? My mother is dead!

'Hello...'

'Yes, I am still here.' *Oh God, why did I leave it so long? Now it is too late.* Her heart felt like it would snap in two. The chance to talk to her mother had dangled before her and just as she was ready to grab it a cruel twist of fate snatched it away.

'Cawa said she sent you a message and she was sure you would contact her and send help. Then she thought you could not have received it, but as time went on some of us doubted whether you were even real or if she had imagined you.'

'I...I didn't get it till now...,' the lie stung her, but she could not admit the truth, 'who I am speaking to, are you a friend?'

'My name is Yasmeen; Cawa was married to my brother. We lived together all these years, sharing whatever Allah blessed us with on a daily basis. She was a good woman, may Allah have mercy on her, and may she never know hunger and thirst where she is now.'

'What happened?' *The tape had said she was sick. She should have sent help instead of dwelling on her own hurt... Allah, forgive me.*

'We were running out of clean water and I am sure Cawa had taken to drinking the scarce, dirty tap-water instead of the bottled water. What she could get off that she saved for Haweya. Her money began to run out and she could not afford enough for them both.'

'What will happen to Haweya?'

'Allah hasn't blessed me with any children of my own and I look upon Haweya as such. Where I will sleep and where I will eat, so will she.'

Hamdi's eyes clouded with tears. 'Thank you, Yasmeen, I know times are hard and I would like to send you some money every month. Please accept this, if not for yourself, for Haweya.'

Hamdi knew the pride of such women as Yasmeen. Her dignity and spiritual wealth came across even on the crackly line. Her every sentence referred to Allah. Hamdi did not want to wound her or demean her.

'Oh, Hamdi, may Allah bless you ten times over,' said Yasmeen, her voice thinned with emotion. 'I have never asked for charity even though I have lived in poverty most of my life, but I must accept, as you say, on behalf of your sister. I do not know where the next drink of water or bowl of rice is going to come from. She is too young to send alone to the charity station and I am lame.'

Hamdi couldn't speak. Her chest heaved.

'Do not cry, my child. With your help and whilst I live, Haweya will have a good life. I will see to her education and take her out of this camp. I have a cousin who will take us in, but I could not afford to pay someone to take us. Now with your help and Allah's guidance, I can.'

Hamdi fought for control. 'Do you have a *dahabshiil*, or any other money transfer service in Garrisa?'

'Yes, child we do. There is a *dahabshiil* here. Whatever you give I hope Allah returns it to you, if not in money, then in blessings.'

They exchanged details and Hamdi gave her address and telephone number. 'Please contact me if you need anything, anything at all for Haweya or yourself. Please promise, Yasmeen. And, Yasmeen, make sure Haweya has my contact details. Tell her I will always be here for her.'

'You are a good girl. Your mother said you were. I am sorry Allah did not spare her for this day. He must have seen she could not wait any longer, but he was safe in the knowledge that good worked inside of you and your sister would be okay. I send a thousand blessings to you, Hamdi.'

When the phone went dead, Hamdi buried her face in her hands and wept years of pent up tears. *Why, why... Oh why hadn't she rung sooner? Now she would never know the sound of her mother's voice or what they would have talked about.*

Images of her mother, dying, like those on the TV, and hoping and praying for the phone to ring, assaulted her mind whilst questions battered her conscience: did she keep asking at the office if a phone call had come for her? Did she check the mail with shaking fingers praying and praying that today would be the day she received something? What did she think when the answer was always, no?

Dropping to her knees she implored Allah, *Why must life be so hard! If it is to punish me, then do so, but not a young girl who doesn't even know me or a tired woman who had to take tough decisions all her life.* She sat back on her heals. It seemed every time she took one step forward something pulled her two steps back. *Will she ever truly escape her from her past?* A desolate misery descended on her. *How much more could she take? Why must God pile so much onto me?*

What do you really have to complain about? A little voice inside her asked. You're not the one living through a drought, you eat and drink at your pleasure, so what has God piled on you that is so hard to bear, Hamdi? Wasn't it Him who took you out of the situation you were in and brought you to this country? Did you deserve that chance more that the others who never received it?

'*Shut up, shut up! Leave me alone...*' She stood up. She ached in her body and in her mind. She wanted to tear her hair out or bang her head against a wall to block everything out. But she had to pull herself together. She had to get to the ATM and put the transfer in motion.

***

The journey on the underground passed without Hamdi noticing. When she came out of Whitechapel station her route took her past a grocery shop. Its lime green and orange stickers displaying the special offers on booze beckoned her. She needed to get drunk, fast. The 'three for a fiver', small bottles of wine, should do the trick and wasn't too heavy to carry. Twisting the top off the first one gave a satisfying smell, one she was becoming more familiar with of late. She swigged a large mouthful. Her palate rejected the bitter, cheap taste. She swallowed it down anyway. The next gulp didn't have the same tang and went down easier. By the time she reached her destination she'd almost finished the first bottle.

The money-shop door stuck as she pushed it. But when she put her shoulder to it, it gave way too easily and catapulted her inside. She stood there, the clanging of an old fashioned shop bell ringing in her ears, wobbling like one of those Russian dolls with a rounded bottom for a stand, trying to regain her balance. Five pairs of disgusted eyes looked from the bottle in her hand to her. They all judged her; guilty. She didn't care. Finishing the wine she dumped the bottle in the bin, it made a satisfying clonk as it hit the bottom. With her head high she sat down.

Soon the last of the jury members had gone and the call of: 'Next,' applied to her, she leaned over the counter with her £200 and gave the details. The religious type sitting behind the counter, wearing a khamis and sporting a beard, recoiled from her alcohol breath.

'I'm not asking you to kiss me, am I? Just wire the money and I'll get out of here.'

She walked out into the street. None of her guilt had lifted with the payment. *Two hundred lousy quid! She'd spent double that on her last pair of shoes.* But she consoled herself with the thought of the difference it would make to her little sister. The difference between life and death. Once more she prayed to Allah. *Let what I have sent save my sister and her guardian. Praise Allah; let them find a place of safety. And may Haweya have good thoughts about me so she can see a time she will contact me.*

The second empty bottle found a home in a rubbish skip she passed on her way back to the station. As she opened the third, she put her head back and laughed, *'Ha, I've kept Allah busy today. He never hears from me and then all at once I'm begging him and knocking on his door.'* The giggle started in the bottom of her stomach, but never reached her heart; it dissolved into tears. Silent tears. Tears wept from her very being. *Today she had become an orphan.*

Chapter Thirty Three
Reaping what we sow

The halogen light lit up the step where Hani snuggled up to Izzy. The same step they had shared their first kiss, their first argument and which led to his flat. Even though spring remained shyly around the corner, only showing small signs – the odd leaf unfolding, a brave daffodil trying to burst from bud to flower and the sounds of birds fighting over territory as to where to build their nests, the evening held a warmth, which had lured them outside.

'Where do you think we'll be in the next twelve months, Izzy?'

'It worries me to think about it. I sometimes feel I climbed a ladder but before I got to the top the rungs began to give way and I slid back down again.'

'But not all the way down, you're still in a good position.'

Winning the Mercury Prize had increased his album sales and bought him into the forefront of the public attention for a shorter time than he had anticipated. Now all the hype had quietened down, they had resumed their easy, loving relationship uncomplicated by any problems of her not accompanying him on public outings. But for Izzy it meant his struggle to make it to the top just got harder.

'I didn't tell you, but that precarious position just took another nose dive, babe. The mainstream radio stations have refused to give significant air play to the latest single. They want either hard-core rap or soft hip hop with an R&B hook and Street Stories isn't it.'

'Well, fuck them. You can make it without them. Get writing material for your next album. You know yourself there are a lot of artists out there having massive sales of albums and sell out concerts, but you never hear of them on mainstream stuff or the see them on the tele. They are different, they aren't for the masses, and this is the niche I see your music in.'

'You have a point there'

'I do, all the recent stuff has been good. It is getting you known, especially the concerts where you are a supporting artist, as they reach the right audiences. We need to tap into the internet a lot more, get some music up for free downloads. I know you don't have time to update your tweeter and facebook accounts, but maybe the label should hire somebody for that.'

'Hey, you want the job as my manager or what?'

'Not your manager… Oh, Izzy, I wished things could be different for us. I love you so much.'

'You can be so cute sometimes and I love you but, sweetheart, you are the stumbling block. You've just sorted my professional life, what are you going to do about my personal one?'

Izzy leaned back. He'd always had dread-locks but short neat ones, now he sported them almost to his shoulder and they fell away from his face and tickled her cheek.

'I still can't get used to this Damien Marley look. It's too scruffy.'

'Don't change the subject. We need to have a conversation. We should have moved on a tad by now, babe. Living together, maybe even sharing the same last name...' he said softly

'If that is a proposal, then it is a poor one,' she joked.

'And if it is, what would be your answer?'

Hani held her breath. Izzy wanted to marry her? Brief excitement was squashed by old fears, 'I can't answer that, I'm sorry. We're okay aren't we? We don't have to do any of those things right now. I stay here a lot now things have settled down at home.'

'You live two lives, Hani, and I don't really exist in any one of them, how do you think that makes me feel? I would choose you over my family any day. They'd have to damn well accept my relationship – my choices, or do the other thing. What are you scared of? What could happen to you if you went against your family's wishes?'

'You already know the answer to that...'

'I don't, Hani. All I know is it is a choice and you have chosen them over me.'

'No, I want you both, but I don't see a way I can. You ask what could happen, well, you know about the pain it would cause my mother and sister, but my fear had always been my brother...'

'They would get over it and Salim is gone now so...'

'He's gone but he's not dead. He'll find out in no time, and then what would he do? He's so radicalised, who knows what he's capable of now?'

'He's not coming back. You can't live your life always looking over your shoulder, Hani'

'You don't understand and you never will!' she said, her frustration with the conversation showed. 'It's about culture and tradition. Those things matter to us...They are bred into us.'

'But they don't make you happy, they imprison you, and yet, you defend them whilst kicking against them. Now, don't protest, Hani, you being here is proof of it.'

'I can't change things, Izzy; they built up over thousands of years. I lean more towards this culture at times and than towards my own, but I have no right to inflict the pain of my choices on those I love. You saw what happened to Zuleka and what it has led to for her.'

'Fucking rubbish and fucking insulting... You say you love me, but you inflict hurt and pain on *ME*. And as for that friend of yours, breaking free has given her a licence to live the good life. Okay, she took a beating, but nothing more has happened. Her family have just abandoned her. That's all.'

Hani stood up. 'I think it is time I left.'

'No, please don't leave… Hani, I am sorry. Shit, I'm a fucking idiot sometimes…' The grip he had on her arm stopped her progress. She looked at the ground. A war waged inside her; a war with the basis of the truth hurting, as some of what he'd said hit a chord.

'Fine, but let's give this conversation a rest, shall we? I don't think you'll hear what you want from me anytime soon.'

'Okay, we won't discuss it again until you're ready.'

His arm came around her, 'It's getting cold out here, let's go back in.'

Some of the magic of the evening had gone. Izzy tried to get it back by kissing her as soon as they'd closed the door on the evening, but it all seemed forced now and though it wasn't the right time, locked in the arms of an illicit lover, Hani sent a little prayer up: *'Please, Allah, forgive me, and grant me a solution to the conflicts in my life.'*

***

Walking towards AA the next day with Hamdi, it seemed everyone she knew had joined forces against her. But it took the biscuit for Hamdi to put herself up as the one with all the answers. She needed some herself, and quick; she looked ready to crack.

'Hamdi, stop this. Leave my problems, love, and concentrate on doing something about your own. I can see you're suffering. You have to let it out sometime. Release all that pent up feeling… Cry if you must, scream and kick and smash something up, but don't bottle it. That is not good. Why not do as Tariq says and go for some counselling, eh?'

'Because that would make me feel like some looney.'

'I thought you had more intelligence than that, Hamdi, you take the piss out of the piss sometimes, look at you. You haven't slept in weeks, you hardly eat, you've passed size zero, you're skeletal, and that ain't pretty. Get real. Recognise your grief, give it some space. It is natural... Oh, love...'

Hamdi's frail body had collapsed onto a bench. Hani sat down beside her and took her in her arms. Feeling Hamdi's bones didn't give a comfy cuddle and set a dread inside Hani, if this carried on her dear friend would become seriously ill.

'That's right, cry. Weep your heart out. I'm only harsh with you because I love you. We are all worried for you. Zuleka and I even held a prayer session for you.'

Hamdi looked up. Her watery smile didn't touch her eyes, 'You did what? Bloody hell that should work then! As if Allah would listen to you two...' Her mouth quivered and the tears flowed again, 'He hasn't listened to me. He's punishing me, Hani, and you. You're in love, but can do nothing about it and have all that responsibility of your family. And, Zuleka, too... She has lost her family and her dignity. Only Ayan out of us all has reaped His reward. Her emails tell of her happiness. And, you know what? She is the only one who deserves it. She didn't become a sinner and lose her way like we all have.'

Shock at Hamdi's words, and the small element of truth in them stunned Hani.

'Look, Hamdi, Allah doesn't work like that. He isn't this revengeful being sitting up there striking this one down and that one and rewarding only the good. The good are okay, He doesn't have to worry about them. He does worry about us and listen to us. But, we do have to meet Him half way. Yes, man has made a lot of conventions and added on to His law, but I have a peace in me. I am not a bad person. I do not steal or hurt anyone. I haven't taken anyone's husband or murdered, cheated or defiled and nor have you. We are young; we want some of the fun everybody around us seems to be having. And that is all we are guilty of.'

Hamdi shivered, 'And, Zuleka?'

'I know, but all we can do is to talk her. That's all Allah would ask of us. For us to be there, ready to pick up the pieces. I pray He will keep her safe and then when she graduates, she will find she can channel her life away from herself and into helping others. I really believe that will happen.'

'We don't help though, Hani. We love all the money she has to spend and she enjoys having it to lavish on us.'

'Well, that has to stop. Without hurting her, we will have to find a way of showing her that we love *her*, not what she can give us. I mean… I know she knows that, but…'

'You're right, we'll figure it out. We have to try to get our lives in order. Ayan is a role model for us, so we must become that for Zuleka. I think that is what Allah is asking of us.'

Hamdi brightened. It was if she had a mission and that is what she needed, but concern weaved its way into Hani's mind. She didn't want Hamdi to change too much. For her to become a religious person, with Allah on her every breath would be a disaster. Find a level ground, yes. They all needed to do that. But in her experience, those who found religion late, like Salim had, sometimes took it to the extreme.

'No more talk of Allah and what He might and might not want or do. He can take care of his own plans. We need to get us some good smoke, lady, then I am coming back to yours and cooking us a special dinner, one of my mother's recipes. And you, lady, are going to eat every morsel I put on your plate, right?'

'Right. But, Hani, I am going to make some changes…'

'Hamdi... I'm warning you! If you go all religious on me once more today I'll put poison in your food.'

'Okay.'

Though Hamdi laughed, Hani couldn't deny something different had occurred in her friend. Their problems halved when Zuleka joined them. None of them had to put up with what she did and her appearance reminded them of that. Hani thought she looked even worse than Hamdi.

'Z, for God sake what's going down with you? You look like shit!'

'Thanks, Hamdi, can't say you look good either, and Hani, you've lost your spark too, girl.'

'Well, we all have things that are not right in our lives and we all know what they are. I think it's time we re-grouped and had us a plan to get back those three beauties that started out on this trail.'

'I know, Hani, it's all gone wrong. We thought we chased a dream, but the dream turned out to be a nightmare, didn't it?'

'It did. Come on; tell us about it, love.'

'It's the Sheikh, he really is going to another place, I can't do anything right, he criticises me and never misses an opportunity to have a dig. The latest is that my skin is too dark and I need to keep out of the sun. Ha, that's a good one, as if I get the chance to sit in it, if it does shine!'

'I suppose we all knew Arabs have a preference for lighter skinned women, but you are a gorgeous ebony colour and no darker than when he met you, so what's his problem? Besides he has a very dark swarthy skin,' Hani felt her anger rising. How dare this so-called Sheikh, undermine Zuleka in this way?

'That's what I told him, I said: "You Arabs amaze me it's like you are caught up in a requited love affair with the West. The more you admire it, the more they despise you and bomb you into the ground. You're an embarrassment to the Muslim world, full of hypocrisy and no guts. Look at you, for example, paying me for sex while walking around with your beard pretending to be something you are not! It's insane! And you want me to shade from the sun so I can be what, more white?" Then I laughed in his face.'

'Hence the cut on your eye, Oh, Z...' Hani couldn't find words. She wanted to go down on her knees and beg Zuleka to leave him.

'He went mad, and yes, he slapped me so hard I lost my balance and my head hit the doorframe. Then he shoved me out screaming at me to leave.'

'Well, that's good, come back to mine, love. I know it's cramped but we managed before. You'll be safe there and you can study while I am out at work.'

'I'll think about it, Hamdi, thanks, but he has gone back today. I knew he was going so I waited at the end of the street to see if he did and his car came and picked him up. I went back into the flat and nothing seemed amiss. So I'll go back for a while. It's not so bad when he isn't here. I'll just wait until he phones and see how things lie. It could just be a glip as I tried his credit card and it let me have money, I mean, cancelling that would be the first thing he would do if he meant to have me out of his life, he has told me that.'

'It's not worth it, Z, leave now. It's the only way.'

'I do have a plan, Hamdi, trust me. I have some savings, but I need more and he owes me big time. He once said he doesn't even check what I spend. He has an arrangement to clear my card debt at the end of the month and that is that. I'm going to clean him out in the next few months and save the money before kicking him out of my life for good. My finals start next week and with how my work has improved whilst he is away, I have good forecasts to offer. I intend to look for a post up

North, Manchester, or Liverpool, they both have excellent teaching hospitals, and the city's are almost as vibrant as London. I have the other one secured if I don't manage it, but if I do, he'll never find me up there.'

'I don't blame you for that, girl. Get what you can, while you can. But no more big spending. Me and Hani spoke earlier and we don't want you to treat us, not any more. It was okay whilst you were happy and living your life how you wanted, but you're not now and it wouldn't feel right for us cashing in on your misery.'

'You got it, girl, I'm not going to spend anything other than to fund a quiet life while I concentrate on my exams. That way, even if he happens to change his mind and check up on me he won't see anything amiss. I have clothes, shoes, and jewellery I haven't even worn... Funny, but the thought of that doesn't give me pleasure anymore.'

Hani looked at this new Zuleka and felt glad. She had turned a corner and woken up. Her future looked bright, and it was a good future. *All it needed now was for her own and Hamdi's situation to sort out.*

Chapter Thirty Four
Crashing dreams

Izzy's phone rang its normal tone, but the way it cut into the silence that had fallen between them Hani thought it sounded like a ring of doom. Everything between them hung on such a thin thread. Their love had no questions hanging over it, nor the passion for each other, which consumed them both, but they had begun to learn you cannot build a future on these things. The divide between their cultures wouldn't allow it.

'No, man... No, give me another chance, please. I'm working on some great...'

Hani held her breath. This sounded bad.

'Fuck... Fuck... Fuck!!!'

'Izzy?'

'They've dropped me. Can you believe it? After everything... They've fucking dropped me.'

Something like a sob caught in his throat.

Hani waited. She watched in disbelief as Izzy crumbled in front of her, when he didn't say anymore she asked, 'The record company?'

'Yes, Oh, Hani...'

He flopped back on the bed; his hands still covered his face. 'Fucking radio stations! Applauding my originality and then refusing to play my shit because the mainstream public isn't ready?! They hold all the power. If they don't give it air time, then it is dead in the water.'

Hani didn't know what to say. She reached out her hand and tried to take his, but he resisted, 'it seems nobody wants me, not the woman I love, not the music buying public, nobody...'

'I'm sorry...'

'Shit happens; I guess.' he picked up a joint he'd rolled earlier and lit it blowing rings of sweet smelling smoke into the air. Lying back down, he gazed at the ceiling. A tear crept from the corner of his eye.

Hani's heart cracked in two. To see her sweet, adorable Izzy brought so low, it didn't bear thinking about. Guilt assailed her. She was in the equation of things that hurt him and could do nothing about it. She tried encouraging him, 'We can try other labels. It should be easier this time around. People actually know you; I mean you won the Mercury Prize for god sake!'

'It doesn't mean shit. These fucking station managers are too busy salivating over American artists, meanwhile something real is happening right here and they just don't see that!' he stood up and slammed his fist into the wall. A dent appeared in the plaster.

Hani shrank back. She wished Tariq was there, he would have known the right things to say. 'There must be something we can do. Don't give up…'

'Just leave it, Hani, don't even pretend you care.' He grabbed his coat and his keys and slammed out of the room.

The pillow had often taken her tears, this time it took her desolation as she sank her face into it and sobbed the hollow sobs of her grief. There had been something final in his tone and the way he hadn't bothered to say goodbye or see you later or anything. She had lost him, he hadn't said so, but she knew it was true.

After an hour she woke, not even realising she'd dropped off to sleep. She unfolded her stiff limbs and made her way across the room and opened the door. She couldn't hear a sound anywhere in the house. Getting her things she walked out and went home.

***

After a week and Hani hadn't heard from Izzy or had any answers to her texts she contacted Hamdi and Zuleka telling them she needed some of their time. Both knew what had gone down and had left her alone for a while thinking she and Izzy needed some space.

'I haven't seen Izzy, nor heard from him or anything. He... well, he put me into his pot of things that have gone wrong in his life, there just didn't seem anything I could do, but wait for him to work it through, only he hasn't,' she told Hamdi when Hamdi rang her.

'I didn't know that, babe; I haven't seen Tariq for a few days. I needed to get my head straight a bit, too. Anyway, I've spoken to him now and he said Izzy just needs time. The news was tough on all of them, but worse on him. Tariq thinks he'll come around eventually. He always does.'

'I'm willing to give him that, but I don't see why he has to cut me out altogether and not text or anything. As I see it when the chips are down couples stick together and see it through, not dump each other to get on with it alone.'

'Hani, you know what's wrong in that department. He doesn't feel your loyalty, he... Well, he said he feels used by you and it isn't going anywhere so why should he seek comfort with you. He said he'll work it out his way and then, well... Look, I'm sorry, Hani love, but he said he might call it a day and sort out a new future for himself, one you don't figure in.'

'Oh, Hamdi...'

'Don't cry, love...'

'I'll be alright. I'll meet you and Zuleka in about an hour. Thanks for telling me, I needed to know, it kind of tells me where I'm at.'

Once she put down the phone she could no longer hold back the tears. No one would hear her; both her mother and Luul were out. She could vent her feelings.

She had no choice, huge sobs wracked her. Her world had come to an end.

'Hani? Hani, daughter what is it? My own sweet daughter, no. Tell me. Tell me what troubles you, Hani dear.'

'*Hooyo*. I… I thought you were out…'

'I was, but I have come back. Talk to me, sweet one. I know things are not well in your life. You have troubles you do not share. What is it?'

'I can't, Oh, *hooyo*, I am not the good daughter you think I am…'

'Yes you are. Is it a man? Have you fallen in love with an unsuitable?'

Hani felt her mouth drop. Her mother's words only held concern. Not anger. Not hurt. Not even a longing for her to say no. Should she tell her? She looked into the loving eyes and nodded her head.

'So, this man, he is not a Muslim?'

'No, but how did you know?'

'I am your mother. I am not blind. I see the signs in you. And, I see the conflict inside you. If he had been a Muslim you would have presented him to us by now'

'He says he will convert for me, but I don't want him to, *hooyo*, it wouldn't mean anything to him, he is not religious at all, he doesn't believe in it.'

'Well, that is better than someone who does. Some other faiths clash in fundamental ways to our own and that would cause you unhappiness'

'You don't mind? You are not angry?'

'My daughter, you cannot help how you feel. I know. Something happened to me when I was a girl. It was a man who delivered goods to my father's house. He was of a different clan to us so would never do, but it did not stop our feelings. I had no choices, father and mother knew, I think, so they married me off as soon as they could. They chose well and I came to love your father and still miss him. I did get over my first love. But, you are older than I was and I think you will not get over it. Things are different for you.'

'But Salim, he would never allow it…'

'He may, if he knows the man has converted. Why not let him convert for you, Hani?'

'I can't. It wouldn't work. It's hopeless, *hooyo*.'

Arms strong and loving took hold of her and held her, in a quiet voice her mother said, 'then you may have to give him up, my daughter, for Luul's sake. When you have some distance between you, I can do what my parents did and find you someone special to fill the gap in you.'

'Oh, *hooyo*, I couldn't bear it…'

'You could. You are strong. I did and I am not strong. Then, like I said, I did fall in love and everything was fine, I was very happy, your father became my soul-mate.'

Knowing it was no use arguing but finding peace in knowing she now had her mother's confidence and her love remained full for her, Hani regained her composure, 'Thank you for not going mad at me. I thought when you knew it would break your heart or you would beat me with a stick or something.'

'No, not at all. Most mothers, even very strict Muslim ones, understand their daughters, after all they are women too, you know. Father's and brother's, they are different. And when the man in the household takes a strict line most women have to stand by and let his word be law. But they don't always want to, they are afraid to do anything else.'

Hani thought of Zuleka and wondered if the treatment she received at the hands of her mother was because her mother was afraid of her husband. It could have happened that way. Didn't she seek Zuleka out, wanting her to tow the line? Was that because she loved her and wanted her back in the family and safe, well, at least she could think of her as safe? A small part of her hoped it was.

'What would my daddy have done?'

'Your father was a kind man. He had a great understanding about life and relationships. He understood when I told him about how I felt about my first love. He didn't condemn me and he knew I told him the truth when I said the boy had left my heart and I loved him, my husband. But, he was a devout man. This would not have made him happy. He may have come round with the conversion of your young man to Islam, but not in any other circumstances. But, daughter, though he may watch over us, he isn't here. Nor is Salim. Try to come to a conclusion, little one. And one that won't bring gossip down on us and reach Salim.'

'I will, *hooyo*. I will.'

As her mother left the room Hani lay back. Her mind a turmoil of pain mixed with a funny feeling of having everything in the open. *Did any of it matter anyway?* Izzy didn't want anything to do with her and she couldn't blame him.

When she reached AA Hamdi and Zuleka had been there some time, but they understood. Neither of them waded in with 'I told you so' or any other criticism of her or Izzy. Hamdi offered her the pipe she'd just drawn smoke from and as she exhaled she said, 'double apple. Yea, I know, but you need some strong stuff to get through all that pain, girl.'

'You're not going to believe me when I tell you the next twist in the tale,' Hani told them as she sat down and took the pipe.

'What gives, girl, you're not giving a clue with your face. Have you heard from him?'

'No...,' She related what had happened with her mother.

'You're kidding!'

Hani wasn't sure which one said it first, but the same utterance came from both. Their faces showed their shock.

'You're one lucky lady to have a mother like that, Hani... I miss mine so much. If only she had stuck by me...'

Hani looked towards Hamdi at Zuleka's words, not sure which one to console. Each had issues when it came to mothers.

'I think both of your mom's would have acted the same if the circumstances had been the same as mine. My mother said that most mothers would, but they have to follow their husbands. She even said, though my father was a kind man he would have been angry and Izzy would have had to convert to stand a chance with me. And she indicated that is how she would like things to proceed, so there isn't a lot of difference.'

'I don't think my mother would have cared either way...'

'You don't know that, Hamdi. Out of them all I think she would have had the most understanding. Don't forget what you said, she had to live with the choices of the male members of her family. She never had a say and was forced into making wrong decisions.'

'I know what that feels like'

A silence fell at Zuleka's words.

'Well, you're taking steps to get out of it, and then, you can live your life how you want to again.'

'I can't, Hani. I will pull together a good life, but never like I wanted it to be. I always thought there would be a time when sneaking around behind my parents back would come to end, that I would settle into the role of a good daughter when the time was right, that I would meet someone who is well off, and marry with my parent's consent, because he would be suitable. That's never going to happen.'

'Look, none of us can see into the future, Z. You will become a doctor and will meet someone and be happy,' said Hani, 'Hamdi, you and Tariq should make a go of things. You're compatible in every way, even down to him being Somali. The world is your oyster. And me? Well I will have to look at my options and go from there. But, I know one thing. This is the pivotal moment for us all. We all have to take steps that will set the path for the rest of our lives.'

As Hani finished this little speech Zuleka's phone rang.

'Shit, it's the Sheikh and on his UK mobile. Fuck, he must be back!'

Fear crossed her face. She'd managed well whilst he'd been away. Her bank balance was healthy. Her finals were in the bag and she was looking forward to hearing back from the Northern hospitals she'd applied to. But she'd hoped to have some time before he came back to pack and get out.

She answered her phone, 'I'm in a café with my girlfriends...No I am not, for fuck sake; I'm just around the corner. You can have your man pick me up if you like and you will see for yourself! Why the fuck do you do this? If you had let me know you were coming I'd have been all ready for you.'--'Well, that's your prerogative, but a little trust would go a long way!'--'Oh, don't start. I'm on my way back. You will know by me being there in five minutes that I am telling the truth!' She rang off.

'Oh, my god, he's back?!'

'And wants to pick up where he left off after what he did last time? I'm coming with you, girl.'

'No, Hamdi. I have to do this alone. I'm going back there and I am going to finish it.'

'But will you be okay? What if he hits you?

'He won't, I'll tell him that I have told you to ring the police if I don't ring to say everything is alright in an hour's time. That should work. He's terrified of the police getting involved in anything to do with him. No, girls, after tonight I will be a free lady, and you will have this bitch back on your sofa, Hamdi.'

'Three cheers to that!'

Zuleka laughed as Hani and Hamdi clicked their glasses, 'here's to freedom and to our futures, whatever they may hold.'

They all hugged. A hug that held the love and concern they had for each other. Hani felt it went on and on, but she didn't want to be the one to let go of the others. Zuleka did that. She kissed them, then gave them her lovely smile and left.

Chapter Thirty Five
Paying the ultimate price

His silence and sinister look ground the fear into Zuleka deeper than she'd ever felt of him before. An outburst would have been easier to deal with.

'I do not know what you expect of me, Abbas; I do not go to nightclubs since it displeased you. I stay in most of the time, but I need my friends and they need me. Meeting them for a smoke and a chat now and again is something I must do or I'll go mad.'

'Why do you always go where men will look at you? Why do you dress in that provocative way? You lie. You think that while I am away you can betray me...'

'I don't...I...'

His voice hadn't raised, its menacing tones brushed the hair on her neck.

'Don't even think about denying it, whore'

'Whore I may be, but I am your whore, you use and abuse me. You pay for my pleasures, so what does that make you? Scum, that's what... No!' Her arm came up to stave off the blow. 'No more, do you hear me, no more...' His face inches from her, his rancid breath warm on her cheeks, his eyes black with evil told her he'd reached a point of no return. A blow she did not see coming sank into her stomach, the air left her lungs and her knees buckled.

'Don't you ever talk to me like that again! Do you hear me?!'

He lifted his foot. She rolled away before the kick could land.

'If I don't ring my friends within an hour to say I am alright they are going to ring the police. And don't even think you can get away, because my friends know exactly what you do to me. How you hit me and everything about you. I left your credit card with them so you can be traced'

This last proved a stroke of genius, though a lie, it registered with him. He turned from an aggressor to a hunted man.

'Why have you done this? Don't you know I get angry, but I calm down? What time is it, how long have you been here? Make the call. Tell them you are okay.'

'But I don't feel okay, how can I? You looked murderous, you have scared me like never before.'

'Here, let me help you up. I'm sorry. Look,' He'd lifted her and lay her on the sofa she'd thought of as the ultimate in luxury, but now cringed at the feel of the velvet cushions. So much had happened to her in these rooms that now they all closed in on her like a dark prison cell. 'I have you a present. You have been a good girl.'

He fetched a long royal-blue box and opened it. The diamonds glittering at her threw sunrays around the room; their size spoke of thousands of pounds. How once she would have coveted them, now they made her feel sick.

'It isn't presents I want, its freedom. I want out of this relationship, Abbas, I have to move on. I am not good for you, you said it yourself, I make you sin.'

'No, I was angry. I love you, Zuleka, beautiful Zuleka; I cannot live without you in my life. I am sorry for hurting you, I will change, by god I will, just don't leave me. I'll give you anything…'

A tear trickled down his cheek. Some compassion entered her. Maybe it would be best to say everything is fine and sit this visit out then escape when he leaves.

'I just want you to trust me. Allow me time with my friends. That is all.'

'My dear, yes, I will do that. Ring your friends, tell them all is okay, and tell them I will arrange for them to come out with us one night like I promised. We will give them a time to remember. Take them shopping after hours, dine them and then we will book them in to one of the top hotels so they can have a luxury spa for the weekend. How would that be?'

'Sounds good.' His face had softened as he'd warmed to his theme. His eyes now held love for her and all her fear left. Her plan was the best one. And because she knew she was leaving him she would be extra special to him.

She rang Hani's phone. 'Hi, just checking in. My sheikh loves me again. He was cross, but he isn't anymore. He wants to take up the offer he made before of treating you and Hamdi.'

'Well you can tell him to stick it. We don't want anything from him, thanks.'

'I will, speak tomorrow, babe.'

'Zuleka...Z... You are not...'

She disconnected Hani, there was no way she could enter into an argument with her over the wrongs or rights of her decision. Her plan was good.

Something came from behind and jarred her head back. It tightened around her neck. She put her hands up and tried to release it.

'You lowlife, you think you had me fooled, eh? I know your plans. Appease me, get me into your vile body, pleasure me, then when my back turns you go. Well, that isn't going to happen. I will not allow you to leave me, I would rather you were dead!'

The ligature tightened. She couldn't breathe. Her eyes swelled. *Allah, help me... Help me...* Her mother's face came into her blurred vision. *'My child I warned you.'*

'Hooyo, hooyo, do not abandon me...

Darkness fell over her. Her lungs burst inside her as strength seeped out of her body. *Not like this, dear god, not like this. I am not ready to die.* After what seemed like an eternity his hands moved away from her throat. She gasped for air before collapsing to the floor.

Chapter Thirty Six
The light of life goes out

Hani decided she could bear Izzy's silence no longer. Before going to work in the morning she passed by his flat. She would go round to see him and discuss their future. This limbo state drove her mad and the unfairness of it made feelings of resentment boil inside her. Izzy behaved like a child who couldn't get what he wanted and yes, she understood his disappointment, but to throw a wobbly of this proportion just did not become him. She'd think better of him if he tackled his problems in an adult way rather than go into this cocoon of sulks and shut everyone out.

When she reached his house she didn't feel quite so determined. What if he said it was over? It took all of her courage to knock on the door. Tariq answered. His greeting gave emphasis to her name, which triggered Hamdi to come from the living room. Tariq stood aside.

'Babe, what are you doing here this early, are you okay?'

'Yes, I'm fine, Hamdi, but I am not standing for this wall of silence any longer. This is my life too. Either he wants me or he doesn't, but I need him to be man enough to tell me which it is so I can move on.'

Hamdi took her in her arms, 'Babe, are you ready for rejection, big time? I mean the boy has plans…'

'I can speak for myself, thank you, Hamdi.'

'Well, it's about fucking time you did. How dare you leave me like this? It's fucking cowardice not to mention childish.'

Hamdi bowed out at these words from Hani. She went back into the living room taking Tariq with her.

'If you have come for an argument, then I should turn around now, I am not going to enter into a slanging match with you, Hani,' he said, looking weary. 'Yes, I'm bang out of order for not contacting you, but I needed space to sort my head out…'

'So there is only you to sort out is there? You are Mr Big, Mr I am everything, no one else is in the equation. I am appalled at your treatment of me, Izzy; you don't have the right to drop me as though I was a spare part, because you happen to be upset. We have been a couple for over a year and yet you cast me aside the moment trouble arises.'

'I'm sorry. I couldn't deal with it all any other way. It wasn't just loosing the record deal and you know it. In fact I got that out of the way after one day. It was your rejection of me that hurt the most. Both put together it was too much to handle. I had to take time out.'

'You could have given me the courtesy of saying so. But no, I have had to stew in my own juice all this time…' She cursed the sob on her voice and the tear that seeped out of the corner of her eye. *Fuck it, she had meant to be strong and really show him!*

'Look, let's go to my room. I have stuff to talk over with you. I have come to some conclusions. I'm sorry if I hurt you, babe, really, but you never seem to see how you hurt me.'

'I don't have your choices, Izzy. And I don't know how to make you understand that.'

The bedroom reeled her senses. So familiar and the place where their love had found expression, it welcomed her, and yet, prepared her for the worst.

Izzy turned towards her once he'd closed the door. 'Hani, you know I love you. I love you with all that is in me and I want to spend the rest of my life with you, but I am trying to come to terms with the fact that will not happen. If we carry on as we are it may last a couple of years, but soon your mother and family will want to see you married. What will happen then? With the love and respect you have for them, you will allow that. Then, you would leave me. By then I would be broken, babe. I have to act now to save us both. I love you enough to let you go…'

'No… No I don't want you to let me go, Oh, Izzy…' Her sobs wracked her with desolation.

In his arms she found comfort and the sure knowledge this is where she wanted to be. 'I love you, Izzy. I love you…'

'I know you do, but I can't ask you to give up everything you hold dear for me. My love is big enough to step out of your life and stop this conflict inside you.'

They stood clinging on to each other, both crying, both in the worst place they'd ever been.

'Hani, I am leaving. I have contacted my mother. She went out to live near to her sister in the states a few years back. My aunt's husband is an American, he's the manager of the KMPG's office in New York and he's offered me an entry level job. It means I'll have papers to live in the US and pursue a deal over there. I intend to throw my whole life at my music and out there I will stand more of a chance. '

'Oh …' shocked, she moved away from his arms. She was stunned into silence. He was leaving the UK? When? Why? She hadn't expected this. She hadn't come to say goodbye.

'It will be hard for me, too. I don't know how I am going to do it. These last couple of weeks have been hell, like I am burning away without you. But I can't have you, so it is only right we allow me to take some steps in building a life away from you. I am sorry I didn't discuss it with you earlier.'

'When are you leaving?'

'Tonight.' He said, looking uncomfortable and avoiding looking her in the eyes, 'I was planning to drop by your work place this afternoon...'

'What?! Seriously? After everything we that went on between us, this is how you choose to end things? You booked a flight out of the bloody country and you didn't even tell me! I have been going crazy over you and all the while you couldn't wait to get away!'

'It wasn't like that.'

'What was it like? Never mind, I really don't want to know. Have a good life, Izzy, It was nice knowing you.' She turned to leave. He blocked her way. *How could he do this to her?*

'I was angry at you, okay. Cutting you out maybe wasn't the adult thing to do, but I honestly had no friggin clue about what to do. I tried everything with you, Hani, and you wouldn't even budge to meet me halfway. I feel like throughout our whole relationship, I've just been chasing you while you prioritized everybody but me. How do you think that made me feel? I guess a part of me wanted to hurt you back.'

The pain in his voice made her wince. There was a truth in his words that she couldn't deny. She had put her family and her friends before him each time. He had made her the central part of his life while she had banished him to the shadows of hers. He had loved her completely but she had failed him, she didn't deserve him.

'Oh Izzy....I am so sorry. I am sorry for everything I've put you through. I am sorry I disappointed you and I couldn't be that girl for you'

'You are that girl for me, you just need time.' He pulled her into a tight embrace and kissed her forehead.

Hani didn't want the hug to end. She closed her eyes and inhaled the scent of him. Inside she willed time to stop so they could stay like that for a long time but she knew her thoughts were in vain. She'd lost him.

As she came down the stairs Hamdi came out of the living room. 'You knew?'

'Not until late last night, hun, and Izzy promised he would come to see you today so I didn't want to jump in before him. If I thought he had no intention of telling you I would have contacted you, but I thought it right and proper to let him tell you himself. Come on, love, let's go for coffee, eh?'

'I suppose you think he is doing the right thing? Oh, Hamdi, I…I…'

'I know. It's one of the saddest thing to have happened to any of us. One of us falling so much in love, but with the wrong guy. I… I mean, it couldn't go anywhere, Hani. You are not the kind of person to leave your family, nor could you ultimately abandon all of your values…however small they maybe. I tried to explain to Izzy. I think he understands though he said it wouldn't stop him living in hope…'

Once outside she linked in arms with Hamdi. In her desolation she was thankful for her friend's support. Izzy had given her the address of where he'll be staying and asked her to get in touch with him when she was ready, but that didn't make her feel better. A break up was a break up. He loved her now, but the memory of her would grow dim with the excitement of being in a new country and meeting new people. *And who knew when she would be ready, or if she ever would be?*

She still had an hour or so before she had to be at work so she was glad to have some time to compose herself. Starbucks wasn't far and she managed to find a somewhere to park quite near to it.

'Great, I'll leave you to manoeuvre the car and go in and order for us.'

'Thanks, love, I'll have a mocha with extra cream' The thought of the steaming hot, sweet drink had her hoping it would bring her some comfort and settle the wobbly feeling in her stomach, but she'd hardly sat down when her phone vibrated. Her heart did a flip. Had Izzy changed his mind? She flicked it open with eager anticipation only to find the number showing was unknown to her.

'Hello, who is this?'

'This is WPC Clarkson, I am afraid there's been a tragedy, ma'am. Are you a relative of Zuleka Abdi? Her phone shows that the number she last dialled was yours'

'What do you mean the last number? Is she okay? Is she in trouble?'

'I need to know who I am speaking to first, ma'am'

'I am her friend. Now tell me, what's wrong? Where's Zuleka?'

'I am sorry. Your friend… Well, look, do you know the girl's family, we need to contact them. We need a formal identification before we can give out any facts about the case.'

Hani's mouth opened, but nothing came out.

'What is it? Hani… Hani…'

Hamdi jumped off her stool and took the phone from her. 'Hello, who is this? What has happened?'

Hani recovered enough to pull Hamdi closer to her and have the phone between them so they could both hear. The voice came again, but as if from a long distance. 'I am WPC Clarkson, are you with the girl who just phoned, what are your names?'

'Why, why do you want to know them?'

Hani forced herself to stay calm and listen but her stomach twisted in a knot and her mind would not give her the truth of what she knew. Everyone and everything around her stood still and yet went in and out of her vision.

The voice carried on, 'There has been a serious incident, and we need to contact the family of the girl we believe to be your friend, Zuleka Abdi.'

'Is...is she hurt... where is she?'

'Please try to understand, I cannot give information over the phone, I need identification from the family to establish that the girl here is your friend.'

'You say here, are you in her apartment?'

'Yes, we are...'

'We're on our way...'

'No, don't do that. This is a crime scene and you cannot enter. If you will not tell us where her family is, we will have to follow up other enquiries...'

'Is... is she dead...?'

'I cannot tell you anymore until we have a formal identification. Please give me the address of her family.'

Hamdi gave the address.

'Thank you, now I need both of your details, please. You may be required to make statements.'

Hamdi answered all the WPC's questions. When she'd finished the WPC said, 'We'll be in touch, thank you.'

The phone went dead

'Oh, my God! Is she...?

'Oh, Hani, no... No...'

'We have to go... We have to...'

'But she said it was a crime scene... She said we can't... Oh God, Zuleka...'

'I don't care what they said, come on...'

Hamdi raced after Hani. Saw her rummage in her bag for her keys. Heard the click of the locks as the remote released them, but though it all registered her mind screamed her denial at her. *It has to be a mistake. Z can't be dead! They had only seen her last night – spoke to her on the phone- she said everything was okay... Please God don't let it be right. It didn't make sense...She couldn't be dead! She couldn't be...*

In no time Zuleka's apartment block in Sloane Square came into view. The police cars parked outside told her she was wrong. Before the car even came to a full stop, Hamdi opened the door and jumped out. She pushed past the police cordons and into Zuleka's apartment. Forensics and plain clothed officers tried to bar her way, 'Ma'am, ma'am, you're not supposed to be here!'

When she raced into the living room she saw Zuleka on the floor. Her unseeing eyes stared into space, her mouth open as if she was about to exhale told her there hadn't been a mistake. Zuleka, their beautiful Zuleka was dead.

The realization hit her in the gut with a sudden and concentrated force that buckled her knees. She crouched on the floor. A sharp pain tore through her stomach. Everything before her blurred and shook as if a violent earthquake had struck. Her distraught mind could take no more. She went into the blackness that descended over her.

Chapter Thirty Seven
A spiritual reunion

Hamdi woke first. She looked across the room to where Hani lay in her bed. They had hardly left each other since the dreadful night of the murder. Sometimes they stayed at hers, but for the last couple of days they'd been at Hani's.

Two weeks had passed and still the police could give no indication of when they would release her body for burial. All they knew was that it had been the cleaning lady who came in twice a week who had found her in the morning and called the police.

The thought of fun loving Zuleka confined in a freezing box night after night added to Hamdi's nightmares. Riddled with guilt, her grief manifested itself physically. She'd stopped eating. Her body weight had dropped. Her hair came away in clumps when she combed it leaving it thinned and wispy.

Now she knew for certain Allah's punishment knew no bounds. She thought of her mother. Dead... Dead - just like Zuleka... *No more, Allah, no more... I will change, I will.* Her body trembled with the intensity of her resolve.

'Hamdi? Come on, love.'

She hadn't realised that whilst she'd had her eyes closed, Hani had woken and now stood over her.

'Hamdi, love, maybe you will feel better after we have dealt with this. You know we have to co-operate with the police. They'll get him if we help...'

'How? What do we know about him? We don't even know his name or where he comes from, or anything, what can we tell them? Oh, I can't bear it. I can't bear it, Hani...' The duvet felt as though it would suffocate her, she threw it off and sat on the edge of the bed. Hani sat down next to her.

'I know, but we must. We have to be strong that is the only way we will get through.'

'I can't, I don't have it in me. Allah has taken everything from me...'

'Not everything. You have me, and Tariq, and Nimo and you have your sister...'

'She doesn't want me, Hani. She has never contacted me...'

'But, she is a child. You must contact her. You are the adult. What means does she have of contacting you, anyway? She knows your phone number, but how hard is it for her to have access to a phone? Hamdi, don't do this. You were just getting well again, don't regress, Z wouldn't have wanted that.'

Hani's words didn't penetrate her bewildered mind. Nothing of Hani's love or the love she reminded her she had from others touched her. Allah had shown his displeasure, and that would have to take priority over everything. She must do her penance. She would fast. Pray. Stop seeing Tariq – cut him from her life with the sin she'd committed with him. Even Hani must go. Hani didn't believe. Not properly, she justified her sins to herself and tried to make her do the same. But she could no longer deny her own wickedness, she must atone for it. She could not do that around Hani.

'I am leaving, Hani. Don't try to contact me. I will go to the police and after I have told them everything I know I am going back to Nimo's. She will help me. She has never abandoned me, not the personified me nor the spiritual me. I need to marry those two together once more. I cannot do that around you.'

Hani's shock could not have been deeper if Hamdi had said she had murdered Zuleka and was now going to murder her. But she felt unable to move against Hamdi's decision. She watched her dress, then leave without saying a word.

Reaching for her phone she dialled Ayan's number. Checking her watch she realised it would be around 1pm there, a good time to catch her.

Choosing her words with care, she confessed her own guilt over Zuleka's death to Ayan. Together they cried, finding it difficult to talk.

'But, Ayan, something almost as bad has happened to Hamdi. I don't know what to do.' Gaining some control she told Ayan all that had transpired in Hamdi's life and how that and this terrible tragedy had affected her. 'She needs help, Ayan. She could have a complete breakdown. Her mental and physical state is so fragile. She just said... She... She said she doesn't want me in her life...'

Her sobs brought her mother to her door. 'What is it? Oh, daughter, what is distressing you once more?'

'I'm sorry, Ayan, I have to go.'

Ayan told her she would ring later, when she'd had time to speak to her husband. 'Try not to fear too much, Hani,' she'd said, 'this is a knee jerk reaction, a panic flight. Once her mind settles and she can take it all in, Hamdi will come back to you.'

Telling her mother all that had happened released some of Hani's pain and the burden she'd carried with her. Her mother did not condemn, 'it seems you and your friends lost your way. One of you has paid a tragic price. I am so sorry for you, my darling Hani. Hamdi is suffering too much grief for her to cope. Zuleka, allowed herself to go from her parents protection. If only she had listened...'

'*Hooyo*, don't talk like that. At heart Zuleka was a good girl. She cared about others. She wanted to qualify as a doctor and once she did she would have given up the life she led. Her parents failed her. When they found out about her they gave her an impossible ultimatum. She did not act according to them so they cast her out. They left her to flounder. Yes, inside she craved material things, but even that would have gone in time, I know it would, if only they had remained protective of her. You did not abandon me when you found out about the man I love.'

'No, this is true, but things would have had to be different if your way of life had been exposed whilst Salim was still here, you know that. As it is, I am aware of your love for a non-Muslim, but I did not know how you have conducted yourself, partying and dating and alcohol. I am shocked, my daughter. Shocked and hurt. You have deceived me and, as you say Luul knew, you have set a bad example to her, too.'

'I'm sorry, *hooyo*. Please don't be angry with me. It is all over, Izzy left for America. From now on I will try to be a good Muslim and to make you proud. I want that. I want to follow your example. Drinking has never been a big thing with me and I can do without it.'

'I do forgive you, Hani. But only because I know you will change and you have a good future in front of you.'

She promised to try and she would. She knew she was blessed to have a mother like hers. If only Zuleka's parents had a little more understanding perhaps things would have turned out differently. She knew one thing. If she became a mother, her daughters would never live in fear and she would never impose an identity on them. They would know they could talk to her openly about their feelings and would be free to make their own choices.

Chapter Thirty Eight
Zuleka laid to rest

Ayan reunited Hani and Hamdi.

Hamdi clung to them both. Hardly able to stand, weak from not eating or sleeping she'd had to remain in her seat to do so.

'You must forgive yourself to receive Allah's forgiveness, Hamdi'

'I cannot, Ayan. I failed Zuleka as a friend. I had judged her, and then, like a hypocrite I enjoyed all the trappings that her lifestyle had to offer with none of the risk. Guilt is killing me. I punish my body daily but cannot rid myself of my sins.'

'You are rid of them. You have changed your ways, you are about to marry a Muslim boy, who has also vowed to change. Allah can ask no more of you.'

'What are you talking about? I haven't seen Tariq…'

'No, but we have. He loves you. He wants to help you to get better and he wants you as his wife. He says he is ready to make everything halal.'

'But, how can we…?'

'Look, you need to talk, Tariq is out of his mind, but he is willing to wait until after the funeral tomorrow. He has some ideas of how he would like to go forward, but he doesn't know how you will feel about it all.'

'Oh Ayan, I just can't bear to be happy when I think of Zuleka. I can't bear to think of it. It's unfair! Why did she have to die? She's alone now.'

'She is not alone, dear. From Allah we come and to him we return, Inshallah, she is in a better place.'

'But her sins, Ayan…?'

'Hamdi, you are still judging her and that is not your place. You know how her heart lay. In the manner in which she died she would have had time to know her death was imminent. I know she would have cried out to Allah and in His infinite mercy He would not have abandoned her. She would have known she needed to ask for forgiveness and she would have received it.'

'How could He forgive her?'

'In order for you to heal and to take up your faith again, Hamdi, you need to believe in Allah's great capacity for forgiveness. You need to trust His love for us. Once you have done that, you will be accepted back into His fold and know His mercy.'

The sincerity in Ayan's words cracked the misery that tied Hamdi's mind in fear and something in her loving eyes soothed her. A wonderful peace descended into her heart. *Allah could and would forgive her. He did not ask her to punish herself. Just to change her ways and be sorry for her old ones.*

'Did you mean it…, all that you said about Tariq? And what about you, Hani?'

'Yes, it is all true. We have all had to think hard about our lives and how we want to live them, Tariq feels the same. Zuleka did that with the sacrifice of her life, it woke us all up. Allah will credit her with that, I know He will.'

'That's beautiful. It makes Zuleka's existence worthwhile. We must tell her parents that…'

'No, we cannot, Hamdi. At least I cannot. My mother is coping well with learning how her daughter has behaved, but if anyone in the community knew, she would be devastated. I have done enough harm as it is. Let us just know it - the three of us - it is a fitting tribute to our friend.'

'Yes, you are right. Enough people have been hurt.'

The police had, with the act of releasing the body, effectively closed their investigations. They had not caught the Sheikh, but they knew his identity and his guilt without doubt. Whether they would ever be able to bring him back to face the British justice system remained an open question, and one with an almost impossible answer, other than a negative one.

Standing outside Zuleka's house ready to go in to pay their respects the three girls held hands. They walked into Zuleka's home. Inside, next to a beautiful picture of Zuleka stood a framed headed-letter from the university, on it they read how Zuleka had obtained a first and the condolences of her tutors.

Hamdi felt a sense of pride as the words sank in. Yes, it was a waste, but Z had shown her family that she had not given up on the dreams they had for her. She had gone it alone and succeeded. The thought set a worry in her that this might consume them with remorse at their treatment of her, and she finally knew this shouldn't happen. Like her, they had not made the choices for Zuleka. She had made them all and gone the way she had wanted to in life. None of them could have stopped her. But she also knew Ayan was right and Z would have asked for forgiveness and it warmed her heart to know without doubt Allah would have given it to her.

They walked into the living room. The family had moved the big sofas to the side and replaced them with rugs where the women sat and prayed. Incense filled the room; giving it a heady aroma while suras of the dead from the holy Quran played from the stereo.

Zuleka's mother sat in the corner, surrounded by family and friends. She looked small and her face etched with grief. Hamdi remembered Zuleka telling of her last encounter with her mother when her mother had told her not to come to her funeral or that of her father; cruel fate meant her words were prophesied.

When it was time, the house emptied as people made their way to the local mosque where Zuleka's body lay;

washed, clothed and ready for burial. *No fancy designer clothes this time Z, just a plain white cotton shroud.*

Sitting on the women's side of the hall, they couldn't see the coffin that was placed in front of the men. They sat on the carpet and waited in a trance-like state as the Imam conducting the service reminded the congregation to observe the daily prayers before it was too late and prayers were said over their own coffins.

As people began to supplicate for her, Hani broke down, accelerating the tears flowing over Hamdi's cheeks. Ayan, good, kind, strong Ayan took up the position between them and held them close to her.

At the end of the prayers the Imam finished with a short Dua:

> *'Oh Allah! Forgive those of us that are alive and those of us that are dead; those of us that are present and those of us who are absent; those of us who are young and those of us who are adults; our males and our females. Oh Allah! Whomsoever You keep alive, let him live as a follower of Islam and whomsoever You cause to die, let him die a Believer. Amen.*

As they came out into the sunshine Hamdi saw Tariq across the road looking out for her. When he spotted her he came towards her. She nervously adjusted her head scarf. This was the first time she had worn one in his presence.

'Are you alright, Hamdi? Are you ready to talk?'

'Yes, Tariq. Where can we go?'

'I have my car just along there. Will you come home with me?'

She looked at Ayan and Hani. They nodded. She took hold of their hands and told Tariq, 'If I do, you must know that you cannot touch me again until we are married.'

'Oh, so you are going to marry me?'

'Yes, I love you, but...'

'You don't have to say anymore. I know how you want things and I am in full agreement. But, we do have so much to discuss. How about I pick you up at around seven and we go out for dinner?'

'That would be nice.'

His eyes held hers for a long moment. In them she saw a love deeper than anything she'd ever thought anyone would ever feel for her. 'Oh, Tariq...' He'd turned to leave, but he looked back. His face held worry, 'I hope you know somewhere where they give big portions. I'm starving!'

His laughter matched that of herself and Hani and Ayan. Her two friends hugged her. At last she felt ready to heal in her mind as well in her body.

***

At the airport two days later, Ayan promised to return for Hamdi's nikah, no matter that Hamdi insisted it was just going to be a small affair. 'And, make it soon. I won't be able to fly after August for at least four months.'

'What, why...?'

Hani cut Hamdi off in mid question, 'Ayan, you're pregnant! Oh, my God, that's wonderful. Are you okay? You should take care. Sit down...'

'Yes, and it is, and yes I am, but I do not need to sit down, I am not ill. I have never felt better.'

With her bags checked in they made their way towards the passport control. The hustle and bustle, children crying and others jumping around with excitement and posh voices announcing different flights, all passed them by as they stood a moment looking at each other. In other times they would have gone to AA the night before to smoke and say their goodbyes in style, but instead they had spent a quiet evening together at Hamdi's drinking soft drinks.

'You never said last night…'

'I know, Hani. I thought I would wait until the last minute. I didn't want you both going all gooey over me. You needed me to be strong and I couldn't have done that if you were trying to protect me. But, I am so happy. I have never been happier. I want this kind of happiness for you both.'

'And it is going to happen, too. I didn't tell you something either.'

'Well, whatever it is it better not be the same news as Ayan's, Hamdi.'

'No, it isn't. I have already contacted Nimo and she is arranging my wedding in six weeks time…'

'That's wonderful…'

'Yes, but I didn't say because afterwards, Tariq and I are going away. We are going to help out in Somalia. We are going to volunteer with Islamic Relief, they operate in Puntland and it's relatively safer in that part of Somalia.'

'Oh, Hamdi, Somalia! I just don't know what to say, how soon after?'

'We don't know yet, but not long…'

'You are not doing this to punish…'

'No, don't even think that. It is something Tariq wants to do and when he told me, I knew it was what I wanted, too. We'll pass by Kenya so I can meet my sister; while I am out there I can do so much good. They are crying out for someone with my organisational skills.'

'Hey, slow down. I can't take all of this in. I have a flight to catch you know.'

'Neither can I. Hamdi, your life will change so much, but do you know what? I think you are the ideal couple to do this.'

'Thank you, that means a lot to me.'

'So, see you in six weeks then. I can't believe it. It'll be wonderful to all be together again, but this time for a celebration. And, Hani, promise me you will keep positive as I know something good will happen for you, too. We all have a happy future ahead of us, I know it. And that is true even of Zuleka, as we have to hold on to the fact that she is resting in a blissful place.'

A silence followed Ayan's words, but it didn't last long as she said, 'Let's make a pact. Whenever we can we will attend each other's family occasions, but in any case, we will keep in contact every week and meet up at least once each year. Agree?'

'Agree.' Hamdi and Ayan said together.

'Right! Group hug,' Ayan had no need to say this as it happened as a spontaneous reaction to them agreeing their future plans to meet up as often as they can.

As Hamdi and Hani walked out of the airport hand in hand Hamdi turned to Hani and said, 'Zuleka's sister asked you about deleting the photos on her facebook account, you are going to do it aren't you, Hani?'

'Yes. It will be difficult as they chronicle her life as we have known her.'

'You have to do it for her, Hani. Remember that night in Blue Bar when she panicked and she thought she would die there and her father would find her in those hot pants? I told her that if that was the case I would change her into the jeans I was wearing and clothe her exposed body. This is the same thing, she's gone and some of those pictures are in compromising places and she's not wearing the right things. We don't want anyone judging her now she is not able to defend herself.'

'I will, don't worry. I have it planned for tonight. Oh, Hamdi, it's so good to see you looking better and to know you have your life worked out. I know you and Tariq will be happy.'

'Maybe you will too, Izzy is going to be best man at our wedding. He's coming back, Hani.'

Hani stood still. Her heart skipped a beat and brought a smile she had no control over to her lips. Her eyes shone with determination... *Izzy was coming back.*

The End.

Acknowledgments

I would like to thank my family and my husband, JAI: without their support and encouragement, I would not have finished this book. I would also like to thank my creative writing editor, Mary Wood, who added flesh to my work and helped me mould my characters. It was great to have someone who cared about the early manuscript almost as much as I did, thank you, Mary.

Thank you to all those people who subscribed to the blog, 'liked' the Facebook page and kept demanding more and more chapters: I was very worried about the initial reaction the book would get, but your messages of support and appreciation helped me overcome my reservation about publishing this book.